As an innovator and author who admires and has written about the iconic Edison, I can't think of a more creative treatment of his genius. This brilliantly-crafted book will keep you turning the pages until the final twist. Enjoy the ride!"

Lorraine Marchand, General Manager, IBM Watson Health and author of The Innovation Mindset (Columbia University Press)

Hang onto your history books! Only David Church could make Thomas Edison an action hero and populate his adventures with rich characters and brilliant plot twists rooted in actual events. It's the most cinematic and satisfying read I've devoured in years.

Larry Dean Harris
Artistic Director, Strong Words

THOMAS EDISON
AND THE
PURGATORY EQUATION

DAVID CHURCH

This is a work of historical fiction. While based on fact, the names, characters, organizations, places, events and incidents within the narrative are either products of the author's imagination or are used fictitiously.

Published by Ferrisville Publications
Palm Springs, California
ferrisvillepublications@gmail.com

Print: ISBN # 978-0-578-32484-5

Ebook: ISBN # 979-8-9855761-0-8

Library of Congress # 1-11008427241

Cover Illustrations by:
Richard Kilroy
Kilroy Arts

Publishing Consultants:
Enhanced Communications, LLC
Tender Fire Books

For Phyllis and Manson

He created the electric light…
…the phonograph…
…and motion pictures…
…achievements that confirmed Thomas Alva Edison as the most extraordinary inventor of all time.
Yet, for decades, Edison toiled over what he believed would be celebrated as his greatest invention – a machine designed to penetrate the boundary between life and death.

In February of 1918, as the United States prepared to enter the Great War, Edison and John Dawkins, his stalwart young assistant, along with their accidental companions, Emily Auburn, a Ziegfeld Follies showgirl and her rehearsal pianist, the teenage George Gershwin, vanished.

When they re-appeared a month later, Edison disavowed his creation and, to the end of his life, refused to reveal the events of that mysterious winter.

This is what happened.

THE EVENTS AS THEY OCCURRED

Prologue

SÉANCE

1887

"Every failed experiment," proclaimed Thomas Alva Edison, "is still a step forward." It was a noble maxim and expressed with regular determination by its celebrated author. Yet, on those rare occasions of crippling doubt, his fine words seemed little more than a pose. Edison prayed that today would not be one of those occasions. To be precise, the seventy-third day of a relentless exploration into his latest invention, the fluorosight; a fusion of fluoroscopic screens and cathode ray lamps that corralled the new phenomenon of 'unknown' or 'X' rays in a quest to discover the cure for blindness.

Now on the cusp of his fortieth year, Edison had re-invented the world time and again with an assembly of miraculous inventions, the most prominent being the phonograph and the incandescent light. In turn, he had been universally hailed as a genius, and while he reveled in the hurrahs, a nagging watch-cry of doubt never strayed far from his mind: *The natural habitat of genius is failure*. It was a lesson he had been hard taught, first as a boy whose eccentricities were judged to be those of an imbecile, then as an aspiring inventor who was mocked as a shiftless dreamer.

With his first successful creation, a telegraph repeater, he experienced a sudden reversal from derision to praise and grasped a keen understanding of the tenuous skin that separated the two. Destiny was arbitrary. The grindstone of failure was rarely leavened with success, and it had reduced many of his peers into sorry figures of resignation or even madness. But not him! At least, not yet.

Alongside a team of his most trusted assistants, including Charles Batchelor and the Ott brothers, John and Fred, he had toiled nonstop at the laboratory these past months with only a few hours each night devoted to rest on a nearby cot. It was his nature to drive himself in so dogged a fashion, but now his experiments were fraught with additional pressures. Outwardly he remained the same as before and refused to be seduced by the gross affluence that usually infects the nouveau riche. His only real interest in money was to make enough to make more inventions. However, he was no longer a mere tinkerer flirting on the edge of 'what if?' He had realized his promise and the pressure to do right by his extraordinary gifts proved to be a crushing duty. What steadied his path was a wary disposition that could best be termed as that of a 'pragmatic optimist.' He expected nothing yet hoped for something. Today, as on every day, he hoped for a breakthrough.

By sunset his hopes were diminished. He had spent the day examining some three dozen subjects from a local home for the blind. The afflicted had caned a path to his door to confront a gauntlet of fluoroscopes and willingly subject themselves to the eerie glow emanating from the electrified tubes as the X-rays parted the veils of their flesh.

Between sessions, adjustments were made to the amperage

levels, equipment repaired, and the biography of the next subject reviewed for any unique characteristics. On occasion, the process ground to a halt when a subject jubilantly cried, "I can see!" Further investigation proved the opposite, for the subject had merely been captive to the desperate hope that the 'Wizard of Menlo Park' could perform his magic on their behalf.

Edison was preparing for their next subject when a figure adorned in white appeared in the laboratory's doorway. It was not an angel. It was Twain. Yes, that Twain. Mark Twain. The two friends – Twain the sage mentor, Edison the aspiring arrival – greeted each other warmly for they were bound by the common bond of success and the repercussions that came with the kudos. Twain had achieved popular acclaim for *The Adventures of Tom Sawyer*, yet his critics dismissed him as a cracker-barrel scribbler of children's books. As for Edison, the business combines of the world hailed him as a visionary, but had not yet determined how to harness his incandescent revolution for worldwide distribution – or how much they could get away with charging for it.

"Sam, you rascal," said Edison. "What brings you here?"

"Our engagement," snapped Twain gregariously. "Supper at Delmonico's?"

"Oh…yes," fumbled Edison. "My apologies…I forgot…as you can see I…well..." His attention was scattered. Then: "Here... sit."

Intrigued, Twain took a chair as Batchelor briefed Edison on their next subject.

"Mary Bowen, six years, seven months. Contracted rubella fever two years ago, incurred severe damage to both corneas."

Edison nodded and continued to study her chart – so young

– as Batchelor escorted the child into the laboratory. She was a petite brunette with a trusting smile, whose once-blue eyes were now scarred with puddles of milk.

"Hello, Mary. I'm Tom."

"Hello, Tom," she responded politely in a tiny, unsure voice.

"I'm going to examine you now." He guided her to a seat behind the tower of fluoroscopic screens where the Ott brothers gently strapped her in.

"You're going to hear some very odd noises," continued Edison. "You might even feel some sparks. But you're perfectly safe and I don't want you to be frightened. Do you understand?"

The child nodded stoically.

Edison smiled wanly and signaled his team. "Begin."

The surge of high-voltage current flushed into the dynamos and tentacles of electricity flexed menacingly throughout the room. The child gasped in fright and shivered as a violet glow began to emanate from the battery of fluoroscopic screens that surrounded her petite figure.

"Would you like me to hold your hand?" offered Edison.

"Yes, please."

Edison took her palm in his and pressed it reassuringly as the amperage increased to an ear-splitting cacophony and a torrent of sparks erupted from the dynamos, dusting the room with hot flakes of hellfire. Electricity filled a series of Crookes tubes that were connected to a jumble of photographic plates. The plates came alive with a gray fog that sundered Mary's flesh and illuminated the yearning sockets of the child's dead eyes.

Twain observed the proceedings in silent concern. Edison and his men were more than exhausted, they were wounded; scant of breath and hollow-cheeked, their pale skin studded with dark, charring blisters. And this was only now. Who could say how their continued exposure to these strange rays might eventually manifest itself? While Twain admired Edison's zeal in obliterating the boundaries of known science, he was also alarmed. The last prophet who had brought light to the world was Jesus Christ – and look what happened to him.

The experiment ended. The roar of current subsided and the screens withdrawn. The team waited in breathless anticipation as Edison held up a mirror to the child's face.

"Mary, can you see?" asked Edison.

Mary paused, uncertain. She opened her eyes wide and strained desperately against the darkness. Then she retreated, lowered her head with a shame that had no cause to claim her, and hot tears tumbled down her cheeks.

"No." The small voice hung heavy in the twilight.

Edison released the girl's hand. If any of the hundreds he had examined most deserved the gift of sight it was this sweet child.

"Thank you, Mary. I wish I could have been of more service." His voice broke on the word 'service' and then trailed off. He ran his hands through his hair and was startled to find his palms littered with strands of dead follicles.

The child heard the hurt in his voice and, as she was being ushered out, stopped to place a comforting hand on his. "Don't be sad for me, Tom. I remember stars."

'I remember stars.' Her words cut Edison to the quick. He nodded feebly as she departed and then peered up at his men through eyes rheumy with regret. They'd been stricken by this last encounter and John Ott, usually his most stolid associate, ground his knuckles against his mouth to smother his dismay.

"Go home," Edison softly ordered. The men did as they were told.

"You go on, too, Sam" he waved vacantly to Twain. "I'm not a suitable companion for dining. Or anything else." He gestured in disbelief. "I've gone dry."

Twain gave his young friend a long, hard look and then gently offered: "Oh, surely not. The two most important days in a man's life are the day he's born – and the day he finds out why."

"Empty, done, finished!" wailed Edison in defeat.

"You know why," Twain firmly retorted. "You're a born inventor! Never forget it." Then he winked mischievously. "Besides, I've arranged an amusement for this evening's appetizer. A séance with Madame Blavatsky."

Edison looked up sharply, intrigued. "The Russian medium. I've heard tell of her. She summons spirits?"

"Spirits and idiots," amended Twain. "It's all nonsense but do come."

"I believe I will." It was an impulsive decision that took even Edison by surprise. "Give me a moment to…" He crossed to a sink and began the necessary ablutions.

"Certainly," offered Twain. "But don't tarry. Who can say? Perhaps one of the Madame's hobgoblins has a message from purgatory just for you."

Naturally, it was a jest. But Twain didn't realize the possibility of a missive from beyond was the only reason Edison had agreed to join him. Because he'd received such a message once before.

* * *

During the past few years, the trend of spiritualism had rolled across the United States with each burg boasting their own acclaimed fortune-teller, usually a semi-reputable, middle-aged widow. Mrs. Beeson of Hartford. Mrs. Twitchell of St. Louis. Mrs. Cadalver of Denver, and so on. They were pseudo-seers who employed intricate props such as floating objects tied to strings, angled mirrors, black muslin shadowed to trick the eye, and air hoses strategically aimed to raise the hair on the backs of gullible necks. They were aided in their racket by a cast of supporting players. Stone-faced Indian swamis, rictus-grinned Chinamen, and African witch doctors, whose true heritage could usually be traced to deepest, darkest Memphis.

Madame Blavatsky towered above her competitors. An internationally acclaimed occultist, she worked solo and had infiltrated the heady stratums of Park Avenue society by shrewdly promoting what appeared to be a genuine gift – the rare tongue required to speak with the dead. Her current place of business was a Stuyvesant Park mansion that had been placed at her disposal by one of her disciples. She sat silently inside the mansion's library, a stern figure, swaddled in black, listening intuitively to the babble of anticipation just outside the door. This would be her last séance in America. Soon she would set sail for India where she planned to cultivate her 'Society of Theosophists' in a more welcoming environment. She'd already secured the funding for her expedition so why had she agreed to this session? Some pocket money for the road? Or the last chance to impart a crucial message that might one day save the world? Whatever the reason, she was certain of one thing – by the end of the night she'd be well paid. She was psychic enough to predict that.

Madame Blavatsky sat, grunted in readiness, and signaled to a pair of servants. They nodded in mute collusion and unlocked the double doors to the library. The guests, a motley collection of financial butchers who had made their fortunes off the misfortunes of others, loudly sauntered in from the reception hall.

"Repulsive, aren't they?" murmured Twain, delighted to see his cynical view of humanity so nakedly on display.

Edison nodded, affronted by the panoply of crass indulgence. "Their money is tainted."

"Worse. It's twice tainted," complained Twain. "Tain't yours and tain't mine."

Edison laughed, as full a laugh as he'd enjoyed in weeks. Then he observed that, as the guests took their places around the circular, oaken séance table, no matter how grand their station in life, they devolved into a group of breathless children, eager to be astonished.

Madame Blavatsky fixed her guests with an imperious stare, grasped a crystal ball with her claw-like hand, and rapped it three times against a marble base as if it were a gavel. The lights began to dim and the assembly promptly fell silent.

"This is no illusion," she stated in a voice that was both guttural and hypnotic. "The dead live among us. Unseen. Unheard. Untouched. But tonight they shall make themselves known."

The women shivered and the men consoled them as Madame Blavatsky gestured for all present to join hands.

Edison offered a moist palm to Twain, who snorted. Edison grinned and nudged him, whispering, "Let's give it a whirl."

"It's either bunk or Beelzebub," advised Twain as he stubbed out his cigar and took Edison's hand. "And my money's on bunk."

Madame Blavatsky closed her eyes and took a deep breath as if preparing to submerge under water. As she slowly exhaled, bubbles of spit coated her lips and her facial muscles unwound, transforming her imperious demeanor to a blank canvas of flesh. She sucked in a deep breath of air and the tambourine in the center of the table began to rise and rattle rhythmically. Edison smiled in recognition; he'd heard of the floating tambourine. It was a nice touch.

"I sense a man of property," she began. "An older man of wealth who was known in this life as..." She stopped, puzzled, then continued. "Who was known as...?" Again, she paused. "As...Charley?"

Edison gasped, his eyes widening. But before he had a chance to consider her revelation and his response to it, a shrill, indignant voice corrected:

"You're wrong already. His name was Hiram!

Edison turned to see Bessamine Wainwright, a society woman on the itchy side of fifty. Known to her few friends as "Bessie," she had once been a beauty, but was now too blond for her years and newly fat. A slick gigolo sat by her side. Twain suspected she had married, and widowed, well.

The interruption gave Madame Blavatsky a chance to establish a connection with the second spirit in the room and she murmured decisively. "Ah, yes. Hiram."

At that, the tambourine rattled violently and a smoky stream of ectoplasm spiraled up from the center of the table. The guests responded with giddy terror as rumbles of thunder careened around the room and the lights went out. Edison was seized by an irrational fear and tightened his grip on Twain's hand. Surprised,

Twain leaned over to tease his young friend but, sensing Edison's genuine alarm, thought the better of it and returned his grip in solidarity.

A ghostly blue light shimmered in the ectoplasm and curled outward, the fingers illuminating the faces of Bessie and Madame Blavatsky, who spoke again, but now in a contorted, elderly whine. "Greetings, Bessie."

Bessie gasped. "Hiram. Is it really you?"

"I am the spirit you called husband," replied the seer, her jaws jabbering up and down like a nutcracker.

Bessie let out a small yelp and the others gave a collective start as the face of an elderly man appeared in the swirling pool of ectoplasm. Edison and Twain exchanged glances as Bessie recovered from her initial shock.

"I miss you, dearie. You were good to me."

"That is true."

Silence. In death as in life, Hiram proved to be a man of few words and Bessie a woman of many wants. He awaited her request. It arrived.

"I'm lonely, Hiram. I'm going to marry again."

She merrily waggled her thick fingers. One of them sported an engagement ring large enough to be considered vulgar by the other women at the table; a genuine achievement, although it wasn't so much the size of the ring that gave offense as the waggling.

She turned to the manicured escort at her side and smiled expectantly. "Will you give us your blessing?"

"I pray..." The eerie whine of a voice paused meaningfully. "…he brings you the same happiness you brought to me."

Bessie squealed in delight and accepted a supportive kiss

on the cheek from her intended as he tightened his hold on her. Suddenly, surprisingly, Bessie pulled away from him and stared deep into the swirling ectoplasm. "Hiram? Is Heaven wonderful?"

Edison watched intently, and even Twain edged forward in anticipation, as the croaking voice responded in fits and starts:

"I – am – filled – with – warmth."

Bessie rejoiced in the glad tidings, then was suddenly struck by an odd burst of regret. "I suppose I should have been a better wife. If only you hadn't been such an old fuddy-duddy. If only---"

"My time grows short," Hiram concluded. "Fare-thee-well!"

A surge of current erupted from the chandelier, struck the floating tambourine and ricocheted a ring of crackling electricity over the heads of the guests. The library windows blasted open and the storm poured into the room as the ectoplasm evaporated and the lights flickered back on. Madame Blavatsky emerged from her trance and everyone, including Twain, applauded.

"Now we shall retire to the parlor," ordered Madame Blavatsky, "for aperitifs and goodbyes." She gestured and the servants opened the exit doors. Satisfied with their inconsequential glimpse into the hereafter, the guests merrily adjourned.

Bessie approached the seer, embraced her with a husky fervor, and between heartfelt murmurs of "Bless you," pressed an envelope into her hands and proceeded to join the others.

Madame Blavatsky opened the envelope and withdrew a check with a figure more generous than she had anticipated. She was not a woman given to moods, but she indulgently grabbed the tambourine and shook it in delight until she sensed she was not alone. Who could it be? She guessed correctly.

"Ah, my distinguished gentlemen." She turned to confront

Twain and Edison. "You applaud. But you do not believe."

"I applaud your performance, Madame," replied Twain. "But when it comes to your otherworldly powers, I fear…"

Twain gestured for the unsuspecting Edison to move to the opposite side of the circular conjuring table and grip the frame. They pulled.

"…you're nothing but a humbug."

The tabletop split in the center and came apart, revealing a complex effects apparatus beneath, complete with levers, mirrors, and foot pedals to manipulate the elements of the séance.

Edison studied the machinery, intrigued and oddly disappointed. "Smoke and mirrors," he muttered. As always, he'd expected nothing but hoped for something. This time his hopes had been curiously high.

"The tricks of my trade," she shrugged "But I assure you, I am no humbug."

Bessie's frivolous laughter echoed from the parlor. Twain snorted. "Even a damn fool deserves the truth."

Madame Blavatsky barked out an abrupt laugh. "What truth would you have me tell this fool? That her beloved Hiram wishes her the same happiness she gave him which was next to nothing? That the warmth he feels is hellfire?" She plucked a cigar from Twain's breast pocket, lit it, and took a savvy drag. "You see, Mr. Twain, in my craft, like yours, the truth often resides between the lines."

Twain regarded her with new respect and laughed; not at her, as was his custom, but with her. "Then from one humbug to another, my thanks to you and Hiram and…ahem, Charley – whoever that poor devil is – for a memorable encounter."

Twain offered a courtly nod in tribute and joined the others.

Edison, who'd lingered over the mechanics of the contraption, suddenly realized he was alone with the seer. He smiled uncomfortably and turned to go. Before he could make a proper exit, Madame Blavatsky fixed her iron gaze on him.

"Who is Charley, Mr. Edison?"

Edison stopped in surprise and turned back to her wordlessly, his face flushed with emotion. She extended her hands. Edison took them and felt a tingle of shock as his flesh touched hers. He struggled to find his voice.

"My nephew. A promising young inventor. My own children had no gift for my enthusiasms, but Charley was my bright boy."

Charles Edison had been the natural inheritor of his uncle's talents. Following his successful apprenticeship at the Menlo Park laboratory, Edison sent him to Paris to represent his business interests.

However, unlike his uncle's devotion to the rigors of work, Charley was driven by a reckless pursuit of happiness. Spring arrived and Charley fell in love. The object of his affection was a fellow expatriate by the name of D. Murray. Normally, this would have been cause for celebration. However, D. Murray was not a woman – but a man; an American photographer who quickly became Charley's partner in all ways. Only Edison knew the scandalous nature of their relationship. He begged Charley to forsake this unnatural union and return home, but the headstrong youth refused. In a fury, Edison severed their relationship. Charley deeply regretted the break but was determined to embrace his identity. The summer was glorious, the fall even more so. Then, in mid-October, Charley fell ill. The diagnosis? An advanced case of peritonitis. By the time Edison learned of his nephew's deteriorating condition, there was nothing that even a man of his considerable means could do. After enduring ten days of excruciating pain and bouts of shrieking dementia, Charley succumbed from what his shaken physician later described as 'the most wretched dogs-death' he'd ever witnessed.

Edison was overcome with emotion. He rarely told this story and the telling undid him. So it was understandable that he failed to see a sliver of genuine ectoplasm subtly coalescing in the thick air beside him and swirling into the living cameo of a young man.

"He died. So terribly young." Edison took a deep breath. He was about to confess a secret he had never divulged to another living person. "Just before I discovered---"

Madame Blavatsky nodded sagely. "The electric light. Yes. His spirit revealed the missing link."

Edison lowered his eyes to the floor and nodded dumbly.

For months he had experimented in vain with a variety of filaments, carbonizing everything from fishing line and celluloid to wood shavings and coconut hair; fashioning them into a spiral to stabilize the current, but none worked. Not one damned one. Until the night of Charley's death. His prodigal nephew appeared to Edison in a fevered dream. Edison ran to greet Charley but a strange force separated them and he could only look on, transfixed, as Charley bent his hands into the shape of…a horseshoe. A horseshoe! Good God. It wasn't the *type* of filament that empowered the conduit, it was the *shape*!

Edison awoke in a frenzy of revelation, rushed to the laboratory, and looped a carbonized piece of thread into the form of a horseshoe. Miraculously, the revised form allowed the charge to hold and a new light was born into the world.

Madame Blavatsky acknowledged the specter in their midst. She could see him clearly now; a lean, well-formed young man with a sandy shock of hair. Yet no matter how actively the spirit beseeched him, Edison could not see the visage of his nephew.

The seer turned back to Edison. "You have a question for Charley." It was a statement, not a query.

Edison hesitated in disbelief, grappling between guilt and need. "The fluorosight. How can I make it work?

Madame Blavatsky closed her eyes, paused, and nodded. "You will not," she answered candidly. "Perhaps some distant day a machine will allow the blind to see. But the time is not now." She opened her eyes. "You will not be their emancipator."

It wasn't the answer Edison had hoped for. Offended, he tried to pull away, but she held him tight.

"Now Charley has a message for you." The ectoplasm wrapped around both of them as Madame Blavatsky's eyes closed in metaphysical communion and then popped open. She was more startled by the import of the revelation than she'd anticipated; breathless, her body trembling. She chose her words carefully. "A man will enter your life. He will be essential in helping you realize your greatest invention. His name is…John Dawkins."

"Dawkins?" replied the baffled Edison. "I don't know any 'Dawkins.'"

"Naturally," she concurred. "He has not yet been born."

It was too much. Edison broke the connection. An unnatural charge of voltage shocked him and he rubbed his fingers.

"Stuff and nonsense," he responded brusquely and, as he turned to retrieve his hat and coat, walked blindly through the mist of his nephew's yearning apparition.

"It will be as foretold," Madame Blavatsky replied evenly.

"Then I'll believe it when I see it," countered Edison peevishly

"No, Mr. Edison, you will not," she replied in weary regret. "You will not see it until you believe it."

Edison whirled back, unduly agitated and eager to end their interview. "Farewell then, Madame. Making your acquaintance has been quite an adventure."

Madame Blavatsky burst out in delicious laughter and clapped her hands together. "An adventure!" She fixed Edison with a cryptic smile. "Just wait till we meet again."

Speechless, Edison departed, not lingering for food or drink, not even for Twain, who reluctantly took leave of his sherry to follow him.

Edison flew out of the mansion and into the night air that was pocked with plump, swirling snow. He was at odds with himself, defiant and uncertain. He gazed back up at the library. The seer's silhouette moved past the row of windows and then the lights dimmed. He cursed himself.

Twain cantered down the stairs breathlessly. "What the devil's got into you?"

"The devil himself," retorted Edison. "Or not. I don't know."

Twain took a thoughtful drag on his cigar and then exhaled a volley of smoke into the crisp night air. "Nothing that a supper of champagne and chateaubriand won't cure," he prescribed, and set off to hail a carriage.

The street was empty yet Edison was not alone. For Charley's spirit had followed him outside. He must make himself known. Too much was at stake. The determined stream of ectoplasm seized the lingering smoke from Twain's cigar and forged the contours to reveal Charley's face.

Edison gasped in fright, stumbled back on the ice, and crashed to the sidewalk. His fear subsided as he studied the apparition and then gazed wistfully at the specter of his nephew. He reached out to touch the vision but his fingers breached the hold and the smoke dissipated. He considered what he had just witnessed and thought hard. A revelation arrived. "Eureka," he whispered.

The carriage pulled up. Twain gestured for Edison to join him but he begged off. "My regrets, Samuel. I've had an idea."

"For the blind machine?" asked Twain. "Surely it can wait till morning."

"No. It's for something else. Something new."

Twain reluctantly nodded his acceptance. He understood the fragility of inspiration.

Edison shook his hand in solid fellowship and set off into the night, his bustling figure framed by the dual spires of St. George's Church, for the first time in his life assured of the joyous news that the *true* habitat of genius was *not* failure – but the future!

I

WAR 1916

They looked like snowflakes, except they weren't pale. They were dark. In color they would have been a ruddy brown. However, the camera's palette was limited to black and white. The only reason they resembled snowflakes, parachuting lazily down to earth, was because of the slow motion. The cameraman was cranking too fast. He usually held the crank steady and captured the pictorial moment in its natural rhythm. But the blasts had been coming closer; the last one so immediate the ground had fractured and he nearly tumbled into a fissure.

This wasn't a typical shoot. Usually his unit was only assigned to record the action before and after combat; a roster of sabre-rattling rhetoric for the newsreels and posterity. Instead, General Rawlinson had rashly ordered the camera crew into the heat of battle. The Somme promised to be his great victory, a decisive turning point in the grand conflict, and he wanted that triumph immortalized.

Triumph? Fat chance. From the shooter's perspective, behind the lens of a bulky camera that looked like a suitcase with three legs and a Cyclops of an eye, the Somme would be a disaster for the British. Oddly enough, his own instincts of foreboding didn't frighten him. They charged him up with a kind of exuberance. It wasn't the prospect of injury or death that excited him. He wanted to survive, didn't he? Damn right. It's just that the flirtation, the high-wire act with annihilation, made him feel so incredibly present. In fact, he hadn't felt this way since…

He ran out of film. He yanked the old reel out and clapped on a new one. He moved quickly. He'd been trained to be quick. Slow could get you killed and he didn't want 'slow' on his tombstone. Another explosion. A wave of grit fanned across the air. No, this wasn't snow. It was mud drenched in blood.

He wasn't a Brit. He was American. His country hadn't joined the fight and wouldn't for another two years. So how did he come to be here, manning a combat camera for a country that wasn't his? He chuckled grimly to himself. He was here because he believed. In what? Well, hell. Something he used to believe in. Maybe one day he'd remember, if he lived long enough. He was a rugged young buck of twenty-two from Canton, Ohio with a wild thatch of chestnut hair, an athletic physique veined with muscles, a handsome head full of ideals (which wasn't unusual for his age), and an injured heart full of regret (which was). His name was John Dawkins.

John planted the tripod legs, panned across the battlefield, and began cranking. A bomb slammed into a trench row fifty feet in front of him and a dozen British soldiers catapulted into the air, their limbs flapping grotesquely, the life already slammed out of them. Silence. Then the shrieks from the unseen injured, the trench now doubling as their tomb. John stopped, stricken. He felt the urge to do something. But what? Nothing. He wiped the bits of viscera off the lens and lowered his face to the eyepiece.

Before he could advance the film stock, a thick-set figure lumbered into the frame. John bolted up defensively only to discover it was Sergeant Greer, a career soldier with a bulldog face and a family of four back home in Manchester. Myra, Gladys, Lorne, and Gertie. He was a good sergeant. He was even a friend.

"Damn you, Dawkins, retreat!"

John stared hard at the sergeant. The man's ear had been blown off and the socket of his jaw exposed.

"It's all gone to hell!" The sergeant's jawbone see-sawed as he spoke. "Retreat. That's an order." He staggered into the thick fog and disappeared.

Artillery strafed from overhead, followed by more explosions and screams and suddenly John realized the sergeant was right. He didn't know where in hell to retreat to but he knew he had to go and fast. He yanked the tripod legs out of the sodden earth, slung the camera over his shoulder, and took off.

He didn't get far. Just over the ridge he found himself face-to-face with a German soldier who had the good fortune to spot John first. He charged at him with his bayonet, spearing a flesh wound through John's side. He dropped, falling hard onto his back. Over a year in the conflict and he'd never been wounded. Not like this. This was real.

The German charged again, the razored tip of the bayonet aimed for John's throat. He shoved the camera in front of his face, fending off the assault. Enraged, the soldier chopped at the wooden legs of the tripod, trying to sever them from the camera base to reach his target. He succeeded in hacking off one of the legs. It tumbled to John's side and he gave it a scant, unknowing glance as the soldier grunted forward and angled for traction. He continued to thrust his bayonet at John, who, running out of defensive options, cast a second look at the severed tripod leg – this time not scant but knowing. He walloped the camera into the soldier's skull, grabbed the tripod leg, rammed it into his chest, and twisted it out the other side. The soldier promptly expired and then, in a belated reflex, his mouth dropped open in shock.

John turned to confront another German, this one an officer, who formally brandished his sword. John sighed, spent, but gamely gestured 'come and get it' for this time he knew what to do. He cracked off the second leg of the tripod and had at the man. They dueled fiercely, their swordsmanship compromised by the mire of grit beneath their feet. The officer was good, so good that John feared he might lose this fight. His adversary's determination to kill wasn't fueled by rage or fear but by the pride of his station. And 'pride,' as John recalled from his Sunday school days, 'goeth before a fall.' He parried at the officer, spun into a crouch to avoid his return thrust, and slashed the tripod leg across the stays of his military breeches. The trousers fell and the officer, from habit of decorum, dropped his guard to cover himself. John seized the moment and shoved the shaft through his throat.

John started to go when yet a third soldier cried out his vow to avenge his fallen comrades. Why did they always come in threes? Too exhausted to fight, John snapped off the last tripod leg and javelined the make-shift spear between the soldier's ribs. Done. Anyone else? The ferocity of his pre-emptive strike guaranteed no further takers.

John grunted, took off, and was making headway when he heard a shot ring out. He stopped cold, astonished to discover a ball of lead had found a home in his thigh. Then another shot and John dropped, the second bullet piercing his stomach. He collapsed on what looked like a pyramid of mud but was instead composed of the corpses of British soldiers, the most recent addition being Sergeant Greer, his empty eyes wide open in defiance, his pistol cocked for action. John tried to rise but couldn't. A sickening sense of curiosity was all he could manage as a familiar sound drew closer. Click-spit…click-spit. It was the sound of a camera being cranked.

A squat German cameraman approached out of the mist, filming John as he writhed helplessly on the mound of bodies. Looming behind him was another, austere figure that, even in silhouette, achieved the very definition of menace.

This definitive figure was Colonel Wilhelm Skinehardt, a well-constructed man in the vicinity of forty whose striking features were compromised by a sadistic veneer. He had observed John's derring-do and decided this was one kill he wanted to claim as his own. Skinehardt studied John for a moment and John, unsure of what might happen next, let himself be studied. Skinehardt smiled dangerously, loaded a single bullet into his pistol and gestured for the uneasy cameraman to keep rolling. He reached across the table, his voice a mixture of silk and taunt. "I'm ready for your close-up."

He aimed the gun at John's face. John blanched, scrambled backwards up the mound, and spotted the sergeant's cocked sidearm. Skinehardt advanced, his finger flirting with the trigger, and he savored his victim's final seconds of panic. It was an ill-advised indulgence.

John grabbed the dead sergeant's arm, angled it toward Skinehardt, and fired. The bullet blasted the weapon out of Skinehardt's hand and severed his trigger finger. The colonel clutched his bleeding hand in furious agony. John fired again and again but the sidearm was out of bullets. Skinehardt scoured the slop beneath his feet to retrieve his own weapon and found it. Although soiled with spurts of his own blood, Skinehardt desperately tried to reload, now obsessed with reducing John to nothing more than a notch on his belt. The bullet slid into the chamber and Skinehardt took aim.

Then, just like in the movies, the cavalry arrived – in this case the cavalry being a contingent of British Air Support. A trio of Bristol Scouts salted bombs across the battlefield, creating an involuntary retreat from both sides. As more ballasts of grit erupted around them, Skinehardt fired – and missed. The cameraman interceded and dragged the reluctant, cursing colonel into a tunnel of fog where they vanished.

John howled in relief. Skinehardt couldn't have been a more thorough villain if he'd worn a black cape and twirled an oversized moustache. He leaned his head back into the cradle of his fallen comrades, blinked woozily, and passed out.

He awoke some days later in a convent hospital to discover that what was left of his life had evolved into the tools of his trade: a *montage* of film techniques – smash cuts, fades to black, and dissolves. These random clips of lucidness were all he had to cling to for the next few months. The snaggle-toothed smile of an elderly nun. A picture of a rose tacked onto a white-washed wall. Serum spouting from a hypodermic needle. A Christmas orange studded with cloves. A drunken, heartfelt version of "Amazing Grace." And the nightmares. Always the nightmares. That's when he knew he was still alive. The nightmares belonged solely to him.

1918

The advertisement read 'Cameraman Wanted - West Orange, New Jersey.' John stood across the street from a sprawling industrial edifice. He was older, wiser, but less certain of life and his intended role in the big parade. He shoved the ad into the pocket of his navy pea coat and shivered. Was it the February cold or his nerves? Both. He needed this job. Any job. He took a deep breath and entered the daunting halls of Thomas Edison, Inc.

Cut. Print. New reel.

2

OPPORTUNITY

Mr. Meadowcroft, an officious secretary with equal parts of hawk and schoolmarm in his manner, regarded John dubiously from behind his pince-nez glasses. He ushered him down a long hallway that was flanked by a gauntlet of glass display cases featuring the innumerable inventions of Thomas Alva Edison.

John marveled at the collection; the phonograph, the electric light, and the motion picture camera – my God – the multitude of inventions created by this one mind! However, his reverent tribute only served to irritate the prim secretary who snapped his bony fingers and gestured for this latest in a line of never-ending disciples to shake a leg.

As they arrived at the entrance to Edison's private office, raucous shouting was heard from inside. Meadowcroft rolled his eyes in resignation. He had worked as the great man's secretary for nearly eight years and yes, yes, yes, Edison was a genius, but what a fuss day in and day out! In his estimation, a modest intelligence had its compensations. He rapped sharply, waited to see if the din would decrease and when it didn't, sighed theatrically, flung open the double-doors, and admitted John to the inner sanctum – a cluttered rotunda that served as the inventor's lair.

Edison paced behind his desk, fuming into a telephone. Now an eccentric curmudgeon of seventy, he sported a small pot belly and a hot tongue. John watched, both cowed and impressed, as Edison absent-mindedly spun a small, metallic object which appeared to be part gyroscope, part armillary sphere while he harangued the unlucky recipient at the end of the line.

"I've submitted dozens of inventions to defeat the Germans and they've all been murdered! Oh, yes, Mr. President! Strangled in the crib by those assassins in your War Department. The only one with any horse sense is Joe Daniels and sometimes I'm not so sure about him." There was a sputtering pause before the next storm. "Protocol! Then I'll make my own contribution to ending the war – and on my own terms." A second pause and a threatening smile. "Wouldn't you like to know? Good day, sir!"

Edison slammed down the receiver, chortled victoriously, and began mumbling scattershot threats. Mr. Meadowcroft cleared his throat to announce:

"Mr. John Dawkins."

Edison looked up sharply "What? Oh, yes…Dawkins."

Meadowcroft handed John's resume to Edison, relieved John of his pea coat, gingerly hung it on a coat rack as if it were a stool specimen, and departed.

Edison leaned in and took a good, hard look at his newest prospect.

"I've hired several men named Dawkins through the years." John smiled expectantly. Edison continued: "They all quit me."

John dropped the grin. "I'm not a quitter, sir," he vowed.

"Eh-heh," responded Edison, unconvinced. He perused

John's resume and continued to absentmindedly spin the metal whirligig. "What position are you applying for?"

"Cameraman, sir. For your film company. After all, you are the father of the motion picture."

"I'm delighted someone still remembers!" grumbled Edison. John's praise had lit another fire under the old man and he was not to be stopped. "Mayer and Zukor and the rest of those son's-a-bitching trust-busters have high-tailed it out to California," he fumed. "They think they've muscled old Edison out of the game. Nothing doing! I'm going back into production. A whole new slate of two-reelers. Then we'll see. Now, what are your qualifications?"

Distracted by Edison's rant, John hesitated and then plunged ahead. "My major was in science – Ohio State – with a minor in photography."

Edison referred impatiently to John's resume. "Yes, but this says you 'quit' college during your junior year."

John winced. "I took a sabbatical," he replied vaguely.

"For what?"

"The war. I was a combat cameraman for the British Army."

"It wasn't our fight. At least, not then." Edison cocked his head in curiousity, "Why in blazes did you volunteer?"

John paused, trying to find the proper, measured response. "I believed the cause was just."

Edison studied his face intently. "And now you've come marching back home. Don't you believe anymore?"

John dropped his eyes evasively and then leveled with Edison. "It's time for someone else to believe."

Edison considered this. "I see." He noted the time and stood. "I appear to be running behind schedule." The interview was over.

John felt the trickling sweat of failure. He had told the hard truth – why had he done that – and now he'd lost the position. "I have footage I can show you…"

Edison brushed past him. "That won't be necessary."

"But sir, I need this job, I---"

"I'm afraid I'm terribly late," Edison repeated dismissively and slipped into his black wool overcoat.

John took the hint and, downcast, prepared to go.

"But you?" Edison broke into a toothy grin and tossed John his pea coat. "You're right on time."

"You mean I'm hired?"

Edison nodded as he twirled a silk scarf around his neck. "Any man who can survive the Germans *and* the British ought to be able to handle a gaggle of show people." He started out the door and then turned back impatiently. "Come on, come along."

John hurried after him, delighted and perplexed. "Where are we going?"

Edison chortled and slapped John on the back. He could feel the ropes of muscle beneath the worn fabric. The boy was strong. Good! He'd need to be strong.

"To the bright lights of Broadway," the old man exclaimed, and winked raffishly. "To find ourselves a star!"

3

FOLLIES

The top-hat-and-tiara first-nighters were packed into a convivial crush beneath the marquee of the New Amsterdam Theatre as they waited excitedly for the evening's entertainment: the Ziegfeld Follies of 1918. This was Ziegfeld's tenth Follies in as many years and the consensus along Broadway confirmed his reputation as the greatest showman in theatrical history.

However, Ziegfeld's onstage spectacle was rivaled by the display that took place every night before the show, outside the stage door. That particular production starred Emily Auburn, one of the impresario's most glorified American girls. She was routinely delivered to the theatre by a free-wheeling touring car of stage-door Johnnies who were never at a loss for champagne, roses, or diamonds. They constantly showered her with all three and she was worth every single bubble, petal, and karat.

Why? She was beautiful. She always had been, even as a child in the slums of Hoboken. At sixteen, she began her career in vaudeville as the showgirl foil for a pair of baggy-pants comedians. Later she toured the Keith-Albee circuit as a buxom assistant to Harry Houdini. Then, inevitably, Ziegfeld. With each new edition she grew more assured. By the time she landed a star spot, she was a sophisticated lady and a glorious broad all rolled into one. Besides which, she was goddamned fun.

Unlike the standard of the day, her beauty wasn't simply demure, though she could fake it if she had to. It was something rare, even tinged with danger. Her beauty was a dare. Two kinds of men were inclined to take up the challenge. The first was old, foolhardy, and the founder of an old-money bastion. The second was young, foolhardy, and the inheritor of an old-money bastion. It was a game she enjoyed playing, even excelled at, but one she swore she'd give up in a heartbeat if she could find the right man who could go the distance. The score so far? Zilch. All limited engagements. No long runs. In spite of the odds, Emily still hoped that someday her prince would come – but he'd better move his ass. She'd been built for youth and her moment was fleeting.

"Later, boys," Emily ordered the throng of tuxedoed swains. "Mother's got to work." They protested loudly, but not too much, and happily adjourned to the theatre's roof garden for cigars and whoopee as Emily entered the stage door.

Pops Carmichael, the elderly doorman, looked up from his racing form and grinned. "Evening, Miss Emmy."

"Hiya, Pops," she replied as she hiked him a spare bottle of rye and headed to her dressing room through the backstage traffic of stagehands, chorines, and specialty acts.

She heard a nasal voice lifted in song and stopped in the wings to watch as the show's young rehearsal pianist auditioned a new number for anyone who would listen. He hailed from the Russian-Jewish tenements in Brooklyn and this was his first job on Broadway. In Emily's estimation, the reedy, awkward kid (he was only nineteen for crying out loud!) already had the one thing everybody in the business would kill for – the goods. He was born in Brooklyn as Jacob Gershowitz, but on 42nd Street he billed himself as George Gershwin.

Gershwin turned to see Emily and a smile lit up his face. He adored her completely. So what if she'd cast him in the recurring role of kid brother instead of passionate young lover. 'Kid brother' was enough. For now.

"Hey, Emmy, listen to this!"

Swanee
How I love you
How I love you
My dear old, Swanee

"What's the title, son?" asked Will Rogers, the cowboy humorist. Gershwin replied in song:

Swanee,
Swanee,
I am going back to Swanee...

Rogers tapped his boots in tune to the music and a crowd gathered.

"Gersh, it's wonderful," beamed Emily

Gershwin shrugged happily. "You're my muse."

Emily joined in on the second verse:

I'd give the world to be
Back with my folks in
D-I-X-I-E-ven now my Mammy's –

"Whaddaya call that claptrap?" The voice was fat and mean. So was the man it belonged to. As the assistant stage manager for the Follies, Tubby Fisk had just enough clout to make everyone's backstage life more unpleasant than necessary. The crowd began to disperse but Gershwin adamantly played on.

"I call it "Swanee."

"No, no, no," Tubby lectured as he shoved his all-thumbs fingers onto the keyboard and bellowed as he played:

Way down upon the Swanee River...

"Now that's a song," he snorted arrogantly.

Gershwin tightened defensively. "Mine's different." He joked easily about himself but was serious about his talent. In order to open doors, he knew he'd have to break down barriers and was ready to start swinging.

Emily draped a protective arm around Gershwin. "Don't feed the animals."

Tubby hocked up a wad of mucus and rattled a nearby spittoon. "You're late. Again. I'm docking you a week's pay."

"You can't do that," cried Emily.

"It's done."

Tubby tried to make an exit but Emily stepped in front of him, stopping him cold.

"Someday I'll be early," Emily decreed. She gestured to Gershwin. "And someday he'll be a genius. But you, you miserable prick? You'll always be you."

Emily exited and Gershwin signaled her departure with a flourish on the keyboard.

Tubby blustered impotently as the company tittered. He spun on Gershwin. "You're fired!" he roared and waddled off.

Crushed, Gershwin drooped over the keys. His first Broadway show and his career was already over.

Will Rogers laid a sympathetic hand on his shoulder and admitted, "I never met a man I didn't like. Except for that son-of-a-bitch."

* * *

The theater had been a lifelong indulgence for Edison. One might have expected his taste to lean toward serious, probing dramas essayed by renowned authors who were, on the whole, deceased. However, one would have been wrong. Edison adored the musical theatre and wasn't snobbish about the grade; revues, vaudeville, even burlesque when Mrs. Edison was indisposed. It was the sheer exuberance of the performers' drive to entertain that appealed to him and allowed the intensity of his mental prowess to unwind inside the rhythmic cradle of a tune he could hum.

The manager escorted Edison and John to the house box and they took their seats as the lights began to dim. However, it wasn't long before a man in the audience, a feed salesman from Yonkers, looked up and spotted him.

"Hey! Up there! It's Tom Edison!" he hollered.

The crowd turned like a cresting wave and their applause escalated into a roar of welcome. Edison was a legendary figure but, more than that, he had reached a plateau unique in the status of American icons. He had revolutionized the world and lived long enough to enjoy the spoils. While he was not a loveable man by nature, his status commanded something more than respect. It was affection, and he was gratified, even humbled by it.

A crew member turned his spotlight on the box and the crowd wouldn't rest until Edison had acknowledged their ovation. With mock reluctance, the old man rose, raised his hands in a clasp of victory, and then urged the audience to be seated. The conductor approached the podium, offered a courtly bow to Edison and the audience, and cued the downbeat with a drum roll.

4

SKINEHARDT

The drum roll echoed across the ocean to a location the near-opposite of the New Amsterdam Theatre; a place where the sound of tympani didn't signal the promise of an overture but the climax of a finale.

The site was the Reichstag, the parliament of the German empire. Now four years into the Great War, the massive structure served as one of the many wartime enclaves for Kaiser Wilhelm and his entourage of generals. They were all present – Ludendorff, Hindenburg, even the inept Admiral Capelle – each of them pedestaled on a grand balcony overlooking the gardens, dead with frost, as a regiment of soldiers shivered stoically below. The occasion was the dawn execution by hanging of a trio of young soldiers, their pink faces glistening with a slick veneer of snot and tears.

The drum roll, the blindfolds, the cries for mercy, the stricken faces of the regiment witnessing the event; all of these prompted a broad smile on Hindenburg's face.

"A valuable lesson for potential deserters," he counselled the Kaiser.

“Good for morale!” added Capelle; bookend Iagos, the both of them.

The other generals joined in with a chorus of guttural approval. All but one. General Wilhelm Skinehardt.

Yes, now a general. His rise to the high command had been meteoric and wholly based on his willingness to undertake those assignments his peers found beneath the dignity of their station. Yet Skinehardt deemed this exercise in discipline to be an absolute folly. His demurral wasn’t based on sentiment. If anything, the ensuing years had made him even more ruthless. It was simply common sense. The long war had decimated the German fighting force. These soldiers were mere boys; their only crime being that they were too young to know how to kill efficiently. Why not allow them a reprieve to cultivate their capacity for mayhem? The drum roll stopped, the traps were sprung, and the deserters plunged to their doom.

“Good for morale?” muttered Skinehardt cynically. “Good for nothing.”

The Kaiser and his generals retreated into the comforts of the war room, a plush cocoon of gold and velvet where the strategy for battle was fueled by a long marble serving board choked with food and drink. Skinehardt watched with mild interest from an acceptable distance as General Ludendorff, the war’s chief strategist, argued in support of “...a new offensive, beginning in Armentieres and ending in Reims.”

The military men considered Ludendorff’s proposed solution. Although his plan was still lacking in detail, it held promise. By year’s end the war could be over. However, they remained non-committal until the Kaiser passed judgment. The querulous old despot had grown weary of the conflict and its constant intrusion into his practiced tastes for wine, women and song (but mostly women). His sharp teeth wrestled a hank of meat from the bone of a drumstick and he made smacking yips of gluttony as he fretfully shook his head.

"Another year? You told me the same thing a year ago, and the year before that. Ach, it never ends." He tried to lick the goose fat from his considerable white moustache but only succeeded in waxing it into the bristles. "And what about the Americans?"

For a moment, the generals, who always had an immediate, soothing response, were stumped. For years, America had stayed out of the war due to a potent mix of xenophobia and isolationism. However, the torpedoing of the Lusitania had changed all that. True, the Lusitania had been a British ship and, yes, the British claim that it had merely been a passenger vessel was a lie. It was carrying 173 tons of ammunition bound for the Western front. However, the attack had come without warning, and of the 1,198 souls who perished, 128 were U.S. citizens. The Germans maintained the hard line that all waters surrounding the British Isles should be considered a war zone in which any ship, enemy or not, would be destroyed. The price for this hubris was a propaganda disaster that turned the opinion of neutral nations against Germany. President Wilson severed diplomatic relations and asked the Congress to authorize a new policy of armed neutrality that accelerated into a declaration of war. Indeed. What about the Americans?

"Hah!" boasted Admiral Capelle, a ruddy-faced blowhard who ended every sentence with an exclamation mark. "My submarines will sink them!"

"You didn't sink Pershing or his First Division," Hindenburg observed acidly. "They're dry. And in France."

Capelle chewed on his lower lip and tightened his jaw defensively. Hindenburg turned critically to Ludendorff. "And their mobilization has just begun. Two million troops by spring. Won't that complicate your plans?" Ludendorff heatedly joined in and the war of the words escalated.

Skinehardt buried a smile. He enjoyed watching his colleagues carve one another up under the polite guise of debate. However, he didn't let his true feelings show. Truth wasn't a currency of worth in such a toxic enclave. An aide diverted his attention from the squabble by discreetly handing him a telegram. Skinehardt opened it, read the encrypted message with a growing sense of cold pleasure, and gestured for the aide to offer a confidential ear.

"Alert Captain Krill," discreetly ordered Skinehardt. "It's time we paid a visit to Mr. Edison."

The aide nodded and left the room as Skinehardt settled back into his chair and indulged in a moment of ambitious reverie. If the contents of the telegram were correct, then the war might be over far sooner than anyone had a right to suspect. The sharp sound of his own name – "Skinehardt!" – intruded, and he looked up to see the others staring at him intently.

"Your perspective," demanded the Kaiser, "on how to handle the Americans."

Skinehardt approached the serving board and proceeded to answer more candidly than he normally would have dared.

"Their President, Wilson, used to claim America was too proud to fight. Now America is too proud to lose." He speared a hunk of goose flesh, thrust it into his mouth, and savored the seared meat. He understood the power of momentary silence. "Annihilate them," Skinehardt advised matter-of-factly. "Before it's too late."

5

BACKSTAGE

The home-spun wisdom of Will Rogers, the vocal stylings of Marilyn Miller, and the comic golf lesson by W.C. Fields; it all built to the finale starring Emily Auburn in a tribute to 'true love.' She was backed up by the Ziegfeld showgirls who were costumed in an eye-popping assortment of strategically stitched baubles, bangles, and bugle beads.

John watched, transfixed, as Emily commandeered the stage, indiscreetly sheathed in a diaphanous Cupid's outfit that would have made Cupid blush. If Emily's image wasn't compelling enough, her voice, filled with what was known in the trade as 'that come-hither thing,' compounded her star quality.

Baguettes of diamonds
Or rubies
Or pearls by the score
Sparkle, just briefly
For less is truly more...

Everything accelerated now – the pulse of the music, the soaring chorus, and the grandeur of the jewel-box finale, with a multitude of valentine drops embracing the stage. Edison watched attentively as the entire audience leaned forward in anticipation and none more so than John, who was on the edge of his seat. Damn, she was something!

Yes, the most priceless adornment
A girl can acquire...
Is the love of the man

Emily planted her feet downstage center and belted out the finale The entire company echoed her, socking the anthem to the rafters and beyond.

(The one and only man)
She truly adores!

Emily held her final pose amidst the waves of applause. The curtain descended and she was gone, swallowed up by the billowing velour. John bolted up from his seat and triggered a standing ovation.

Onstage, Emily nodded briefly in professional satisfaction and then turned with jaded confidence to the company.

"Truly adores?" Emily snorted. "What a load of hooey!"

Several of the chorus girls nodded with the kind of wisdom that only comes from the hard-knock life, and W.C. Fields wheezed his approval. He liked his women bitter. Then the curtain rose and the waves of hurrahs washed over the cast. Emily accepted the accolades with an unbecoming modesty that was less a curtain call and more of a triumph over the cross.

As the curtain descended for a final time, John found himself still shouting bravos. Edison observed him wryly. "I think," he mused, "we've found our star."

* * *

A dresser slung a robe over Emily's bare shoulders as she navigated the backstage babble and found Gershwin parked at her dressing room piano, dejectedly plunking out 'taps.'

"I'm fired," he offered flatly.

Emily clucked sympathetically. "That fat bastard."

"My first job on Broadway and I'm fired. Now I'll never have a career. It's back to Brooklyn for me."

Emily leaned in and leveled her eyes to his. "Don't sweat it, Gersh. Someday you *will* be a genius."

"But when?" moaned Gershwin.

Emily gave him a supportive kiss on the forehead. "Soon."

As Emily turned to the make-up table to peel off her false eyelashes, he touched the imprint of her kiss and gently pressed it to his lips. Then, once again, reality. "Yeah, but today I'm broke."

"I can spare a few bucks." She fished into her bag but only found two ones and a five. She gave him the five. "Sorry. This month I'm cash poor and accessories rich." It was her natural financial state.

Gershwin didn't want to take the money but he needed it so he did. "I'll pay you back when I'm able," he promised.

Emily fluttered her fingers dismissively and poured a glass of champagne. She downed it, poured another and, as she raised the crystal to her lips, gazed at herself in the make-up mirror. It was a shrine framed with congratulatory telegrams, professions of passion, and invitations to midnight suppers. Funny. Why didn't she see the same fabulous creature that everyone else did? She dumped the bubbly, strangely dissatisfied. "I'm sick of champagne."

An enthusiastic knock at the door interrupted.

"Go home, boys," she brayed. "The only body I want in bed tonight is mine."

The doorknob rattled insistently and Gershwin jumped up to ward off the intruders. "Miss Auburn is unavailable---"

Before he could finish, Edison bulldozed his way into the room, with John behind, and they inadvertently pinned Gershwin between the door and a costume rack. Emily leapt up, chastely tugged her robe around her breasts, and cast a furious look at the two intruders.

"My dear, you were enchanting!" enthused Edison as he handed her his card. "A vision *and* a voice." Then to John: "Wouldn't you agree?"

"Damn right!" he vouched.

Emily took the card, but was more angry than attentive. "Who do you jokers think you are anyway, barging in here? This is my dressing room – and I'm *dressing*!"

"Are we intruding?" posed Edison innocently.

"You bet your ass! And if you two don't blow, I'm gonna call the…" The name on card finally registered. "…*the* Thomas Edison?" she exclaimed with a google-eyed double-take worthy of Eddie Cantor.

Gershwin emerged from behind the door, draped with a feather boa and a lop-sided headdress, but he was more intrigued than miffed.

"The one and only, at your service" replied Edison.

Emily smiled fetchingly, poured herself back into her chair, and provocatively crossed her legs. "To what do I owe the pleasure of your company?"

"I'm in the market for a leading lady. And I know just the candidate," he waggled his finger teasingly.

"I'm not at liberty. Not at the moment," she hedged. "But do tell."

"It's a winter's tale of romance entitled *Honeymoon on Ice*."

She considered the title. It could be changed. "Comedy, drama or musical?"

Edison shook his head. "Oh, no. It's not for the stage. It's a moving picture," he proudly responded. "A two-reeler."

He anticipated the small gasp of approval that usually followed his proclamations. None arrived. Although moving pictures had been heralded as a technological marvel they remained, for theatre people, a poor cousin to the stage.

"Oh. The flickers," Emily dourly muttered to Gershwin.

"By my calculations, at a reel per day," figured Edison, "I'd require your services for two, uh, two and a half days at most."

Emily sighed, weighed her artistic integrity against her purse, and cut to the chase. "How much?"

"What would you say to…five hundred dollars?"

Everyone gulped on cue. Emily knew she wasn't worth five hundred dollars, not for a two-reeler. Nobody was. However, experience had taught her never to question the nature of salvation, especially when it appeared in the guise of a rich, elderly man.

"Why, I believe I'd say 'yes'," she accepted, fluttering her eyelashes. "I assume, Mr. Edison, you'll be helming this enterprise?"

The old inventor shook his head. "I am merely 'the money.'"

He pushed the star-struck John forward. "May I present Mr. John Dawkins? Your director."

John pulled Edison in close. "I thought I was the cameraman," he hoarsely whispered.

Edison shrugged. "Director, cameraman – what's the difference?"

Emily sized up the situation. Edison was too legit to be non-legit, so he was a safe bet. The tall drink of water with him – whatsizname – John – he was a fan. She could handle him.

"While I prefer to associate with established artists, I'm always willing to lend a 'leg up' to new talent," she offered grandly. Gershwin hooted and Emily shot him a disparaging look.

She resumed the negotiation: "However, I'll need a guarantee for expenses. Paid in advance."

Edison paused and then nodded in agreement.

"…and I never appear before ten."

Edison nodded again, although this time the feat was more difficult to manage.

So far, so good. Emily decided to go for broke.

"…and I couldn't possibly deliver the performance you deserve unless I had the proper mood music to inspire me."

She shot Gershwin an unsubtle cue. He slid onto the piano bench as if it were home plate and scoured the keyboard with samples of 'happy' and 'sad.'

Edison considered the terms, turned to John who indiscreetly nixed the deal points, and then confronted the expectant Emily. "How much?"

"Shall we say…?" Emily's grandiose tone made a quick descent to the street. "…a hundred bucks?"

"A hundred bucks!" John and Gershwin found themselves exclaiming in unison.

Instead of erupting in kind, Edison merely offered a shrewd smile and clapped his hands together. "Done!"

* * *

A thick fog had crawled into midtown, blurring the lights on 42nd Street. Edison emerged from the stage door, delighted by his casting coup, followed by John, who was still shaking his head over the exorbitant cost; both of them unaware they were being watched from the shadows.

"One hundred dollars?" exclaimed John. "For two days? For mood music?"

"Yes, I know, but pay it no mind." It wasn't that Edison was easy with money. He'd fight like a tiger if he thought a business combine was cheating him. Rather, he'd learned the secret to a happy life was inconspicuous consumption. Besides which, he had an inkling. "Something tells me that young man's of value," he observed. "And Miss Auburn. And you, John. Most definitely you. Well then – until tomorrow."

The two men shook hands and parted. As Edison started off John remembered to ask – "I'll see you at the office then?"

Edison chuckled and shook his head. "My office is where I make money. My laboratory is where I make magic. Menlo Park."

Edison departed into the electric haze of Broadway and John paused to consider his astonishing stroke of luck. As he sauntered down a darkened side street, he softly whistled with a satisfaction he hadn't known since…well…for a long time.

There was a break in the layers of fog and a knife of moonlight sliced through the mist. It was then that he saw it – an enormous figure in a black cloak whose weird visage stopped John in mid-stride. Trapped in a shaft of light, the hulking creature looked up, revealing a violently misshapen face: mangled red lips, open holes where ears should have sprouted, and a dome of white hair standing straight-up as if in shock. The creature unleashed a threatening hiss and the moonlight shut off. John gasped and heard the creature lumbering away. He gave chase and then stopped, listening for the sound of footsteps. Nothing. Then something. Pulsing bulbs from a nearby marquee danced across a puddle of water, illuminating a metal orb the size of a large egg. John plucked the orb from the puddle and inspected it closely. It was painted blue on one side and gold on the other – and both halves were freckled with blood. Strange.

John shuddered involuntarily, pocketed the orb, and continued off into the night. He hoped he'd never see the likes of that 'creature' again.

But he would.

6

LABORATORY

The next day the fog had chilled into a hard frost that covered the Menlo Park countryside. A taxi deposited John in front of a ramshackle collection of weathered buildings. He approached the main entrance and presented his identification to the guard at the front desk, an indifferent old fellow lodged behind a newspaper.

As the guard checked his credentials, John peered through a pair of swinging doors that revealed the inner workings of Edison's laboratory. His enthusiasm stalled. The 'laboratory' consisted of a stale room of stained walls and antique equipment presided over by a trio of ancient, doddering inventors. Oh, well. A job was a job.

The guard returned John's credentials and he started into the laboratory. The guard lowered his paper and shook his head, the shaking accompanied by a hollow wheeze of air. John spotted the blanket of angry scar tissue that covered the man's throat. He was mute. The guard pointed to a side door marked 'Supplies.' John gestured to the door, uncertain. The guard nodded and pointed again, this time more insistently. John entered the supply closet and pulled the chain on the overhead light to discover…supplies. Very funny. No doubt a first-day gag on the new hire by the old-timers. However, when John grabbed the door handle to leave and found it locked, the joke didn't seem so funny anymore. He rattled the knob forcefully and was ready to shout with false good humor that they'd certainly fooled him, hah-hah, when the supply closet began to hum, then vibrate and, unexpectedly, drop. John steadied himself as the room descended and then, just as abruptly, lurched to a stop. He tensed as the humming returned. But this time, it signaled the release of a series of internal locks and the closet walls unfolded, opening onto…

Edison's *real* laboratory, a jumbled technological maze straight out of Jules Verne, populated by a dozen inventors busily at work on a variety of mind-bending machines. John grinned in eager amazement as he watched Edison scurry from experiment to experiment like a busy bee pollinating each creation with a touch of brilliance. Edison spotted John and hurried over to greet him.

"Welcome!" Edison pumped John's hand and noted the splayed walls of the supply closet automatically re-assembling behind them. "The boys upstairs will have their fun" Edison chuckled. "Next time take the stairs."

John grinned in relief and pointed upwards. "I thought *that* was your laboratory."

"That's what you're supposed to think," retorted Edison. "Once you get your name in the papers everybody wants to take a bite out of you. That's my 'camouflage unit.' Keeps out all the nosy parkers. And if the bastards persist, we invite them in to take a good look. After five minutes they're so bored stiff they never come back."

An alarm sounded. Edison led John over to a group of inventors who were gathered around a large, oblong object.

"Your man up there," observed John. "He's been injured."

Edison nodded. "Acid explosion. Ate out his voice box."

"And the others?"

"My 'pioneers.' Blind, deaf, bones crushed, limbs lost. It was the least I could do. Invention, Mr. Dawkins. On occasion, it's exhilarating. Most often, it's mundane. But it is *always* dangerous."

Edison joined his associates at the coffin-shaped water tank which held two miniature submarines at either end. He reviewed the lead team's development report and nodded.

"Very well, gentlemen, let's give it a whirl." Edison threw a switch and the first submarine released a torpedo aimed directly at the other.

John and the inventors watched intently as the deadly tube propelled through the water. Then Edison threw a second switch and the opposing submarine unleashed its own torpedo. As the second torpedo plowed through the water the outer casing of the guide stud split in two and expelled a sheer metal net that was charged with energy. The undulating mesh honed in on the approaching torpedo, intercepted it, wrapped tightly around the tail, and crippled its trajectory. The torpedo sank to the lower depths where it harmlessly exploded. John laughed in surprise as the inventors burst into hurrahs and Edison pumped the hands of the lead team in congratulations.

"My magnetic torpedo net," Edison advised John. "Of course, this is only a test model. I've nearly finished a life-sized version."

"When will it be ready?" asked John.

"When the goddamn War Department figures out why things *will* work instead of why they won't," grumbled Edison. He had submitted forty-two inventions to the government during the past year and all forty-two had been denied. Could the reason be that his weapons were designed to incapacitate rather than kill? Yes. It could.

Edison swept into another room, this one tufted with padded walls, and John followed, astonished to witness three of the inventors riding a trio of vertical cylinders that not only hovered off the floor but traveled across it as well.

"Unbelievable," murmured John as he inspected the machines. They were pulpits of aluminum, solid in front with a chest-high control panel and open in the rear, with enough room to accommodate a standing driver and passenger. The base featured a powerful compressor and panels of high-pressure air jets that lifted the vehicle off the ground and, when shifted, propelled it forward. A canopy shaped like a halo crowned the top of the cylinder, giving it an ecumenical sheen.

"Hover tubes," explained Edison. "An intriguing but, at present, impractical prospect. We haven't been able to engineer the base compressor to lift the blasted things more than six inches off the ground. That's guaranteed to make for a bumpy trip."

"Seven inches," a voice corrected.

John turned to confront a short, wild-haired man in his middle years with pencils behind both ears and Lord-only-knows-what stained on his jacket, who was the dithering personification of an absent-minded professor.

The twittering figure consulted his notes. "As of, uh, last night – at 6:41 p.m."

"Better," pronounced Edison. "John Dawkins, meet Harry Singer, my chief assistant.

John and Harry shook hands and were in the middle of their greeting when Harry spotted something behind him and abruptly broke off the pleasantries.

"Good God!" he cried, and John turned to see someone aiming a bizarre, oversized weapon at them. As Harry approached, the figure lowered the weapon, revealing…the creature from the night before – still monstrous, but now attired in a domesticated outfit of a white shirt, canvas pants and a vest whose buttons had popped off long ago from the mere act of breathing.

Before John could pull Harry back from sure annihilation, the frizzy little man confronted the colossus, who snarled with low menace.

"Give it to me. Now!" The thing refused. Harry yanked the weapon out of the creature's grip and slapped it on the wrist. John gasped in surprise when, instead of ripping the little man apart, the behemoth merely whined.

Edison placed a comforting hand on the creature's arm. "Now, now…you know you're not supposed to play with the machines."

Suddenly, he spotted a calamity about to occur in an adjoining supply area. "Look out there, boy!" Edison shouted, and loped towards a young trainee who was carting an open barrel of white, oily powder. Edison pointed accusingly at the barrel. "Move the concentrated oleum *away* from the water tank – and for heaven sakes, *don't* get any on your skin!" The shame-faced trainee pivoted the barrel to a new location but Edison became even more agitated. "No, no, not by the sugar! Put it someplace safe…next to the cyanide."

John marveled at the dazzling stockpile of exotic chemicals

and minerals, which included a pirate's bounty of precious gems.

"My supply chamber," boasted Edison. "Everything from gold to goldenrod."

John interrupted his wonder to pull Edison aside and gesture discreetly toward the monster "Sir, that 'creature' was lurking outside the theatre last night. And I found this…" John withdrew the egg-shaped orb from his pocket. Before he could give the object to Edison, the creature's huge hand clamped onto John's arm with a vise-like grip, took the orb, and returned it to its rightful place – its left eye socket.

"May I introduce Gaunt," offered Edison. "My personal factotum. Odd jobs and the like."

John was dumbstruck. "This…thing is your employee?" Gaunt growled defensively. Edison calmed them both.

"I found him during a uranium expedition in the wilds of Saskatchewan. The poor fellow was more dead than alive. I nursed him back to health, and he's shown his appreciation in a variety of ways. He's an unusual soul, but I assure you, completely devoted and no threat to anyone I call friend."

Harry Singer rushed up to them, hugging the weapon in his arms. "Set and ready."

Edison nodded and they entered a testing chamber. As Gaunt willingly took his place execution-style against the far wall, Edison confided to John, "My latest, ignored creation for the War Department. It combines electricity with water; cheaper than bullets and far less permanent. I call it the 'H2Ohm,' in tribute to the late, great Mr. Ohm."

Harry Singer, outfitted in goggles and a rubber overcoat, checked to make sure the weapon was fully charged. "Primed!"

The other inventors took cover as Harry aimed the weapon at Gaunt.

Edison nodded. "Voltage!"

Harry activated the weapon and the stream of mist combined with the spirals of current to electrify the giant; an assault potent enough to disarm an ordinary man. Gaunt shivered in pain but stoically withstood the attack.

"Maintain," ordered Edison. He shook his head incredulously. "Amazing constitution."

However, Harry did not maintain. Either he failed to hear Edison above the crackling din of the electricity or was so carried away by the experiment that he allowed the voltage to increase. Gaunt didn't cry out, but his metal eye began to slowly rotate, flashing gold, then blue, until it spun into a blur of color.

As wisps of smoke began to rise up from Gaunt's scalp, Edison realized the experiment had gone too far and severed the power. Gaunt collapsed on his knees with a thud, heaving for air, and his metal eye slowed its rotation, finally resting in an awkward mix of half blue-half gold. Edison checked the voltage levels and was appalled to discover that Gaunt had withstood a lethal amount of current.

"Reduce the maximum output to stun – and lock it," he brusquely ordered the chastened Harry and then offered a grateful hand to Gaunt. "My deepest thanks. Your contribution has been invaluable."

Gaunt moaned his appreciation but, unseen by the others, turned his half-blind gaze to the oblivious Harry. His features contracted into a mask of fury – and the metal eye clicked defiantly back into place.

Edison and John resumed their tour of the laboratory. After a moment, John stopped him, overcome by the magic of the place. "This is all so…it's extraordinary," he sputtered. "You're a brilliant scientist!"

Edison puffed up with mock indignation. "Sir, I'm an inventor! If I was a scientist, I never would have invented anything!" Edison offered a sly smile. "Except excuses."

The young trainee appeared and whispered in Edison's good ear.

"Excellent!" announced Edison. "The players have arrived."

7

REHEARSAL

John and the film crew were assembled behind the camera to record the first scene from *Honeymoon on Ice*, a movie whose title could be construed as either exhilarating or frigid. At present, frigid had the edge.

"And…action," said John.

In the background, Gershwin began improvising romantic music as Emily enacted a melodramatic love scene with her on-screen paramour, Percy Blythestone, a pompous English actor.

"Your lips, your eyes of blue," Percy over-enunciated as he stared past Emily's eyes and into an off-camera mirror held by his dedicated young valet to check the line of his jaw. Not defined enough. He sucked in his cheeks. Better.

"Be careful, my darling, or you'll drown in those pools," replied Emily, trying to lift the ersatz emotion into something approaching true love, but instead overacting.

"Gladly," cried Percy as he gave Emily a chaste kiss.

John regarded them, underwhelmed. "And…cut."

As the hair and make-up team freshened the actors, John

quickly identified the problem. Although Edison had a fine eye for beautiful leading ladies, his choice of leading men was often sabotaged by his ear. Percy was a West End actor trained in the Shakespearean style who had migrated to Broadway due to what Scotland Yard termed "a crime of unnatural ardor" in a public lavatory. Since then, he had enjoyed a middling but consistent career in a series of drawing-room comedies. Percy was, as one critic had observed, 'a wonderful actor from the tonsils up.' His face was still handsome, his dialogue beautifully enunciated. However, he was also short, running to fat, and bald; facts made clear as the crew adjusted his wig, corset, and the riser box he needed to stand on to gain equal footing with Emily.

John rallied. "This time let's try to make it more…"

"Passionate?" queried Percy.

"Real," countered John. "If it's real, it'll be passionate."

John retreated behind the camera. Percy sniffed imperiously. "Well! I've never had any complaints."

Wise to her co-star's deficiencies, Emily thought about the money. "Me neither, honey."

As the set prepared for take two, Percy's valet spritzed his throat with an atomizer of clove-tinged gargle. "Me, may, ma, mo, moo," trilled Percy.

Emily rolled her eyes at Gershwin, who stifled a chuckle.

John took a deep, hopeful breath. "And…action!"

* * *

Above the studio's cathedral ceiling was one of the original buildings in the laboratory's complex, a rambling storage structure that now served as the home for Gaunt. 'Home' was something of a misnomer, for the space was the opposite of inviting. There was a bed, a chair, and a phonograph. However, for Gaunt, the accommodations were luxurious and the space featured something of even greater value – a collection of floor grates that looked down on any number of rooms in the subterranean facility. Gaunt liked to watch. Today he watched Emily. As the sweet sound of her voice wafted up from below, the smitten giant pressed his drooling face against the grate. His metal eye clicked from gold to blue and he moaned longingly.

* * *

Below, John watched another lame, perfunctory kiss in growing frustration.

"Cut. I admit, I'm no deMille. But this is supposed to be a moment of true love and I'm not buying it."

Emily batted her eyes mischievously. "Why don't you show us?" she suggested, baiting him. "After all, you *are* the director. Or is it the cameraman?"

Percy picked up the scent of blood in the water. "Yes, I'd welcome the lesson," he added fatuously. "I'm sure we'd all get the benefit."

John modestly accepted the dare, waited for Percy to descend to ground level, and then took his place in the scene. He kicked the diminutive actor's riser against the wall, pulled Emily into his arms, and bowed his face to hers, breathing in the scent of her perfumed skin. Emily was startled, not so much by John's actions but rather by the speed in which he achieved them. Now here she was, wrapped in his arms and, surprisingly, not offended by the proximity.

"Your lips, your eyes of blue." John stared deeply into Emily's eyes of, yes, blue.

Emily tried to dismiss his amorous intensity but found she could not. "Be careful my darling or you'll, uh, drown in those pools," she gabbled.

John leaned closer, his lips breathlessly caressing hers, his long muscles flexing against her curves in concert with their every breath. "Gladly…gladly…"

John kissed Emily, softly at first, and then with a mounting hunger. In spite of herself, Emily responded deeply as the cast and crew looked on in rapt silence.

"Cut!" Gershwin heard himself exclaim. "For crying out loud, cut!"

John broke the kiss, briskly called, "Five minutes," and released Emily, whose unexpected case of knock-knees threatened to dump her on her ass.

As John left the set with a roguish smile on his face, the outraged Gershwin and Percy flanked the happily-dazed Emily.

"The nerve of that amateur," blistered Percy. "The crust!"

"Yeah," added Gershwin. "Who does he think he is?"

Emily toweled off her smeared lipstick. "He may not be deMille – but he sure can kiss."

The company went on break and, after they'd departed, a faint but injured moan echoed throughout the studio. It was the sound of jealousy, and the spatters of drool dripping onto the set indicated that it came from somewhere above and dangerously within reach.

8

ORE-SEPARATOR

By day's end, all the interior scenes had been completed. Emily was excellent, Percy improved, and Gershwin's underscoring had surprisingly coaxed the appropriate emotions of hearts and flowers from the company.

John adjourned to an isolated area of the laboratory where he was finalizing the set-ups for the next day's exteriors when Harry Singer scuttled around a corner. Harry's furtive manner suggested intrigue and, curious, John followed him down a maze-like hallway of oddball lines and angles.

Based on the sound of Harry's footsteps, John was gaining on him but, as he turned the last corner, ran into the dead end of a brick wall; surprised to find the wild-haired little man had disappeared. Remembering his initial entrance via the storage closet, John checked the bricks for a hollow wall. None. Solid. More puzzled than disappointed, he started to leave and inadvertently brushed against a lighting sconce. It moved. John gripped the fixture, jiggled it from side to side, and then turned it upside down. The action unlocked a vertical seam in the bricks and the wall slid open on opposite tracks to reveal…

Edison's *secret* laboratory. Of course, John didn't know it was a secret laboratory. Edison would confirm that fact at a later date. For now, the differences between this laboratory and the others were as follows: It was (1) isolated, (2) warm, hot even, fueled by a quartet of furnaces and, (3) dominated by a huge contraption in the middle of the room that was covered in a muslin shroud.

John contemplated the masked object and felt the hairs on the back of his neck rise to attention. Why? He had to find out. He yanked the billowing sheet to the floor and stood in astonishment before what appeared to be a life-sized, full-throttled version of Edison's miniature sphere.

The dazzling machine was designed in a collusion of the Victorian and Industrial styles with two unique additions to Edison's pocket-sized model. The brass skin of the machine was studded with thousands of tuning forks that sparkled brilliantly. Also, two tufted passenger seats encased in thick glass bubbles were featured on opposite sides of the gimbal. It appeared to John that the invention was some kind of vehicle. But to where, and to what end?

From the corner of his eye, John spotted a blinking green button. It was housed on a control panel that sat off to the side of the machine. He inspected the buttons and dials and couldn't make head nor tail of the lot. Probably best to leave it alone. Yet the green light continued to pulse and the machine glistened seductively. Intrigued, he punched the button.

The machine shuddered to life. The outer frame and the gimbal began to turn in opposite directions. Tempted, John jumped into one of the passenger seats as the machine began to pick up speed. What the devil was this invention? He was about to find out.

A warning bell sounded and the passenger bubble

automatically locked down, trapping John inside. As the machine continued to accelerate, spurts of electrical current triggered the tuning forks to revolve and hum, faster and faster, until the hum intensified into an eerie, piercing wail. Concerned, John reached for what appeared to be the vehicle's emergency brake and pulled, but the damn thing stuck. As he fumbled impotently, trying to pry the brake into position, the machine kicked into top drive, blurring the room and dulling even the details of the machine itself. The yowl of the tuning forks and sheer speed of the thing were overwhelming. Then he saw it. In the core of the machine. He blinked and strained his eyes. A shadow – shifting, evolving. Suddenly, the machine skidded to a violent stop. John cracked his head against the glass bubble and blacked out.

He stirred, squinted, and saw the hazy figures of Edison and Harry Singer floating above him. The sting of a hard slap revived him and John discovered he'd been pulled from the machine and was lying on the laboratory floor.

"Hells bells, Mr. Dawkins!" cried Edison. "What do you think you're doing?"

John knew he should be embarrassed or even frightened by what he'd just experienced but he was too damned excited.

"I'm sorry, sir," offered John. "I was looking for Mr. Singer and I found this extraordinary invention and…my God, what is it?"

"Oh, well, um…it's uh…uh." Edison faltered. He rarely faltered. "It's an ore-separator. Yes, that's right," Edison unconvincingly decreed.

John recalled the ore-separator as one of the great man's rare failures. In theory, it was a complex maze of magnets, rollers and belts intended to separate precious metals such as gold and magnetic iron ore from common minerals. In practice, the contraption proved to be such a financial debacle that it had all but ruined Edison.

"But I thought that---"

"Young man, what you think has no bearing on the matter. I've been slaving over this, uh, machine, for nearly thirty years. And I tell you, it separates ore!"

John cast his eyes to the floor, shamed, and nodded tightly. Then Edison leaned in with an eager curiosity he could no longer suppress. "How'd she ride?"

John burst into a grin. "As slick as soap!"

Edison slapped his thigh and turned to Harry Singer, cackling proudly. "I knew it!"

John joined in Edison's contagious enthusiasm, and then soberly offered, "But the hand brake sticks something fierce."

"The what? Oh, yes! The, uh, jettison lever. I suspected as much." Edison consulted Harry. "We'll have to re-configure the base to accommodate the release mechanism."

"And why is it so hot in here?" continued John.

"To reach maximum transference, the temperature has to be kept at a minimum of ---"

A warning glare from Harry brought Edison down to earth.

He harrumphed and turned authoritatively to John. "You have no business here, sir. Leave. Now. And be quick about it."

John nodded, chastened. "My apologies." John turned to go and went but Edison continued to harangue him for good measure.

"Get back to work! You hear? And, you are never to enter this room again!"

John left. Edison sighed. Harry sidled up to him.

"Who is this new man? Can he be trusted?"

Edison shrugged. "I don't know. He may just be another 'Dawkins.' Or he might be the one."

Harry cocked his head curiously. "The one what?"

Edison paused. Harry Singer had been his chief assistant for the past year and a half. He was very capable, a bit of an oddball, yes, but then 'oddball' was a common character trait among inventors. Edison trusted him. But not with everything. Not with this.

"Nothing. Never mind."

Harry regarded Edison for a moment, knew there was something he wasn't being told, and accepted it. He nodded slightly and then peered dubiously over his glasses. "An ore-separator?"

Harry tittered, Edison guffawed, and within moments they were both howling like schoolboys.

9

AND...ACTION!

In the early days of filmmaking, weather was not a critical factor when it came to the photography of exteriors. Granted, sunny skies were always preferred but the goal was not the cosmetic purity of the cinematography. It was simply to record the moving images in a recognizable fashion. However, as the company prepared to shoot the final scenes at Black River Junction, the weather proved to be, per the script, bright and bracing.

The cast and crew had assembled on the bank of the frozen river and were all outfitted with skates in order to complete the sequence more efficiently. This served as a boon to John who could navigate the set with speed, as well as for Emily who had skated since she was a child and elegantly etched a figure eight around the other players. However, skates proved a detriment to the hapless Percy, who had to have his riser outfitted with runners, and to Gershwin who, while flailing awkwardly across the ice, oddly never lost his balance. Emily applauded as he haphazardly made his way through a group of extras and skidded into her arms.

"That's the ticket!" she enthused.

Gershwin grimaced. "Ice is for fish, not for travel."

Emily turned to the make-up table, applied a fresh coat of lipstick, and inspected her features in a hand mirror. Lovely enough. However, as she lowered the mirror, she found herself face to face with Gaunt. Startled, she tried to hide her reaction to the creature's misshapen features.

Gaunt offered her a withered nosegay of dried flowers and struggled to speak. "You – are – beauty."

Emily knew what to do. She accepted the flowers, batted her eyes, and smiled flirtatiously. "Thanks, big boy. You're not so bad yourself."

Gaunt whined bashfully and lumbered off. Gershwin was aghast.

"He's hideous!"

Emily gave a jaded shrug. "I've seen worse."

"Places!" shouted John.

The company took their positions. Emily skated to her mark and palmed the mirror off to John with glacial indifference. He frowned and put the mirror in his coat pocket. Maybe he'd gone too far with the kiss but, hell, she'd challenged him, hadn't she? Damn right. And besides, he couldn't resist. She was something else.

Emily joined Percy and watched as John prepared for the first take. She'd been a fool to let him gain the upper hand. She'd lost control, and she made it a point never to lose control. It always ended badly. However, she had to admit there was something thrilling about not being completely in charge, especially when the man sharing the reins was someone you could possibly… Emily stopped thinking. The shoot was almost over and they'd all go their separate ways. It was enough to say he was something else.

John peered into the camera's eyepiece. "And… action!"

Gershwin began playing a waltz as the crew dragged the stationary Percy across the ice and around Emily, simulating a dexterity he did not possess.

"The great outdoors," he trilled. "Bright and bracing!"

"And yet the winter seems warm," responded Emily.

She opened her arms for their final embrace, but the crew misjudged the angle and Percy flew past her and out of the frame.

"Cut," said John, with good-natured resignation. Everyone, even Percy, chuckled at the gaffe.

However, while they laughed and John ordered, "Again… quickly," the eye of the camera registered something they failed to see: three tiny, sparkling objects dancing in the distance.

Emily and Percy took their places. John peered through the lens.

"And…action!"

Percy curled smoothly around Emily. "The great outdoors. Bright and bracing!" He hit his mark, they kissed, and then skated out of frame.

John blinked. In camera, he spotted the three strange objects moving towards them at deliberate speed. What the hell? He zoomed in and focused. The hover tubes! Each one manned by a pilot and accompanied by a gunman; one of whom aimed a dart gun directly at John and fired.

John flinched back from the camera as the dart smashed through the lens, nearly skewering his eye.

The hover tubes attacked, unleashing a barrage of darts that sent the cast and crew crashing to the ice.

John rushed through the chaos to Emily and Gershwin and

shoved them behind the temporary shelter of the upended make-up table.

"This isn't in my script!" protested Emily.

"Is this improvisation?" cried Percy indignantly as he slid by on his riser. "I can't abide improvisation!"

With that, a dart improvised its way into his neck. Percy hit the ice hard and slid to a stop in front of them.

John knelt over the fallen actor and screwed the dart out of his flesh. A thick, green substance oozed from the hollow tip. He checked Percy's vital signs.

"He's not dead," confirmed John. "He's drugged."

A piercing whistle whizzed towards them. John grabbed a film can and thrust it in front of Emily's face, blocking a dart from stabbing her in the cheek. As she gasped in gratitude, he pocketed the dart and tried to formulate some kind of strategy as the hover tubes picked off the remaining filmmakers and circled back, recharging their engines for a second assault.

"Go!" John yanked Emily and Gershwin to their feet and pushed them down river, skating mightily to give them a head start. They approached a double-fork in the river and John gauged the opposite sides of the shore.

"Stay close to the riverbank," he advised. "It'll slow 'em down."

"What about you?" Emily asked.

John committed to a course of action. "I'll take the center of the river and draw their fire."

They'd been spotted. The hover tube pilots gunned their engines, eager for the energy cylinders to recharge to maximum power. With seconds to spare, Emily gave John an impulsive kiss.

John grinned and took off. Emily gazed after him.

"What a man," admired Emily.

Gershwin shrugged. "Aww, you've seen one Adonis, you've seen 'em all."

The hover tubes geared into action. Emily shoved Gershwin in the direction of the east tributary and she took off into the west.

* * *

The pilot on the lead hover tube signaled his strategy to the team. He'd track John and the other two would split their pursuit; one gun on Emily, the other on Gershwin. They parted company and the lead tube accelerated into overdrive.

John saw the leader gaining on him and increased his speed. Despite his prowess as a skater, he realized he couldn't continue to outpace his pursuers. With nothing but ice and more ice surrounding him, he tried to figure a way out, but his concentration was interrupted by the slapping of his coat pocket against his thigh. He reached inside and found the make-up mirror and the dart. John quickly recalled a cardinal rule from his college days on the gridiron: The best defense is a good offense.

He dug the drag picks on his skates into the ice, ground to a stop, and pivoted onto a collision course with the hover tube. The pilot and gunman chortled at his reckless move. The pilot aimed the flying vehicle straight at John and the gunman trapped him in his sights. However, before he could take his shot, John withdrew the mirror, reflected the sunlight into the gunman's eyes, blinded him, and hurled the dart into his chest. It burrowed into the man's ribcage with such force that he toppled off the tube and smashed onto the ice.

The startled pilot circled back to retrieve his fallen partner. However, a crucial defect of the hover tubes was that they were awkward to turn and required a wide arc. The delay gave John the edge he needed. He leapt onto the hover tube and attacked the pilot, who lost control of the machine. As the tube spun wildly the men slugged it out, with John's opponent gaining the upper hand and knocking him to his knees.

Dazed and bleeding, John tried to gather his wits as the pilot withdrew a pistol and aimed it at his head. John slowly raised his hands in surrender and, as he did, spotted the control panel. The pilot muttered something he didn't understand (in German?) and cocked his pistol. That last part John understood. He swiftly secured himself to a rung on the hover tube with one hand and, with the other, switched the power off.

The machine slammed to a stop, the force sling-shotting the pilot across the ice. John righted the hover tube and turned it back on. As the energy cylinder powered up, he examined the other elements of the control panel, which included an emergency button (although what benefit it might provide remained a mystery) and an arsenal of loaded dynamite guns. The cylinder jets recharged, John opened up the throttle and powered down river to save Emily and Gershwin.

10

PURSUIT

Up until now, Emily and Gershwin hadn't been in need of saving. Emily took John's advice and veered close to the riverbank. Since the tubes were limited to a lift of seven inches, they had to cautiously navigate the stray tree roots and fallen limbs that jutted up from the ice. As for Gershwin, while he cut a comical figure flailing across the frozen river, his awkwardness was his salvation because he proved to be a damned hard target to hit. However, they were both growing cold and tired and, more ominously, the two tributaries were re-uniting, bringing them into a dangerous, focused line of sight.

As the forks converged, the gunmen from the two remaining tubes signaled each other, loaded their dynamite guns, and fired. The flaming sticks soared into the air and landed in front of Emily and Gershwin, demolishing the ice on the banks and corralling them into the center of the river.

John heard the explosion and, as he approached the junction, saw the vehicles were gaining on Emily and Gershwin, who navigated the blasts as best they could in spite of the continuing salvos of flying dynamite.

Gershwin turned back to see both gunmen aim their weapons in the same direction and fire simultaneously. A dual explosion opened a gaping hole in front of them. Gershwin knew he couldn't stop in time, so he bravely grabbed Emily's arm and swung her out of harm's way. She spun off as Gershwin plowed into the river.

"Gersh!" screamed Emily. She doubled back to pull him out but a new explosion blocked her path and created a sudden surge of water that sucked the flailing Gershwin under the ice. There was nothing she could do. Nothing but go. With a furious burst of adrenaline, she shot down river, surprising her pursuers. One tube gave chase and the other stopped at the spot where Gershwin had disappeared. The gunman jumped out of the vehicle and found the boy at a break in the ice, holding tight to a branch that was half-submerged, half-exposed. The gunman turned triumphantly to the pilot and they exchanged cruel smiles. Their orders were 'shoot to stun – not kill,' but this young whelp was expendable. The gunman grabbed hold of the branch with both hands and sadistically twisted it out of the ice. Gershwin lost hold of his lifeline and became a captive to the current.

Unsure of what to do, John remembered the hand mirror in his coat pocket. He smashed it, jammed the largest shard of glass into a lit stick of dynamite, and fired. The dagger plunged into the gunman's back. He frantically tried to dislodge the sizzling explosive but his grasp came up short. The pilot leapt out of the tube to help his partner but before he could reach him, the gunman detonated, his innards spewing across the ice.

John pivoted his hover tube past the stunned pilot in search of Gershwin. He spied a large ice bubble that bloated above the lake's surface. Gershwin was beneath the frigid hollow, gulping at the trapped air. Although the current eventually yanked him down river, the saving grace of the air bubble gave John an idea. He began firing sticks of dynamite in front of Gershwin's path, punching a series of holes in the ice that were big enough to provide him with a few sustaining breaths of air.

* * *

Due to years of dance class, Emily was able to scour the ice in a series of leaps and pirouettes that forced the pilot to slow his vehicle to maintain a credible pursuit.

John spotted her dead ahead and considered his options. If the choice between saving Emily or Gershwin wasn't fraught enough, the pilot from the second tube had returned with a vengeance and slammed his machine against John's. The combatants flayed at each other, their vehicles grinding together like flying chariots.

John's dilemma interrupted Emily's focus and her right skate tripped over an exposed tree root. She lost her footing and somersaulted across the ice. Before she could recover, the tube was upon her and the gunman slammed the butt of his rifle against the back of her neck, knocking Emily out. As the pilot helped drag her onboard, Gershwin drifted past, his hands clawing at the ice for any opening, but his determination to survive evaporating.

John realized he'd have to initiate a loss to gamble for a win. He slugged the pilot into a daze, hooked the two machines together, sparked the fuses on the remaining sticks of dynamite, and locked the accelerator. He leapt off and staggered to his feet as the hover tubes careened down river and exploded, blasting a crater in the ice. Gershwin popped up from his frozen tomb and gagged for air.

John pulled him to safety. He was numb with cold but, miraculously, unhurt. John wrapped his coat around the shaking Gershwin and shoved him onto the riverbank.

"Get help," John ordered. He took off to save Emily as Gershwin gamely crawled toward land.

* * *

Emily's captors roped her hands to the vehicle's guard rail. As they powered up the cylinder jets, they failed to see she'd regained consciousness and was calculating her next move. She spied the gunman mentally undressing her. She moaned in response and he lasciviously bent over her body, licking his lips in lust. She thrust her right leg up in a perfect high-kick, dug the serrated skate blade into his chin, and yanked it out. As the gunman tried but failed to stanch the wound, Emily shoved her feet against his backside and toppled him onto the ice.

The pilot aimed his dart gun at Emily but she kicked it out of his hands, fending him off with her skates as she untangled her bonds and he tried to keep the hover tube on track. She looped the rope around his neck and they struggled mightily as the vehicle veered near the riverbank. The base bounced along the uneven surface and an upcoming bramble of jutting limbs signaled catastrophe. The tube slammed into the thicket and catapulted into the air, whipping the pilot out of the machine and slugging the vehicle against the ice where it fell on its side, skidded against the frosted surface, and came to a stop in the middle of the river.

Emily was thrown clear of the machine and appeared to be unconscious but alive. However, the cumulative effect of the explosions had breached the structural integrity of the river's surface, with sheets of ice breaking off into floes.

John was too late. The surface surrounding Emily and the hover tube split off and started to drift down river. He abandoned all caution, gave a running start, and launched himself into the air. He landed on a see-sawing floe, steadied himself, and began the perilous journey of hop-scotching across the crazy quilt of bobbing ice.

* * *

Gershwin staggered up an inland bluff. His legs were still unsteady and his arms felt like lead, but the malady that most concerned him was the rushing sound that rang in his ears, no doubt a side-effect from being submerged in the freezing current. As he reached the top of the bluff, he found no sign of civilization but was rewarded with a majestic view of the river winding its way in a series of curlicues through the countryside. However, he quickly discovered the rushing sound wasn't due to an injury but the roaring waters of Black River Falls, a descent of some thirty feet – and John and Emily were headed straight for it.

* * *

John reached Emily's side and shook her out of her stupor. She revived and kissed him, as much from relief as passion. Then she remembered: "Gersh!"

"He's safe," comforted John. "Can you stand?"

Emily nodded cautiously and he helped her up. She could

stand. She thought that, with a man like John by her side, she could do anything. Then there was no more time for thinking.

The ice floe curled round the bend, picking up speed and, for the first time, they saw the approaching falls in the distance. Emily clung tightly to John.

"We're goners." she whispered.

"Not today," he vowed.

John lifted the hover tube back onto its base and they climbed onboard. He tried to restart the machine. Dead. He pressed the emergency button. Nothing. It wouldn't deploy unless the machine was operational. John pried open the engine's punctured casing and searched through the maze of wires as the ice floe careened closer to the lip of the falls; a drop that ended in a riverbed clustered with razored spears of ice.

"Hurry," thought Emily and then heard herself say it, then shout it.

John fumbled through the guts of the engine. He found a severed wire and knew it had to have a twin. He located the other wire, twisted the ends together and threw the go switch, bringing the machine back to life. He wrapped his arms around Emily and, as the rapids shot them out over the shelf of the falls, pushed the emergency button.

A parachute shot up from the crown of the vehicle's canopy ring and the flooring disc jettisoned with it, carrying them up and away from the hover tube as it crashed, impaled on the spikes of ice and rock below.

The parachute drifted them toward the safety of the riverbank. They leapt into the shallow water and made their way onto a sliver of land where they staggered through a frigid paste of frost and mud. A hand reached out to lift John onto the shore and, thinking it was Gershwin's, he gladly took it. He looked up too late to see that the hand belonged to a bear of a man whose most distinguishing characteristic was his head, bald and pale, the neck ribbed with thick rolls of fat, and the face sporting a sadistic, jack-o-lantern grin. The grin was the last thing John saw before he was fisted with a punch so strong it plunged him into darkness.

II

KRILL

The dream always began with clouds. Most dreamers associate clouds with the sensation of falling. However, John never fell. He rose steadily until he had shed all constraints of consciousness. This time, he'd soared so effortlessly from the pursuit on the ice to the journey inside his mind, he wondered if the clouds were banks of snow. No. They were the same familiar clouds that lurked in his subconscious and propelled him into a personal landscape of nightmares.

The images came at him in sections, with the only difference being now they were framed within the spinning skeleton of the ore-separator. Odd. Most of what he witnessed consisted of the usual combat horrors of mud, blood, and mangled flesh. Then the images accelerated until John found himself cast as a voyeur in a gauntlet of rooms.

The first room was a flophouse. A distinguished but dissolute gentleman in evening clothes sat in a drunken sprawl, polishing a pistol. When the weapon gleamed sufficiently he popped on his top hat, wrapped his lips around the muzzle, and fired. The force of the bullet split his head in two and peeled back the flesh around his mouth like an exploding cigar.

The second space was an elegant bedroom. A hysterical woman thrashed wildly in her sickbed, immune from the attempts of her physician, nurses, and various family members to subdue her. Her frenzy of grief was so intense that it veered into the environs of madness. Suddenly, the woman froze, stared dead ahead at something only she could see, and unleashed a shriek so terrifying it curdled the blood of everyone within shouting distance.

The third room was the parlor of a funeral home. The caskets of the man and woman had been opened and propped up on slant boards, as per the custom of the day, for the final viewing and a photographic remembrance. In repose, the woman retained a beauty her dementia had failed to disfigure. The man was another matter. While one could tell he had an athletic form in life, no amount of mortician's skill could properly reassemble his face which remained a crater of rot. To protect the mourners from such a hideous sight, a velvet mask had been draped beneath his eyes to hide the gaping hole. The ploy failed for it prompted the mourners to imagine even greater horrors beneath the fabric.

A young boy approached, too stunned from grief to weep. Bereft, he reached out and touched their hands, hoping that somehow they would find a way to touch him back. The hands remained lifeless, dead hooks whose only hold was on his heart.

As the boy turned to go, the hands reached out, resting on his shoulders as if to comfort him. He felt their touch and turned back in welcome. They caressed him, his father's palm cupping his cheek, his mother's nails combing his hair. The boy closed his eyes. Content. Home.

Then the caresses became more insistent until the fingers were clutching him into their grasp. The boy shouted and tried to pull away but they had him now, their hands muffling his mouth and sight, except for one eye that peered through a gap in their assault. His gaze settled on a child's coffin. The boy fought, panicked, as the hands carried him toward the silk-lined box, pinned his flailing body inside, and bolted the lid shut.

John panicked, too. As the designated witness to this relentless horror he had the power to make it stop, to wake up, but not this time. He required an intervention.

* * *

It arrived; a second blow that brought John back to consciousness. His eyes burst open to confront the leering grin of the bald bastard who'd slugged him on the riverbank. His assailant's name was Schurke, a professional brute whose only goals in life were to follow orders and inflict pain. He enjoyed his work.

John forced himself to focus, and discovered he was back inside Edison's secret laboratory – drenched, skates still on his feet – and that he'd been chained to the base of the ore-separator with Emily, Gershwin, and Harry Singer.

"What happened?" asked John, still in a daze.

"We thought you were dead," whispered Gershwin.

"All of a sudden you started shouting, and joy boy here paid you a wake-up call," explained Emily. She crooked her head toward Schurke, who guarded a bulky burlap bag at his feet.

John rattled his head.

"Are you sure you're all right?" pressed Emily.

John nodded, groggy but game. "Never better."

Gershwin indicated the half-dozen other intruders in the

laboratory. "Who are these *mamzers*?"

John considered the men. They were dressed in unobtrusive street clothes and dutifully took notes as they examined the ore-separator. He shook his head. He turned to Harry Singer, who was a tangle of nerves.

"Where's Mr. Edison?"

"I don't know," whined Harry. The last thing I remember was…" Harry shakily pointed across the room to a lean, ramrod figure in a black trench coat and a matching homburg hat. "Him."

Captain Gottfried Krill turned to inspect his prisoners. A cruel cadaver of a man, his face boasted three memorable characteristics. The first was a scar that had been gouged from his left temple to his chin, the effect enhanced by a botched surgery that had caved in his cheek and left a string of fissures, suggesting the wound had been stitched with fishhooks instead of sutures. The second were the slivers of metal that studded the soft flesh around his right eye. The captain would have you believe they were the souvenirs from a glorious battle when, in truth, they were the result of a mishap in a steel mill during his youth. No matter. These two keepsakes of non-combat provided him with the unnerving edge he desired in warfare, especially when the conflict was face-to-face.

However, the third item was not an infliction but a device. It was a monocle with a razored orbit attached to a reel line anchored to a metal compartment on the captain's wrist. When required, the monocle fit snugly and painlessly into the metal studs around his right eye. When at ease, the captain retracted the monocle by pushing a button near his wrist. The line would snap, yanking the monocle back into the compartment with a sharp crack that never failed to provide Krill with a shiver of pleasure. However, this was more than John or the others would ever learn. The captain had no intention of explaining the mechanics of his monocle, the myth of his injuries, or the reason for his visit.

Captain Krill's examination of his captives was interrupted when two of the intruders escorted an injured man into the laboratory. John recognized him as the lead pilot whom he'd left stranded on the ice. The pilot had difficulty standing, let alone walking, but managed an uneasy salute as the captain considered his fate.

"You incompetent!" spat Krill. He gestured contemptuously to the captives. "Beaten by these bumblers." The pilot lowered his head in shame. The captain drilled in harder. "Your men are all dead!" Krill turned away in disgust from the lead pilot and then continued with an air of dangerous nonchalance. "And now there's more bad news…"

The pilot looked up in alarm as Krill spun back to confront him.

"…so are you."

Krill flicked the monocle. It whistled across the air in a wide arc and sliced the pilot's throat open. A spray of blood fanned out as if a lawn sprinkler had been turned on full force. The pilot dropped to his knees and bled to death as John and the others gasped in shock.

Heartened by the effective response to his object lesson, Krill turned to the captives and swiftly identified the weakest link in their chain. Harry Singer. He approached the terrified little man, inhaling his fright as if it were an aphrodisiac.

"Oh, mercy, mercy me" twittered the wretched Harry who,

within seconds, was sitting in a pool of his own urine.

The captain wiped the blood off his monocle and gestured to the bizarre machine that anchored the room. “Tell me about this… invention.”

Harry shot a quick look at John and tried to temper his panic by approaching the question as if he was giving a technical lecture.

“The ore-separator? Well…uh, it separates ore and, uh...” Harry began warming to his lie. “You see, there’s a great need for harvesting minerals from the---”

He didn’t complete his thought, for Krill had bent down to evenly scrape his monocle across the terrified man’s cheek, carving an ‘x’ in blood. John struggled against his bonds in an attempt to come to Harry’s aid, but the chains held him fast.

“You do not have the luxury of lies. Do you understand?” Harry burst into tears and tightly jerked his head up and down. “Yah, I think you do. I know the purpose of this machine. My only question is, does it work?”

Harry tried to answer but fear had paralyzed his vocal chords and his words tumbled out as nothing but stuttering yelps.

“Does it work?” screeched Krill.

“I don’t know!” shouted Harry. “We were ready for a test run when you broke in and ruined everything.”

Krill grinned and gestured to the others. “You see? Easy as cake.”

“That’s pie,” corrected Gershwin. “Easy as pie.”

Krill noted the correction, gestured in appreciation, and pressed a button on his wrist compartment that reeled the monocle back in. “Schurke. Say our goodbyes.”

Schurke grunted happily and began dousing the laboratory

with a canister of gasoline as Captain Krill and his men turned to go.

"Where's Mr. Edison?" demanded John. "What have you done with him?"

"Edison lives," replied Krill. "You don't."

With that, the captain left the laboratory. Harry turned in shame to the others. "I'm so very sorry. The rigor of my mind is outweighed by my body's fear of pain."

Emily and Gershwin tacitly acknowledged his apology but were gripped by the deadly consequences of the astonishing situation they'd stumbled into.

"It looks like curtains," whispered Emily.

"For keeps" echoed Gershwin.

Schurke surveyed his handiwork. He had paid special attention to the corners of the room. With luck, the walls, then the roof would collapse, trapping his victims under the rubble as they burned to death. If only he could stay to watch. Perhaps next time. He lit a match, dropped it, and the laboratory erupted into pockets of fire. Schurke hefted the bulky burlap sack over his shoulders and turned to go. As he did, an object fell out of the sack and twirled towards John. It was Edison's model for the ore-separator. Edison was alive and inside the sack! But what could John do? As the sphere danced around the encroaching flames, it gave him an idea.

John stretched out as far as he could from where his hands were chained to the base of the machine. He dug the teeth of his skate blades into the sides of the control panel and slowly, evenly, dragged it across the floor. The others looked on, too puzzled to be hopeful. Harry suddenly realized John's intentions. "You're not going to…you can't!" he protested.

"Brace yourselves," advised John as he raised his right foot, aimed at the pulsing green light, and punched the power button with the heel of his blade.

The machine began to revolve and, as it picked up speed, John honed his metal bonds against the undercarriage of the axis. A shower of sparks erupted from the grinding of metal against metal and soon John was loose. As the others freed themselves from the linked chains, John removed their skates by slitting the laces with his pocket knife.

John beat back the flames, scooped up the miniature sphere, and led the others through the zig-zag maze of hallways. As they reached the central corridor, Harry Singer stopped in sudden realization and abruptly doubled back. It wasn't until they had reached the entrance to Edison's main laboratory that John noticed Harry's absence. Unsure if the intruders were still nearby, he gestured for the others to stay put as he raced back to retrieve him.

Harry was intent on making a retrieval of his own. He returned to the secret laboratory and bravely navigated the conflagration to access a hidden compartment in the far wall. As the machine's revolutions accelerated, he located a set of its blueprints. Posterity demanded as much. Harry returned to the exit only to find his path was blocked – not by the fire – but by Gaunt!

Mangled screams echoed throughout the maze of hallways. John increased his speed only to reach the secret laboratory in time to see the snarling Gaunt lift Harry's jerking body above his head and hurl him across the room where the little man disappeared behind a curtain of flames.

John's shouts of "stop" came too late and only served to direct the creature's attention to him. Gaunt paused, trying to think – was

John a friend or a foe? He snarled. Foe. The monster unleashed a howl of vengeance and charged. As Gaunt bounded across the room, he failed to see the fire had eaten into the floorboards. His sausage-sized fingers were only inches from clamping around John's neck when his lumbering frame broke through the surface and he plunged out of sight.

John froze momentarily, realizing how close he'd come to death and how close to death he remained. He started to go but then, inexplicably, turned to confront the machine as if, somehow, it was beckoning to him. Why? Entranced, he peered through the layers of smoke and flames and saw the shadow again, undulating in the center of the machine.

Then the spell was broken. Fire breached the control panel and the base gears locked. John hit the floor as the sphere shuddered to a stop so ferocious it warped the gimbals. With a horrible groan, the invention caved in on itself and the inferno consumed the machine. John crawled back to his feet and ran for his life – unaware that he was racing from the fire into the frying pan.

12

DEATH MATCH

Emily and Gershwin breathlessly eavesdropped through a slit in the door to Edison's main laboratory as Schurke and two of his henchmen planted explosives throughout the cavernous space. The grand finale to their master plan was to blow the entire complex sky-high. At least, that was the plan until Schurke discovered Edison's cache of precious minerals. Schurke, as previously noted, had two charges in life: to obey and exterminate. However, these credos were outweighed by one crowning vice – avarice. He dismissed the two henchmen. He would finish the job on his own. Schurke abandoned the gunny sack and peeled off his overcoat – it was getting warm from the encroaching fire – revealing a strap undershirt, shoulders bearded with hair, and a gun holstered around his broad torso. He dug his hands into the barrel of diamonds, fisted them into the air with giddy greed, and shoveled the sparkling gems into a satchel.

Emily and Gershwin crouched defensively as they heard approaching footsteps. It was John and he was alone.

"Where's Mr. Singer?" asked Gershwin.

"Dead," John answered flatly. He peered into the laboratory

and saw Schurke hoarding the gems.

"But how?" asked Gershwin. He was startled by the news. His limited experience with death had been one of sorrow and ceremony, and neither were in attendance.

Emily gasped. Something inside the discarded gunny sack began to move. Edison!

John weighed the situation and pulled Emily and Gershwin into a huddle. "We need a diversion."

"Like what?" Emily asked.

John considered their limited options, grimaced, and accepted his fate. "Like me."

He hurled himself into the room, landed on the brute's back, and smashed him to the ground. Schurke's satchel of diamonds skittered across the floor and his gun popped out of its holster, sliding into a corner near the vats of chemicals.

Stunned, both men staggered to their feet. Schurke was surprisingly fast for his bulk and collared John, wiping him across the lab tables. He dunked him into the torpedo tank, where he mashed his knuckles over his face and tried to drown him. John realized he couldn't escape by rising above the waterline – Schurke's weight was too great – so he'd have to find another way out. He spread-eagled his legs and kicked against the tank's glass walls. There was no result on the first attempt and, on the second, the glass only cracked. But on his third try, the walls shattered and the water shot out, flushing the diamonds down the laboratory's sewer grates. Schurke's sudden loss flummoxed him and John took advantage of the distraction by ramming his feet into his gut. Schurke hit the floor but rebounded, fueled by a murderous rage. It was the exact reaction John had hoped to inspire. He danced around the blindly charging man, then tripped Schurke, who smashed face-first into the glass shards of the water tank.

As Schurke howled in pain, John signaled to Emily and Gershwin. They scampered onto the laboratory floor and helped John pull the still-groggy Edison out of the gunny sack and untie his bonds. However, John had not properly evaluated Schurke's capacity for pain and he rose up yet again, his body festooned with shards of glass, but raring for round two.

"Go!" urged John. Emily and Gershwin didn't have to be told twice. They draped Edison's arms over their shoulders and dragged the dazed inventor out of the laboratory. As John urged them on, he failed to see that Schurke had selected a huge pair of beaker claws as his new weapon of choice. He clamped the metal vise around John's neck, strangling him. Schurke gurgled in delight, safely out of reach from John's frantic grasp, and squeezed the long, metal prongs.

Unable to break Schurke's grip, John spotted a lit Bunsen burner, grabbed the collar at the bottom of the tube, and smashed it into his face. Schurke's head ignited. He roared, released the beaker claws, and dropped to the ground, rolling wildly to extinguish the scalding heat.

John sank to his knees and gagged for air as the rampaging conflagration from below began to sizzle through the walls, infecting the laboratory with a creeping virus of flames.

Schurke stopped rolling. The surface of his flesh was charred and still smoking but he had doused the fire. And there was something else. He'd found his gun.

Once John saw Schurke had retrieved his weapon, he marshalled his strength and charged. The two opponents struggled over control of the gun, getting off several haphazard shots as the fire spilled onto the laboratory floor and pools of flame licked at their feet. Time was running out.

John kneed him in the groin. It was a reliable maneuver and this instance proved no exception. Schurke crumpled in pain and released his hold on the gun. John grabbed it but Schurke swatted him across the room and, as he lay splayed out on the smoking floorboards, gazed groggily at the weapon. The barrel had popped open and the chambers were…one-two-three-four-five-six… empty!

Before John could respond to this ironic turn of events, Schurke yanked him off the floor and into a rib-cracking bear hug. As he struggled in the death-grip, John suddenly realized that while *he* knew the gun was empty, Schurke didn't. He slammed the chamber shut and threw the gun into the open barrel of cyanide.

It was a risk. After all, the barrel was clearly labeled with a skull and crossbones as poison, but John suspected Schurke paid little attention to the fine print. He was correct. Schurke tossed him aside and lumbered after the gun. He plunged his bleeding arms into the vat of concentrated venom, fished for the weapon, and triumphantly retrieved it. His mouth split open in a triumphant display of cackling, candy-corn teeth and he aimed the gun directly at John's heart. As he pulled the trigger again and again with no satisfactory result, the cyanide infected his bloodstream. He went into a seizure, his body wracked by a series of violent, neck-snapping spasms, and crashed to the floor, dead.

John stood over the brute's lifeless form, but only for a moment; more to catch his jagged breath than to claim victory. The fire had engulfed the laboratory and the sizzling heat had combined with the storehouse of volatile chemicals to trigger a variety of bizarre chain reactions. John escaped through a gauntlet of toxic gasses, weird eruptions, and shrieking pinwheels of flame.

This time he took the stairs.

13

ESCAPE

John staggered out of the building and gulped the cold, clean air into his lungs as a Model T Ford barreled up to the entrance. It was Gershwin! Emily yanked John inside and he landed next to the still-groggy Edison. The car hobbled across the snow-swept fields until they hit the open road and Gershwin floored it as the ramshackle compound erupted in a chain-reaction of detonations that triggered an earth-shattering display of insane pyrotechnics.

Safely out of the explosion's trajectory, Gershwin slowed the car down to a normal speed in the hope that he could put the brakes on his galloping heart. He was scared, yes, but mostly relieved, and filled with the odd fuel of exuberance and dread that marks a brush with certain death. He glanced at Emily. She was all of the above and more. He nodded and managed a thumbs-up. She returned the gesture and hooked her thumb in his.

In the back seat, Edison roused himself from his drugged stupor. He gauged his surroundings – strange – and tried to recall the final moment before he had ceased to remember anything.

"Where's Harry?"

"Dead," answered John. Should he have told the old man so

abruptly? Yes. The sooner they all faced facts, the sooner they'd know what they were up against. "Gaunt killed him."

Edison's eyes opened wide and then narrowed in disbelief. "That's impossible."

"I saw it," confirmed John evenly. "And Gaunt's dead too."

Edison slumped in his seat, dumbfounded and deflated. "But…they were my friends."

John leveled his gaze to Edison's. "Who's trying to kill us?"

Edison hesitated and then decided to fess up. "Spies. From Germany."

John nodded. He'd expected as much.

"The Krauts!?!" exclaimed Gershwin. "What do they want with you?"

"To sabotage my greatest invention." He gazed back at the roiling inferno. "It appears they succeeded."

"The ore-separator?" questioned John. "All that manpower to blow-up an ore-separator?"

Edison fell silent. Then, like John, he realized the time had come for the whole truth, no matter how perilous it might be.

"It's not an ore-separator," replied Edison quietly. "It's a resurrector."

Emily spun around in her seat. "A what?"

"A resurrector." Edison saw that their puzzled faces required a definition. "A machine that communicates with the dead."

Gershwin slammed on the brakes and swerved the Model T off the road. He leapt out of the car and began striding towards an icicled forest – going somewhere – anywhere – to keep his unstrung nerves under control and get as far away from this crazy old man and his *meshuggeneh* invention as possible.

"Mr. Gershwin!" protested Edison. "Please, come back."

Gershwin turned back to Edison, but kept going. "To the dead I have nothing to say except 'Rest in peace.'"

Emily paused, torn, and then joined her young friend.

"Where are *you* going?" shouted John.

"Back to Broadway," replied Emily.

"Where the only killers are the critics," added Gershwin.

"You're free to go," offered Edison, "and with my blessings. However, the Germans won't stop until we're all eliminated."

Now it was Emily's turn to confront Edison. "Hold the phone, Grandpa." She broadly gestured between herself and Gershwin. "*We* didn't invent anything."

"You're witnesses," retorted John. "Haven't you heard? There's a war on."

"And that's why they destroyed the resurrector," proclaimed Edison. "Because it could end this Great War!" A practiced promoter, he'd learned the benefit of making outsized claims on behalf of whatever his current endeavor might be. It made for good press and the more the rhetoric snowballed, the better the wheels of inspiration (and investment) were greased. Edison topped himself with a unique boast: "Why, it could end war for all time!"

John blinked. He didn't follow this line of logic, but it stood to rights that the Germans *had* destroyed the machine and most assuredly had tried to kill them. Their odds for survival only increased if they stuck together. But would they?

Emily and Gershwin studied each other silently. They had no arguments left – but no answers either. "So what do we do now?" asked Emily.

"There's only one thing to do," responded Edison. "We're

going to Florida!"

Gershwin's mouth popped open in disbelief. "That's how we beat the Germans? *By going on vacation*?"

Edison chuckled and shook his head. "After a lifetime of fraud and patent theft, I've learned when you create a new invention you damned well better make sure you've got a copy. There's a second resurrector at my winter home in Fort Myers. The only way to save ourselves is to complete the experiment before the Germans find us." Edison paused gravely. "Are you with me?"

One by one they considered the odds. Emily nodded, Gershwin followed suit, and John reached into his pocket to offer Edison the miniature model of the resurrector. They were with him.

Edison nodded decisively, touched by their allegiance. "All right then. Let's give it a whirl."

* * *

Pennsylvania Station was a modern miracle of mass transit. An extraordinary Beaux-Arts edifice of pink granite colonnaded in the Doric order, it transformed common commuters on the Pennsylvania and Long Island railroads into adventurers with its breath-taking expedition into the refinements of travel. As a wag once quipped, "Civilization deserves what it's willing to pay for," and civilization had come out ahead on this particular investment. However, in addition to the travertine adornments of the grandiose hub, Penn Station had one other attribute that Edison found beneficial: It was easy to get lost in.

Since he realized the bustle of the public would help camouflage his movements, he decided against a local departure from Middlesex County and took the risk of burrowing back into Manhattan. Besides which, he had an unexpected resource up his sleeve.

For his part, Captain Krill wasn't one step ahead of Edison but on the same footing. When Schurke failed to appear at the rendezvous point, he knew the mission had been compromised. True, they'd destroyed the resurrector but their prime directive had been to deliver Edison alive. Now he was on the loose, with or without the three remaining witnesses who, as far as Krill was concerned, were now accomplices and would be exterminated upon discovery. He knew enough about Edison's shrewd intellect to suspect he'd attempt to hide in plain sight and that his eventual destination would be some place other than his usual haunts. But where? His undercover agents were searching each of the remaining trains under a variety of innocuous guises: a pious nun whose specialty was strangulation by beads, a blind man whose white-tipped cane doubled as a stiletto, and a homicidal dwarf camouflaged in a child's Buster Brown suit.

Captain Krill was fortunate to have such a practiced entourage of murderers at his disposal but it was no less than his nefarious reputation warranted. He attributed his success to a life lesson he had learned at the age of ten when his bastard of a father had mysteriously burned to death in a kiln accident. The moral was this: If you're prepared to be more ruthless than those around you, you can achieve your heart's desire.

Krill's nostalgic reverie was interrupted by his lieutenant, a rail-thin man with a nervous mustache.

"There's no sign of them," the lieutenant reported.

"Then you will search the next train and the next," replied

Krill testily.

The lieutenant flinched in dread. “Sir, we’ve searched all the trains and we’ll search them again. But the final departures are scheduled for any moment. What if they’re not here?”

The captain withdrew his monocle, spat on the glass, and wiped the flecks of dried blood from it. “Look on the bright side,” his tone brightly menacing. “The alternative is too dismal to consider.”

“All aboard!” cried the stationmaster, a large, ruddy man with a walrus moustache whose gregarious nature didn’t mask the fact that his trains, by Godfrey, ran on time.

Krill winced. “How many trains are left?”

“Seven. Then no more till morning.”

“Assign an agent to each train.” Krill surveyed the station. “Edison is here.”

The lieutenant hurried off to execute the order. Krill tightened his mouth and nodded sharply, as if to confirm his own decision. His agents would find Edison. Or more likely, one of the old man’s traveling companions, who would do something foolish and condemn the others to their fate. However, a sliver of doubt gnawed at the captain. The hunt was taking far too long. Had Edison outfoxed him?

He had. In fact, if Krill could have seen how close he was to his quarry he would have contemplated the German equivalent of hari-kari. As the midnight run for Richmond sounded its steam whistle and began to pull out of the station, Krill scrutinized the departing passenger cars, then the coal car, then the caboose. Nothing. He burned silently and cursed.

The captain had been well-schooled in mayhem, but a primer

on geology might have provided him with a clue. Coal, when placed under enormous pressure, is transformed into diamonds. Edison had borrowed that principle to forge a unique invention of subterfuge; a private coach disguised as a coal car, masking a sumptuous interior designed in the ragtime style and, on the outside, tinted nuggets that doubled as one-way windows.

Behind the deceptive shell of soot, Edison and company were safe and sound. Emily and Gershwin huddled warily, unsure if Krill could see them or not. Edison bolstered their courage with a round of champagne and they offered a toast to the oblivious captain as the train chugged past him and out of the station.

However, John wasn't prepared to declare more than a minor victory. He'd encountered men like Krill on the battlefield. They were the grade of warrior you were advised to kill quickly and well, lest they rise up to wreak havoc another day. He didn't know where or when their paths might cross again but of one thing he was certain. While Krill may have been momentarily outwitted, he wasn't remotely close to being stopped.

14

MEANWHILE...

Mina Edison was an unlikely social arbiter. Nothing in her staid New England background had prepared her for the public rigors of being Mrs. Thomas Edison. The private challenges alone proved daunting enough, especially in the beginning.

Edison's first wife, Mary, had died at the age of twenty-nine from 'congestion of the brain' the clinical term of the time for the mystery that was mental illness. Although she was a fairy-tale bride, the union had not been a happy one. Mary provided Edison with three children but little else. The coquettish qualities that had captivated him during their courtship soon became tiresome. He grew bored with his wife's infantile passions and came to consider her as little more than his oldest child. As the months dulled into years, Mary's girlish figure ballooned into the kind of obscene weight that suggested something not right; a precursor to the illness that eventually corralled her mind and ended her life. While he mourned Mary's death, Edison realized her passing had provided him with a second chance to find a mate who could not only be a decoration but a true partner as well.

That partner proved to be Mina Miller. She was the seventh

of eleven children from a family of means; a beautiful, slender young woman with lustrous black hair and sparkling eyes. In addition, Mina possessed a keen intelligence which made her all the more attractive to Edison, and he pursued her with a zeal that rivaled that for any of his inventions.

However, once they returned from their honeymoon, Mina discovered that Edison, having achieved his matrimonial goal, turned his attention to other experiments. While she dutifully hired a governess for the children, a cook for the kitchen, and a staff for the estate, Mina remained despondent. Who could she engage to assure her place of worth in her husband's eyes? Eventually, a hard look in the mirror solved her problem. Mina listed her husband's deficiencies (anti-social, ill-tempered, abstract) and dedicated herself to filling those voids as best she could (social, conciliatory, plain spoken). In addition to being the little woman behind the great man, she chiseled her own niche in society through charity and the arts. The result was that Edison adored her. Apart, they were both free to pursue their personal bliss. Together, they were as one – and unbeatable.

So, social, yes. Arbiter, reluctantly. The role of judge-and-jury was automatically thrust on her for, as Edison had advised, she was destined to be the biggest animal in the zoo. Her current menagerie was Fort Myers, Florida, a last-stop boomtown on the gulf coast. They had wintered in the sunshine state since 1895 and considered the area their second home. Edison purchased thirteen acres on the Caloosahatchee River and constructed a house and a nearby laboratory to continue his work. The laboratory mirrored Edison's usual ramshackle affair, but the house was spectacular. Christened 'Seminole Lodge,' the estate was nestled in a botanical paradise and featured two buildings, the main house and the guest house, with a connecting pergola, that looked out onto a vista of expansive waterways.

However, if Mina was the genteel elephant in the parlor, the other beasts in this particular zoo were the members of the local Music Appreciation Society. Mina had agreed to hostess a series of recitals and, while they could be a chore, they were also a way for her to encourage the fine arts and introduce a degree of the big city into small town life. For their part, the locals admired Mrs. Edison. Marriage had assured her renown, but her own democratic decency had earned her the reputation of a great lady and, even more rare, a real person.

A teenage girl with pimples as pink as the bows in her hair sat at the parlor piano and struggled through "Clair de Lune" to the admiring clucks of several dozen club ladies. Guided by the measured pace of the metronome, the child survived Debussy (although the reverse could not be claimed) and concluded her rendition with an inappropriate roadhouse flourish that bemused Mina, but bought a rapturous round of approval from the ladies.

Suddenly, the metronome began to tick wildly off-beat as if it weren't a metronome at all, but a telegraph. And so it was. Mina's eyes narrowed in concern and she leapt up before the next dubious prodigy could lay claim to the keyboard.

"Exquisite!" she exclaimed too enthusiastically as she maneuvered herself in front of the metronome to discreetly strangle the waggling wand. "And now, an intermission. There's punch and shortcake in the gazebo." The ladies hesitated. Mina fixed them with a tight smile and trilled, "Proceed."

They adjourned and Mina opened the base on the device to

read the hidden ticker-tape message inside.

Dearest Wife – Stop
Prepare Captiva Laboratory – Stop
Love – Stop – T.A.E.

Mina sighed, her concern tinged with intrigue. “Oh, Al. What fresh hell is this?”

* * *

Commandant Karl Henke, a stout, blustery man with a paintbrush goatee, stood at attention in the cold, whipping wind, but beneath his uniform he was sweating bullets.

Prior to the war, Henke had been an assistant manager in a wood pulp factory in Dusseldorf where he thrived as a lick-spittle supplicant to his superiors. In life he would never have moved beyond the middle. However, war is that curious institution where both the cream and the clots rise to the top. Thus his current station as commandant of an exclusive military base in Luxembourg near the village of San Quentin. It was a unique facility as it was anchored by an elegant, three-story chateau and served as home to a squadron of ace pilots and their state-of-the-art aircraft.

At the beginning of the war, air power had been used for reconnaissance missions. Planes flew over an enemy camp and, in turn, the enemy sent up planes of their own to give chase. The only weapons involved were pistols or, if a co-pilot could fit one onboard, a rifle or shotgun. Once the military discovered how to mount the planes with synchronized machine guns, the era of close-range aerial combat commenced.

Dogfights quickly gained fame as a noble, gladiatorial contest between swashbuckling adversaries, and several of the air ‘aces’ (‘ace’ being the universal designation for five or more kills) became immediate icons. Names like Rickenbacker and von Richthofen inspired both reverence and fear for two key reasons. The first was that, no matter the bravado, aircraft were certified ‘coffins with propellers.’ The question wasn’t if a pilot would expire but when. The second reason combined both a fact and a feeling. The majesty of flight proved undeniable, and to see a plane with your country’s colors soar overhead was enough to bolster the spirits of any soldier. After centuries of fable, the *Deus ex Machina* had literally arrived.

By 1918, the concept of the gallant dogfight had become a quaint luxury that neither side could afford. The new lines of aircraft piggybacked racks of fragmentation bombs in order to maximize the kill ratio of as many ground troops as possible.

While Commandant Henke was dazzled by such a massive deliverance of death, in private he harbored misgivings. The casualness of this sort of destruction seemed the opposite of noble. However, he took solace in the fact that it didn’t matter a damn what he thought. That was the true comfort of war.

Then why was Henke so discomfited? Because company was coming; a senior officer scheduled to remain in residence for an indefinite period of time. Since becoming commandant, Henke had been able to retire his talent for toadying. But now, once again, he could feel the wood chips beginning to dig beneath his fingernails.

The troops saluted smartly as a staff car, followed by a convoy of trucks, barreled through the main gate and braked to a halt. A pair of spotless, shimmering boots swung out from the rear of the vehicle. General Wilhelm Skinehardt surveyed his surroundings – it could be worse – and exchanged a perfunctory salute with Henke.

"Welcome to Luxembourg, General," greeted the commandant effusively. "I trust you'll find everything as ordered."

"*Danke*," replied Skinehardt curtly.

Commandant Henke watched enviously as the trucks, laden with camouflaged cargo, rolled toward an aircraft hangar that was segregated from the rest of the base. The verboten area had been commandeered by Skinehardt's retinue nearly six months ago. Why, even Henke – the commandant – had been denied admission. Outrageous!

Skinehardt started toward the chateau – he was tired and wanted to refresh himself for the work ahead – but the commandant steered him in the direction of an apple-cheeked child from the village, a sweet girl with a hopeful, gap-toothed grin, who presented him with a bouquet of flowers. As a rule, Skinehardt despised children and flowers as both died too easily. However, when he spotted the base photographer preparing to immortalize his arrival, he realized the beneficent lie of public relations.

"Ach, the human touch." He shrugged good-naturedly. "Why not?"

Skinehardt accepted the bouquet and approximated gratitude for the camera. Propaganda concluded, he turned on heel and continued to the chateau, with the servile commandant falling in behind.

A messenger bicycled awkwardly through the mud, intercepted them, saluted, and thrust a telegram under the general's nose.

"For you, sir. Confidential." The messenger, an attractive but feral young man, displayed a curious sense of self-possession for a soldier whose name was less important to Skinehardt than his ability to fetch. He snatched the telegram out of the underling's hand and read the contents with unhappy surprise.

"That wily old bastard," he muttered in tight acknowledgement. Then he exploded, raking the welcome bouquet against the chests of the commandant's senior officers.

As the pink petals frittered into the mud, the messenger nervously hazarded a query. "Sir! Is there a reply?"

Skinehardt leaned in and hoarsely whispered: "Find – Edison – Now!"

* * *

Snowflakes began to fall and the Middlesex County Fire Chief signaled to his men. Time to call it a day. They were long overdue for their suppers and Mother Nature would help smother any ambitious cinders of kindling at the now-defunct Edison laboratory. The locals swore there hadn't been so much activity at the old place in years but, since Edison himself was rarely in residence, the chances were good he was safe and sound. The same couldn't be said for Edison's staff and a group of moving picture people. They'd been laid out like logs in a supply hut down by the river, all of them doped up on some kind of drug the county medical examiner had never seen the like of. The good news? They'd live. The bad news? None of them could remember a lick of what happened.

Sometime after the fire brigade had gone and the site had been abandoned a creaking sound echoed from beneath the earth. A mound of charred debris shifted, moved again, and then a trap door clanged open in a blast of sparks. A figure emerged. Gaunt. He howled like an animal does when its spirit has been wounded and the hunger for revenge blots out all other instincts. Gaunt repeated the howl until the nature of what he was saying became evident. The howl was a cry for "Edison!" Gaunt lurched off into the night, determined to discover whether the man he had once called 'friend' truly was a friend. Or a foe.

15

THE PURGATORY EQUATION

John woke up with a start, his face peppered with sweat. However, there was no shout, no scream of terror. It was the dream again, as always, but this time he'd been able to take control. This time he escaped before he was buried alive.

Where was he? Right. The train. Nearby, Emily and Gershwin slept in a pair of pull-down Murphy beds. At the end of the car, a single lamp illuminated Edison at his desk, still at work, revising his schematics for the resurrector. John wiped the remains of the nightmare from his face, got up from the divan, and joined his employer.

"Don't you ever sleep?"

Edison chuckled. "When I was a boy telegraph operator I worked the graveyard shift. So I learned to take my rest in small doses. Besides, there's work to be done."

John poured himself a mug of coffee and remembered a quotation of Edison's. "Genius is one percent inspiration – and ninety-nine percent perspiration."

"I said it," vouched Edison. "And I'm sorry to say it's true, even for me." He opened a cupboard that contained a larder of foodstuffs, including a cold bottle of milk and an apple pie. "Would you care for a piece of pie?"

John nodded his thanks. He'd heard tell of Edison's odd working habits but didn't know that apple pie and milk were his meal of choice, especially when he was embroiled in an experiment. As the old inventor cut each of them a wedge of pie, John marveled at his whereabouts. Here he was, face to face with one of his boyhood idols. He shook his head in giddy admiration. "The Wizard of Menlo Park!" he exclaimed.

Edison grinned indulgently. "That's the common wisdom. And it's good for business. Though I've never much cared for the 'Wizard' part."

"Why not?" wondered John.

"It sounds like 'abracadabra' and that's all she wrote. Invention's not that simple. I prefer 'conjuror.' Conjuring takes work."

John regarded him in confusion. "But you *are* a genius," he countered.

"Oh my, yes," replied Edison. "But it's the ninety-nine percent that wins the race." Edison gave the miniature sphere a hopeful spin. "Magic is a dream you have to build."

John studied the old man, intrigued. "Why'd you invent the resurrector?"

Edison mused as he savored a bite of filling. "To comfort

people. To let them know they don't have to go through life so terribly afraid."

"You said it could end the war," recalled John. "How?"

"By proving to mankind there are eternal consequences for our actions here on earth." He warmed to his soapbox. "Why, if people could pay a visit to the hereafter, I guarantee it would eliminate fear, turn sinners into saints, and end war for all time."

John's eyes widened at the claim. "How does it work?"

Edison slid the schematic over to John and pointed toward the top of the page. "My 'Purgatory Equation': Speed + Sound + Shock = IDTrans."

"What's 'IDTrans?'"

"Inter-dimensional transportation," replied Edison matter-of-factly, as if he was sharing a recipe for flapjacks.

John swallowed hard.

Edison explained: "Speed. The velocity of the centrifuge to mimic the rapid vibrations of the afterlife. Sound. The tuning forks – thousands of them – to create the portal. And finally…Shock. A climactic burst of energy from the core that triggers our entry into the unknown."

Edison looked up to see John was overwhelmed. "Think of it as opening a door. Speed to find the door, Sound to unlock it, and Shock to step inside."

John remained politely unpersuaded.

"You don't believe me, do you?"

"In you, yes," replied John. "But in all this other…"

Their discourse had aroused Emily, who listened silently.

"Purgatory…Heaven…Hell," queried Edison. "The sweet hereafter, the great beyond?"

John's eyes met Edison's. Honest and direct. "No, sir. I don't."

"Oh, yes," remembered Edison. "You were going to be a scientist." He paused. "But instead you went to war. Why was that, really?"

"I wanted to make a difference." He hesitated, stymied, because he didn't want to admit he *hadn't* made a difference. No one had. Who could? He returned to the previous subject. "But I believe in the tenets of science and science requires proof. After all, seeing is believing."

Edison wryly considered this without comment. Then: "Why did you choose science?"

John smiled at the memory. "When I was a boy, I wanted to fly to the moon."

Edison shared the smile. "That's a commendable aspiration." He paused and added in all seriousness, "When do you plan to go?"

John laughed in disbelief. "I don't. Space travel's impossible."

It was the cue Edison had been waiting for. "Nothing's impossible, John. And you're wrong." He leaned in to drive his point home. "Seeing isn't believing. It's believing that allows us to see."

John dropped his eyes to the floor to avoid Edison's gaze and when he looked back up his face was flushed with conflicted emotions.

"You're a great man. And I'll do all I can to help you. But I've known more death in my life than I hope you ever will. So take it from me. There is no life after death. It's all death."

Edison nodded soberly, accepted John's declaration, and

returned to work. John abandoned his half-eaten piece of pie and tried to go back to sleep. Emily watched him as he sprawled out on the divan. She was deeply touched by his vulnerability and surprised to find herself bedeviled by a curious sensation; a warm, disruptive feeling that someone not of science might call 'love.'

16

PAPA ABALADI

As night gave way to day, so did the barren flatlands blossom into the tropical climes of Florida. The train had begun to slow its pace some ten miles out from the station, signaling to Edison and the others that it was time to pack up and prepare for the next installment of their adventure. Surprisingly, they weren't filled with dread but a fluttering kind of excitement. Even under their precarious circumstances, it was a luxury to escape the cold blast of winter for the balmy skies of Florida.

"Sun kissed beaches, here I come," enthused Emily as the train stopped at the station and Edison activated a hidden door that split the facade of the coal car and provided a walkway onto the platform.

Emily eagerly exited, stopped, and screamed – for blocking her path was an ominous Indian warrior attired in a fearsome ensemble of buckskin and metallic inlays, who wielded a staff studded with razor-sharp shark's teeth.

John and Gershwin came to her defense, but Edison blithely tut-tutted the three of them aside and greeted the savage with startling warmth. The two men embraced in a sort of ceremonial lodge clasp and Edison introduced: "Papa Abaladi, the Chief of the Seminole Indians."

Papa Abaladi's stone-faced countenance didn't flinch but his head bent slightly in acknowledgement and he addressed them in a mis-accented greeting. "How do you do?"

The others exhaled in relief and Emily summoned up what she thought might be the proper amount of protocol for a tribal chieftain. "Better," she half-curtsied.

Edison realized he should have briefed his party on the particulars of his Florida estate in general and Papa Abaladi in particular. A pocket history on the Seminoles might have been a good start. 'Seminole' translates to 'runaway,' and while they were descended from the Creek tribes of Georgia and Alabama, the Seminoles parted company from their rambunctious brethren to forge a more peaceful, independent path when they migrated to Florida in 1770. From that time on, they were beleaguered by any number of adversaries, including President Andrew Jackson, who initiated the first of three American wars against the tribe. The third and final confrontation ended in a highly unusual manner. Since the government was unable to formally engage with the Seminoles to present them with a peace treaty, the tribe never officially surrendered. The United States had lost too much blood and money in the campaigns and the new President, Buchanan, saw no value in pursuing a dwindling race of savages whose sole asset to the republic was a bog. So, the government simply decided the Seminoles didn't exist and the tribe earned their reputation as 'The Unconquered People.'

Edison was intrigued by the Seminoles from the start. Following a frigid New Year's Eve, he vowed he wouldn't spend one more winter up north and booked passage on the Florida Special, with orders to take him as far south as possible. When he and Mrs. Edison arrived in Fort Myers, they were delighted by the lush vegetation and the warm, silken breezes that cosseted their weathered skin. In short, the climate was nectar and, as Edison set about building his estate, he found no better workers than the Seminoles. They were an industrious, outwardly reserved people who also exhibited a unique sense of creativity and color, from their spangled dress and architecture to their spiritual ancestry. Edison admired them, for they represented the best of what was past. In turn, the Seminoles revered Edison, because they saw in him the best of what might come.

He should have told all this and more to his traveling companions. Yet they were no longer just his companions. Destiny had marked them as his collaborators, whether they liked it or not. For now, the less they knew the better.

Papa Abaladi pointed his staff and gestured for them to follow. They did so and eagerly. So much so that they failed to notice the other passengers who had disembarked; conventional travelers with the exception of a child in a Buster Brown suit, who aimed his large, spiral lollipop at them and snapped a covert series of photographs.

The child was one of Krill's agents, a dwarf whose true identity was Hans Gudegast, a former star performer of the Sarrasani Circus. His specialty in the center ring was a knife-throwing act so spine-tingling it garnered him acclaim throughout Europe until an unfortunate incident involving a novice assistant, a bottle of peppermint schnapps, and a rare case of bad aim, expelled him from the world of entertainment and brought him, hat-in-hand, to the attention of the military's espionage division. The little man smiled with malicious pride. His mission was half accomplished. Now to find a room, have a proper meal, and plot the demise of his soon-to-be victims.

17

BILLIE & AL

Papa Abaladi drove the touring car through the dusty streets of Fort Myers; Edison and John upfront, Emily and Gershwin, along with the inventor's hodge-podge of scientific paraphernalia, wedged in the rear. John couldn't help staring at the chieftain. He wasn't a tall man but his aura projected a larger-than-life persona. At first glance, he was a dubious candidate to pilot a Ford roadster but, given the sharp-elbowed way he navigated traffic, John thought he'd make one hell of a New York cabbie.

For his part, Papa Abaladi realized that John and the others were still puzzled about his exact role in Edison's life. The two men had been friends since they first met. In a society where Indians were dismissed by the locals, Edison was unique in that he approached all human beings in the spirit of true democracy. He was as decent to you as you were to him. Over the first few months they performed small kindnesses for each other. One day Mrs. Edison fainted from a bout of food poisoning and Papa Abaladi carried her to the nearest doctor. After an especially parched growing season, Edison returned the favor by providing the tribe with a wagonload of foodstuffs. And on and on, until these last few years when their destinies had become even further entwined as…

But that revelation would hold for another time. For now, all Papa Abaladi offered by way of explanation was to turn briefly to John and proclaim, "Edison is *ahessi*. Good friend to Seminoles. We see eye to eye."

Edison cackled. "Indeed we do!"

Papa Abaladi steered the car into the Edison estate; a compound surrounded by a tropical paradise of bougainvillea, fruit trees and an alphabet of other exotic plants. Edison leapt out of the car and hurried to the rear veranda where Mina bustled out and opened her arms in homecoming.

"Al!" she cried.

"Billie!" he responded joyously, and the two embraced with a passion that is rarely seen in the elderly, with the exception of those older souls who remain defiantly young in spirit.

"Billie!" exclaimed Emily.

"Al?" queried Gershwin.

Papa Abaladi folded his muscular arms and grunted sagely.

* * *

Mina had prepared a sumptuous breakfast for the weary travelers and, ravenous, they plunged into the meal of seafood omelets, rashers of bacon, fresh crullers with strawberry preserves, cinnamon coffee and, for Edison, a homemade apple pie topped with rum cream. Edison patted his stomach in satisfaction, snuck a kiss onto Mina's cheek, which prompted a blush and a giggle, and then took note of the time.

"A wonderful welcome, my dear," decreed Edison. "But

now, I fear, farewell."

Mina pouted in protest. "But you've just arrived. You can't be going so soon."

"Not I, dear Billie – but you," replied Edison.

Mina's mouth dropped open in surprise. After all these years, she'd learned that 'surprise' was one of her husband's few constants, but on occasion she was startled by the timing. This was such an occasion.

"You're off to our nation's capital," continued Edison. "If you've had no word from me by the time you arrive, you're to deliver this to President Wilson."

He handed her a formal letter that had been sealed with wax and embossed with his insignia. Mina reluctantly accepted the missive but wondered, "Why not simply call or telegraph?"

"My last conversation with Woody was…contentious," admitted Edison as he speared a forkful of pie into his mouth. "Besides, the walls have ears."

"Oh, surely not in the White House," chastised Mina.

Edison guffawed. "Especially in the White House. Although at that particular residence, the walls listen but rarely hear."

John, Emily and Gershwin watched the two of them volley back and forth, as if engaged in a verbal game of ping-pong. They were a genuine pair, Billie and Al; nicknames dually employed for argument and endearment.

"Is it really that important?" Mina disliked Washington, D.C. It was merely a swamp of a different nature.

Edison leaned across the table for dramatic effect. "My dear, the fate of mankind may well rest in your hands."

"Very well," sighed Mina. After all, what was the fate of

mankind as weighed against her druthers? "I'll do my best."

Edison clapped his hands. "Wonderful woman," he exclaimed to the table and the others concurred. However, Mina used the occasion of tribute to take a good, hard look at her husband's traveling companions, especially Emily.

"But what about you and your…associates?" she asked too sweetly.

"We'll be hidden away…" replied Edison absentmindedly as he scoured the pie tin for one more bite of filling, "conducting, uh, various experiments."

Mina shot a look at Emily's *décolletage* which, given the abrupt circumstances of their flight, was even more revealing than usual. "No doubt," she added dryly. She fixed her husband with a pragmatic stare. "You do still love me?"

Edison hooted, deeply touched by her jealousy. "My darling, my heart belongs only to you!"

"It's not your heart I'm worried about," she rejoined. Then, dead serious, she reached out her hand. "Are you in danger?"

Edison took her hand in his. "Dreadful danger."

Mina frowned in acceptance. "Then be careful. And once you've finished your business, come home to me in one piece." She turned to John. "You'll see to that, won't you, young man?"

John smiled warmly at Mrs. Edison. "Yes, Ma'am. I will."

Mina believed him. For the first time since their arrival, she added him up with the young woman seated next to him. Perhaps they were simply strangers thrown together by fate, but the lurking matchmaker inside suspected that fate might have cast her in the role of witness to a budding love match.

As the men retired to the porch, she leaned in and touched

Emily's arm with sisterly care, confiding: "Marriage to a man of invention. It's not remotely sensible. But it's never dull."

18

SWAMP

A moist veil of sunrise fog hugged the water's surface as Papa Abaladi navigated a narrow flatboat down the Caloosahatchee River and toward the mouth of the Gulf of Mexico.

With the exception of sharp slaps at greedy mosquitoes who had suckled so much blood they could barely stay aloft, Edison and the others maintained a vigil of silence. The open water was dangerous ground. If the Germans had tracked them south, it was an optimum spot to intercept them. Their safety would only be assured once they reached Edison's laboratory on the Seminole stronghold of Captiva, a sliver of an island several miles off the mainland's coast.

This last item prompted some confusion. First, Gershwin was startled by a 5 a.m. knock on his bedroom door by Papa Abaladi who advised him to "shine and rise." Emily was surprised to find that, before her own departure for Washington, DC, Mrs. Edison had laid out a safari ensemble for her to wear during the days to come, complete with jodhpurs and knee-high boots. Finally, John was taken aback when Edison excitedly roused him to prepare for the arduous journey to his laboratory. Arduous journey? Wasn't the blasted thing just across the street?

Well, yes and no. Edison had built a modest laboratory on the grounds of his estate which was protected from prying eyes by a cluster of banyan trees. Although he used the space for a variety of experiments, it was more of a retreat; a place to putter, snooze, and be at home in his mind. However, for an experiment as game-changing as the resurrector, Edison required complete secrecy; a place where no man dared venture. Or at least, where no white man dared venture.

Captiva Island. The name alone summoned the allure of exotic mystery and the facts were equal to the musings. Some six thousand years before, Capitva and its larger, sister island to the south, Sanibel, had been created when centuries of storms propelled beds of sediment up from the sea. The original inhabitants of the island were the Calusa Indians, a remarkably sophisticated band whose existence was first recorded in 1510. They were later visited by Ponce de Leon, who dropped anchor while searching for the fabled 'Fountain of Youth.' Instead of youth, he discovered nothing but death; his own demise from a fatal wound in battle, and the tribe's eventual decimation due to an influx of European diseases such as yellow fever and measles.

Following the extinction of the Calusas, Captiva and the other barrier islands became known as the 'Buccaneer Coast' – a safe harbor for blood-thirsty pirates, including the dreaded Jose Gaspar. He provided Captiva with its un-Christian name when he constructed a prison to cage the innocents he shanghaied for ransom on the 'Isle de los Captivas.' Gaspar met a fitting fate in 1821 when, captured by the U.S. Navy and faced with life in prison, he draped himself in chains and leapt overboard, anchoring his corpse as the island's eternal prisoner.

The islands remained deserted for decades until 1884 when the first lighthouse was built on Sanibel and served as a beacon, not just for hardy pioneers, but to those wealthy vacationers who sought release from the constraints of civilization and embraced the beachcombing life – for at least two weeks a year. However, if Sanibel evolved into domesticity, Captiva remained wild – and eventually became the adopted homestead of Papa Abaladi's wandering Seminole tribe.

As the sun breached the mist, it created a shimmering glare. In the distance, the wavering bleat of a white-tailed deer was heard, then the hiss and thrash of a swarm of ravenous alligators, followed by the panicked bawls of their prey. John and Edison took the shrieks in stride but Emily and Gershwin, whose interaction with animals was limited to cats, dogs, and dressing room mice, were breathless with fear and grateful for the bright mask of the fog.

"What in hell was that?" whispered Gershwin, his heart thumping so hard his shirt fluttered.

"Survival of the fittest," replied Edison with a pragmatic grimace. He had always been a realist about the behavior of the species and couldn't help but wonder about his intrepid crew and the perils they'd soon face. Who would be eaten? And who would live to develop an appetite?

* * *

Papa Abaladi steered the flatboat through the marsh that fronted the eastern shore of the island and oared it as close to land as possible. He signaled for them to disembark and pointed his shark-tooth studded staff due west. Emily quickly came to appreciate her boots; the thick water hugged her calves as she sloshed clumsily through the muck. As for Gershwin, he was no better in water than he was on ice. His toes kept searching for a foothold of cobblestone or brick where none existed. Edison mopped his brow with a calico kerchief and popped a straw hat on his head as he and Papa Abaladi forged ahead. John brought up the rear, helping Emily and Gershwin as they waddled through the mire. John studied them with amused admiration. They were a sight, but they were game.

While the show folk appeared to be comic, fish-out-of-water figures, they both harbored reserves of strength their companions had yet to discern. Although Emily's beauty had opened many doors in her life it had also occasioned a multitude of dicey, even dangerous, encounters. As for Gershwin, while he presented an outward portrait of the sensitive young artist, inside he closeted a hidden self who hungered for the thrill of adventure. He was a dutiful son, kosher in the tenets of his faith, and a devotee of the classics. However, slipped between the covers of his composition books were tales of fantastic action by H. G. Wells, Jules Verne, and, his favorite, Edgar Rice Burroughs, the creator of the iconic Tarzan of the Apes. True, the adventure in Gershwin's life was mostly bound to the intersection of Broadway and 42nd Street, but here he was, plunging heedless and headlong into the brazen wilds of…well, Florida. Yes, it was only Florida, not Africa. And he wasn't Tarzan but a pale, lithe boy from Brooklyn with a reddening case of sunburn. Yet he felt strangely at home. He whistled a snatch of melody and plowed through the swamp, imagining he was someone's indomitable hero.

Edison and Papa Abaladi reached a bluff and Edison called

for John to join them. He bounded past Emily and Gershwin who fell into a causal saunter, as if they were strolling along the rialto instead of a high-brush bog infested with alligators, wild boars, and serpents; all of them scrutinizing the new arrivals and waiting.

"Somehow this all seems familiar," observed Gershwin.

Emily shot him a disbelieving look.

"The blistering heat," he continued. "The nauseating smells…the man-eating animals…" He paused in thought and snapped his fingers. "I've got it!"

"What?" Emily asked.

Gershwin smiled triumphantly. "A Saturday matinee in Poughkeepsie."

They both laughed, silly barks of laughter that fed off one another and provided them with a welcome intermission of relief from the stress of confronting the unknown.

Gershwin stopped in his tracks, convulsed in giddy amusement, until he noticed… "Emmy? I'm shrinking."

Emily turned to look at Gershwin. He wasn't shrinking. He was sinking; his feet, then ankles, disappearing into what appeared to be a circle of solid earth but was instead---

"Quicksand!" she shouted.

Gershwin panicked. He'd read enough adventure books to know quicksand was a deadly trap in which secondary characters invariably perished and, let's face it, in this adventure he was definitely not the lead. He flailed helplessly and tried to pry his feet out of the thick gruel, but the sand was so densely packed that the effort to lift one foot was akin to pulling an anvil out of a tub of molasses.

John leapt down from the bluff to determine the best course

of action. Based on the wide circumference of the bog and the rate of Gershwin's descent it was a deep snare, and if he couldn't break free he'd be sucked under and drown. Thankfully, John had learned a thing or two about quicksand in his sophomore geology class. The density of the average human body was half the density of quicksand. Theoretically, there was only one way to survive those odds and now he'd have the chance to prove a textbook theory in real time.

"Stretch out on your back and float," ordered John.

Gershwin shot him a look of utter disbelief. "Are you nuts?" he cried. He was up to his thighs in grasping sediment and there was no way – no how – he'd commit the rest of his body to the clutches of the quicksand. "Throw me a rope – or something – for crying out loud – help!"

Emily had already scampered up the embankment above the pit in search of a large, strong vine she could toss to Gershwin. Most of the limbs were dark gray and brittle, they wouldn't do. Then she found a thick brown vine that felt sturdy enough to do the job. She pulled it – and was surprised when it pulled back. Unfortunately this particular vine was not a vine but a snake, specifically an Eastern Diamondback rattlesnake. The serpent lunged at Emily and she avoided the strike but inadvertently hurled it onto the surface of the pit.

"Swell!" exclaimed Gershwin. "Now I've got a choice of agonizing deaths."

He was right. The threat of a vise-like demise by quicksand was on par to an encounter with this slithering predator. The Eastern Diamondback was the most dangerous reptile in the southeast, boasted fangs a full inch long and, according to the rare survivor, had a bite that felt like being hit with a hot skillet. The venom was potent, assuring the collapse of all appendages and a fatal seizure of the heart – and all within three minutes.

"Sorry," offered Emily. At least she was sincere.

John leapt onto a log that jutted out of the far side of the pit as Gershwin struggled against the soup of grit that was now up to his belly and the snake skittered across the surface, circling its hapless victim.

"Lay on your back," John ordered evenly.

"I'll go under," protested Gershwin. He never thought it would end like this. He had so much to live for. He wasn't exactly sure what, but he'd always hoped it would be something glorious.

"Do it," commanded John.

Gershwin gulped. He trusted John. All right then. He spread out his arms and arched his back, settling his head into the bog. The wet sand tickled his ears and clung to his chin like a slimy beard.

"Good," said John. Now, very slowly, lift your legs."

Gershwin did as he was told. Miraculously, with the pressure of suction relieved, the water was able to mix with the thick sediment and created a kind of lubricant that loosened his feet from the sand. Within minutes he'd be free!

Sadly, minutes would be too late. The rattler had skirted up Gershwin's thighs and nestled on his stomach. It vibrated its tail in warning and Gershwin was surprised that the sound was less of a rattle than a buzzer. How strange that this should be his last thought as the reptile bared its fangs, drooling with venom, and reared back to strike.

A sharp whoosh was heard as an arrow shot through the

air. It skewered the rattlesnake through the brain in mid-strike and flung it across the bog. The reptile hung lifeless, impaled on the trunk of a palm tree where it would soon serve as luncheon for a family of warthogs.

Everyone turned to see the saving shot had come from Papa Abaladi. The Seminole chief tossed his longbow to John, who stretched it out to Gershwin. He grasped the upper limb of the weapon with both hands as the others joined forces to pull him to safety.

Once on shore, Gershwin collapsed, his clothes weighed down with muck and grit. Emily wrapped a comforting blanket around him and he surrendered to his nerves.

"I can't go on…" he sputtered dramatically. "I can't…"

"You don't have to, my boy," proclaimed Edison. "We've arrived!"

He pointed to the bluff and, as they made their way to the top, the village of the Seminole Indians appeared before them; a collection of colorful, thatched huts arranged in concentric circles and anchored by Edison's island laboratory.

19

RAW FOOTAGE

A trio of German attack planes roared over the Luxembourg countryside, their maneuvers serving as an unofficial reveille for the soldiers in the military camp below. Still half-asleep, the young messenger hurried across the airfield where a zeppelin had arrived with a special delivery package that had been three days in rush transit. He signed for the goods – marked for Skinehardt's eyes only – and made straight for the general's quarters in the chateau. He had always dreamed of being part of something larger than himself and thought the military might fulfill that ambition. It hadn't. Not yet. But this intrigue with the general and his secret agents and the great Thomas Edison, this smacked of high consequence.

Commandant Henke and General Skinehardt were finishing their breakfast in a private dining room as the messenger entered, saluted, and presented the confidential documents.

"From Captain Krill, sir." The commandant snatched the private dossier out of the messenger's hands and proffered it to Skinehardt as if it were a ring on a satin pillow. The messenger remained at attention. No one thought enough to tell him to assume a position of 'at ease.'

Skinehardt sliced open the package with his butter knife, withdrew the report, and perused it, his poker face offering no hint of a reaction. The commandant was eager to know the results of the report but remained circumspect. However, the messenger was beside himself with curiosity; so much so that he demolished protocol by asking, "Did they find Edison?"

Both the messenger and the commandant knew immediately he would have to be disciplined for his outburst. The level of punishment meted out would be determined by the general's response. Fortunately, the news was good. Skinehardt dismissively snapped his fingers at the commandant who sent the insubordinate soldier on his way with only a swift kick to the backside.

Skinehardt finished the communiqué and his lips split in satisfaction. The commandant waited anxiously for him to share his findings but the general remained silent and sipped his coffee. Outrageous!

Skinehardt sensed Henke's dismay and relented. After all, supplicants *did* have to be encouraged and he preferred to have the commandant as an ally (or at least, an audience). This former pulp mill manager seemed eager to prove his subservience and, if events veered into more complicated territory, he boasted the added benefit of being easily disposed of. Like wood chips.

"Edison is alive and in Florida." Skinehardt announced, mispronouncing Florida with a long 'i.' He was not a tourist. He tossed the report to the commandant who slavishly rifled through the files as he continued:

"He's built a second laboratory." Skinehardt paused, ruminating quietly. "And no doubt, a second machine."

However, the commandant did not hear this last remark. He had discovered an addendum to Captain Krill's report and was eager to relay it in such a way as to suggest that he had compiled the intelligence.

"He has acquired three traveling companions."

One by one, Henke offered Skinehardt the photographs taken by the shutterbug dwarf at the Fort Myers train station. "Emily Auburn, a performer with the Ziegfeld Follies."

Skinehardt perused her photograph appreciatively. "Exquisite."

"George Gershwin or rather, Jacob Gershowitz," the commandant continued. "A musician."

Skinehardt snorted in contempt. "A Jew."

"...and John Dawkins. He appears to be Edison's new assistant."

Skinehardt skimmed John's picture, dismissed it, and then paused. He picked up the picture again and studied it, intrigued. The photograph was of John's profile and, taken in transit, slightly blurred. However…

"I know this man," recalled Skinehardt dimly. "But from where?"

He brought his hand up to his chin and stroked it lightly in contemplation. After a moment, Skinehardt paused and stared hard at his right hand or, rather, at the void left by his missing trigger finger.

* * *

Late that rainy night a second special delivery package

arrived, this time from Berlin. The messenger scurried through the downpour, clutching the parcel – a round tin of metal. He made his delivery and then a quick exit. As the commandant remained firmly opposed to revealing any confidences in his lowly presence, he decided not to invite more discipline.

The commandant entered a conference room that had been converted into a make-shift cinema. He withdrew a reel of film from the package, fed the celluloid into the projector, and dimmed the lights. Skinehardt sat expectantly. He'd been rankled with a gnawing expectation all day long and now the moment had arrived; the chance to witness the evidence that memory had dulled but film held intact. The footage from the German war office unspooled, revealing a battlefield, circa 1916. The subject was John Dawkins, who stoically filmed the carnage around him.

"He *is* brave," deemed the commandant in admiration. Then: "For an amateur."

"Perhaps," responded Skinehardt. He didn't doubt John's courage, of that there was no argument. Yet there was something else. Something curious. He seized on it.

"You see," gestured Skinehardt insistently, as John fought his way through the trio of attackers. "He's not defying death. He's inviting it." Skinehardt paused decisively. "Very well. I shall grant Mr. Dawkins his wish. The sooner, the better."

"Surely, you don't find him a threat," soothed the commandant. "He's not a real warrior. Not like you."

The general would have none of it. "No. If this man ever stops looking at life through a lens, at a remove, and embraces his destiny..." Skinehardt admiringly took his adversary's measure. "He will be unstoppable."

The men continued watching as the reel unspooled, both consumed with such rapt, fateful attention that they failed to notice a pair of eyes peeking in through the rear window. It was the messenger, who had seen and heard everything.

20

CAPTIVA

The past few days had been a marathon of grueling labor. Once inside the Captiva laboratory, Edison had to implement all the advances he'd made to the resurrector during the past seven months. Luckily, the improvements were more cosmetic than structural and the work went without incident. While Emily screwed the thousands of tuning forks into the frame of the invention, John and Gershwin secured the wooden struts that would hold the machine in place.

This resurrector was different from the Menlo Park version in that it was smaller and made of raw metals and whatever support materials were at hand. The laboratory was unique as well. The exterior was a variation on the 'chickee' style of the Seminole's huts; a frame of cypress logs layered with palm thatch leaves that allowed it to blend in with the community. However, the interior was a dual-level cement bunker; the upper half framed with a circular staircase that hugged the interior wall and descended to the laboratory floor below.

Edison plugged the last of a dozen salt-water generators into the control panel and nodded in hard-won satisfaction at the enormous progress they'd achieved. He owed these young people more than he could say. He only hoped they'd live long enough for him to repay the debt.

"Excellent," he decreed. "We'll begin our trial run tonight."

"Why not now?" asked John. "We're nearly finished."

Edison shook his head. "The generators have to be fully primed for the journey."

"Journey?" exclaimed Gershwin. "Whoa, wait, I thought you said this thing *communicated* with the dead."

"It's not just an aural experience," explained Edison. "The resurrector is a conveyance, like a train or a roadster. We need to travel through the constraints of this world to engage with the afterlife." He slapped his palm against his forehead. "I almost forgot…" He pointed to the two passenger bubbles. "Symmetry is essential to the journey, so one of you will have to ride across from me. George?"

Gershwin looked up, startled. "Who, me? No! I mean, I'm flattered but why not use a couple of sandbags?" He leaned in confidentially. "I know where you can get a lot of sand."

"Human symmetry," replied Edison. "Spirit to spirit."

"Take me," John interrupted. "If you're so hot for me to believe in all this mumbo-jumbo, let me go."

Edison was tempted but shook his head. "If the Germans are onto us, I'll need you in this world to protect us." He opened a faux bookcase that revealed a stairway to a subterranean tunnel. "And help us escape."

John accepted the rationale. "Just save me a ride."

"You can bet on it," cackled Edison.

"Then who's going to run the machine?" piped up Gershwin.

Edison was stumped. "Oh, dear." He hadn't thought that far ahead. "I, uh, I haven't the foggiest, I…"

As he stammered absent-mindedly, Emily struck a tuning fork for attention. "I'll do it," she volunteered.

"You're kidding?" mocked John.

"I never kid a kidder, kid," replied Emily with wry defiance. Whoever had written that ditty about girls being 'sugar and spice and everything nice' deserved a good sock in the jaw.

Edison scrutinized her over his glasses. "Are you sure, my dear?"

"I was Houdini's assistant for a whole season. I got tied up, disappeared and sawed in half six shows a day. If I could handle his hocus pocus, I can handle yours."

Edison clapped his hands together. "You're hired. Now go. I'll see you all tonight at seven o'clock sharp." They hesitated and he waved them off good-naturedly. "Go on, go out. Enjoy your day."

Relieved, they raced out like school children at the final bell. In fact, they were gone so quickly none of them heard Edison mutter an ominous disclaimer:

"While you can."

21

PARADISE

John, Emily and Gershwin emerged from the laboratory into the daily life of the Seminole village and strolled among the natives with a growing appreciation for the simple but productive society they'd established. The men would hunt and build, the women cook and sew, the children help where needed and, depending on their age, train for their eventual role within the tribe. Strangely, there was as much play as there was work and the Seminoles appeared to enjoy both equally. None of them were dressed in full ceremonial attire like Papa Abaladi, but even in their scant clothes of buckskin and sawgrass, the Indians exhibited the earmark of any true civilization: accessories. A shell necklace, a gold bracelet, bits of multi-colored beads woven into their cloth or hair. This infusion of color and style prompted a sense of personal pride in each member of the tribe. Although white society branded them as heathens, John found it ironic that their village was squarely modeled on that most stalwart of Christian tenets: 'Love thy neighbor as thyself.'

As for the natives, all they asked from their guests was a fair shake and, having received it, welcomed them as immediate, if temporary, members of the tribe. The men were eager to share the spoils from their hunt with John and the women delighted in advising Emily on native dress. As for Gershwin, well, they weren't sure what to make of Gershwin. It wasn't prejudice. It was just that there was something special about him; so special it seemed familiar.

The trio stopped to watch a group of young hunters practicing their archery. One by one, the arrows dug into their target, a dead tree some twenty yards off with a series of circles painted on its trunk. Strive as they might, the boys couldn't score the bulls-eye.

"I always wanted to try that but I never did," Gershwin sighed wistfully.

"Why not? Did your mother say you'd put out an eye?" teased John.

"*My* mother?" replied Gershwin. "*Both* eyes."

One of the young hunters noticed Gershwin's interest and offered him a bow and arrow. He begged off, but the smiling boy persisted and Gershwin awkwardly accepted the gift. An expert on weaponry might have characterized the bow as a variation on the Mongol version. It was made with a mixture of animal horn, sinew, and wood – and the upper and lower ends were of equal size, which increased its range and accuracy.

Gershwin knew none of this. In fact, he didn't have the faintest idea how to work the damned thing. He haplessly turned to John who stepped in to mentor him as Emily looked on in subdued amusement.

"First, a steady stance," instructed John. Gershwin followed suit. "Then aim, pull back, aim again, and let fly."

Gershwin anxiously lifted the weapon into position, fixed on the target, pulled back on the arrow – he could feel the tension, it felt good – and then released the arrow. It whistled through the air and landed in the heart of the bulls-eye.

There was a moment of silence. Then the sound of jaws – John's, Emily's, everyone's really – hitting the ground. Gershwin turned back to John with the irritating naiveté of a Christian with three aces and the fourth within reach.

"Like that?"

John nodded dumbly. "Just like that."

The young men erupted in cheers and wrapped their arms around Gershwin in congratulations. He modestly accepted their acclaim and was buoyed up; not only by his unexpected achievement, but even more by the spirit of acceptance.

The native women presented Emily with some beach wear – two loincloths for the men and a two-piece ensemble for her that might charitably be called a bathing suit, but only on the Minsky circuit.

"Anyone for a swim?" she offered.

"You two go ahead," replied Gershwin. He was otherwise engaged. The smiling boy pressed the bow and arrow back into his hands and urged him to try again. Gershwin shrugged happily. Stance, aim, pull back, aim again…

John was tempted by Emily's offer but begged off until a second celebratory cry went up from the hunters. Gershwin had topped himself, not only hitting a second bulls-eye, but by splitting the stem of his first arrow. John shook his head. His work here was done. He turned to Emily and smiled broadly. "I'll race you."

* * *

The sand on Captiva was unique from the mainland's beachfront property in that it was a shimmering white instead of the standard tan because it wasn't sand so much as a landscape of shells that had been pulverized over the centuries into fine, bleached bone. The exotic combination of white shoreline and azure water reached its zenith at a secluded cove that featured an aromatic grove of fruit trees, a pristine beach, and a diving rock that jutted out over the languid waves.

Emily sat on a grass mat as she watched John tackle the diving rock by jackknifing into the air and execute a perfect entry into the gulf. She applauded as he emerged from the water, the bubbles of foam on his body popping to reveal the engine of muscle and skin underneath. He was, she mused, one hunk of a man who could do almost anything and do it well. Anything? Everything? She intended to find out.

"You have hidden talents, sir," congratulated Emily.

John flopped down on the mat next to her and toweled off his body, sopping up the saltwater from the soft, brown hair that dusted his chest. "The talent's due to my summers spent diving in quarries," he responded. "The 'hidden' courtesy of my Ohio upbringing."

"Presbyterian?" guessed Emily.

John nodded. "Modest to a fault."

Emily grinned ruefully. "If I'd been modest, I'd still be slinging hash back in Hoboken."

"But you're not."

"Nope. I'm on the lam with some nutty inventor who thinks he can talk to the dead, which is all we're going to be doing if the Krauts get wise to us."

She stretched out on the mat. John snuggled down on his side next to her.

"Are you scared?" he asked.

Emily laughed sharply and shook her head. "Hoboken was scary. When you're born on the wrong side of the tracks there's only two ways out. For a man, it's his hands. For a woman, it's her legs. You either kick 'em or spread 'em. I kicked. I've been kicking ever since."

Emily paused, amused by her self-analysis. She considered the elements of the scene; the rhythmic crash of the waves, the aroma of the citrus trees, the sight of John's body; his skin glistening into a freckled tan. Her fingers touched his forearm.

"It's hard to be scared in a place like this," she offered.

"It's beautiful," he added.

"So…do you think opposites attract?"

John wasn't sure how to handle her question, so he approached it from a professorial perspective. "In some cases. Science tells us that magnets are opposites that attract," he lectured. "But electrical currents are opposites that repel---"

Emily grasped his jaw between her thumb and forefinger and forced his eyes into hers. She didn't need a lesson. "Not science, you dope. Us."

She kissed him. He responded then hesitated, pulling back. Was she sure? Because this time it wouldn't be for the camera. This time it would be real. She rolled her eyes in exasperation, like a straight man waiting for a tardy punch line. John pulled Emily into his arms and kissed her with a release of passion so unbridled it took her breath away. She joined the campaign and their limbs entwined as they struggled to become one. It was a good fit. They were home.

* * *

Edison's tinkering had come to an end. He couldn't think of anything more he could do to ensure the experiment's success except wait for the generators to reach their full potential and that was nearly four hours away. He offered up a silent prayer to 'do right' and put on his coat to step outside and enjoy an afternoon stroll.

He was amused to find Gershwin had gone native. The young composer had lost his shirt, acquired some tribal markings and head feathers, and was captivated by the unique beat being coaxed out of a strange variety of instruments from a combo of Seminole musicians. None of them had attended Julliard, let alone heard of it. Nevertheless, they produced a sound that was both primal and sophisticated.

Edison approached, bobbing his chin in time to the music. Gershwin caught sight of him and interrupted his reverie long enough to exclaim: "Fascinating rhythm!"

From a distance, the anxious chatter of some natives was heard and then grew insistent, punctuated by several screams. The music died out and all heads turned to see Papa Abaladi emerging from the swamp, an enormous albino alligator waddling alongside him. The creature was renowned as 'Long Tooth, King of the Reptiles,' an ancient figure who was rumored to have been the first inhabitant of the island. The natives fell to their knees as a sign of honor. They had developed a respectful relationship with the animals on Captiva but no one had seen Long Tooth in years, so to witness two species of royalty side-by-side was a historic event.

Papa Abaladi struck his staff on the ground. Long Tooth accordioned his torso, and hocked out an oblong object some three feet in length that landed with a wet thud in front of the villagers.

Papa Abaladi and Long Tooth turned to each other, appeared to bow, and returned to their respective tribes.

Several of the more daring warriors poked at the strange object and rolled it over. It appeared to be a child and a few of the women, who couldn't locate their own offspring, cried out anxiously. The youngsters scampered quickly to their mothers' sides, unharmed and accounted for. Then who in the world…?

Edison knelt near the body and checked for a pulse. None. Dead. He wiped off the mask of sawgrass and drool from the figure's head. On first look, it resembled a child's face, but the skin around the neck was wrinkled, even wizened. It was a dwarf! But who was he and how had he died? There were no bite marks, no evidence of mangled bones. A few stray dots of a red stain around the lips prompted Edison to open the midget's mouth. The tongue was discolored and a strand of chewed berries sprouted from the dwarf's esophagus.

The berries were seeds from the rosary pea, one of the most deadly plants in the region. Deceptively attractive, the seeds caused nausea, an erratic pulse, and rectal bleeding if chewed. If swallowed, instant death. Edison knew the 'how' of the midget's demise, now to determine the 'who.' He opened the dwarf's safari jacket. Both sides of the interior were sheathed with a collection of razor-sharp knives. There was no identification on the body except for a ring. Edison tugged the bauble off the midget's finger, which was already seizing up in rigor mortis, and read the inscription: a sweetheart's sentiment in German. Suddenly, he recalled a glimpse of a child at the train station; an odd youngster who moved with an awkward gait that Edison had attributed to rickets. This assassin had been disguised as that child and tracked them to Capitva. His weaponry revealed he meant business and was prepared to claim as many casualties as possible; a goal he would have achieved, if he hadn't made the fatal error of failing to pack a lunch.

Edison gazed up at Papa Abaladi and, as if on cue, a wave of threatening clouds crept across the horizon and blotted out the sun.

"The enemy," predicted Papa Abaladi, "is near."

* * *

John and Emily lay blissfully in each other's arms, spent from a marathon of love-making that had run the gamut from nurturing caresses to primal thrusts and back again. Neither of them had ever experienced this kind of union before. If there was such a thing as soul mates, they had achieved the enormous good fortune of finding one another before circumstances dictated otherwise.

"What's happening to us?" mused John as he twirled his fingers through her hair.

Emily snuggled closer, draping her thigh over his. "Everything," she murmured.

The same bank of clouds that had erased the sun on the other side of the island now pulled a curtain of dusk across the sand. They sat up as the beach fell strangely silent. The effect was eerie and the portent ominous. John leapt to his feet and pulled Emily up beside him. Paradise was over.

* * *

Papa Abaladi and the village elders gathered around a fire circle inside the council house to perform 'The Ritual of Destiny.'

They mixed powders and potions into the embers in order to divine the wisdom of the tribe's ancestors. The flames erupted in sizzling, multi-colored flares and pungent scents that, to Edison's mind, were as theatrical as they were hallucinogenic. That being the point – to determine the best way forward in the living world, by momentarily taking leave of it.

The ritual was complete. Papa Abaladi opened his eyes. Words were unnecessary. The elders nodded as one, and committed to the course of action that lay before them. Papa Abaladi emerged from the hut and solemnly addressed his people.

"*Soletawa,*" he declared in his native tongue and a triumphant cry rose up from the tribe. They scattered to prepare for the siege ahead and Papa Abaladi turned to brief Edison and Gershwin as John and Emily arrived to join them.

"Two enemies arrive tonight." He pointed to the swamp. "One on earth." Then he gestured out to the gulf where the dark clouds had obliterated the horizon. "One on air. Seminoles stay. We fight."

"Your people are strong," countered John. "But they're no match for the Germans."

"John's right," endorsed Edison. "My friend, I'm sorry it's come to this but, please, don't make my trouble yours."

Papa Abaladi considered this and nodded in appreciation of their concern, but the message from his ancestors was unanimous. "We will defend our land." He paused, and the hint of a knowing smile played on his lips. "And our land will defend us."

22

ASSAULT

Night arrived, and the island appeared to be deserted. However, the members of the tribe were strategically positioned in an assortment of hiding places: surveillance platforms in the tree-tops, camouflaged trenches along the perimeter and stealth compartments in the hollowed-out trunks of mangrove trees.

John and Papa Abaladi shared a sentry tower, a circular platform that hugged the upper branches of one of the island's sturdiest trees. In the distance, a tympani of thunder rumbled and winds gusted through the palm fronds creating a low-pitched whoosh that signaled an encroaching storm.

Papa Abaladi sang a soft, rhythmic chant in communion with the spirits of his ancestors. Then the music died in his throat and his eyes opened wide.

"They come."

* * *

In the laboratory, Edison pushed himself against the rapidly approaching launch time as he executed a series of last-minute adjustments to the resurrector. Gershwin assisted him as best he could – a wrench twist here, a squirt of oil there – but he was nervous and when he was nervous, he chattered.

"When you invented, oh, I don't know, the phonograph or maybe the electric light, did you ever have a 'eureka' moment? You know, where you actually said, 'Eureka!'"

Edison half-considered this. "Not as I recall."

"What about 'Jumpin' Jehoshaphat' or 'Hot-diggity-damn?'"

"No and no," he peevishly replied.

Emily gave Gershwin a dig in the ribs to lay off but he bounced right back.

"What happens if this thing doesn't work? What if it's a turkey? What if it's a big, fat flop?"

"Young man, even a failed experiment is a step forward," retorted Edison, who joined Emily at the control panel. "A hundred percent RPMs – that's revolutions per minute – then initiate the core," he instructed. "Once initiated, ninety seconds duration, no less and, most critically, no more."

Emily nodded as Edison pivoted back to Gershwin and led him to one of the passenger bubbles.

"Ninety seconds, huh?" tittered Gershwin in relief. "That's not too long."

"It'll all be over before you know it," confirmed Edison as he strapped him into his seat. "Now, if my calculations are correct, the afterlife's a different experience for everyone. More importantly, portals to the past – or the future – might intrude." With that, he produced a blindfold.

"B-b-blindfolds are for executions," Gershwin stammered.

"It's for your own protection," pressed Edison, as he tossed him the mask and added a final, confidential warning: "To visit the dead zone, we may have to die a little."

Gershwin gulped. "Make sure it's on tight."

Edison grinned, adjusted the blindfold to confirm Gershwin's sight was cut off, and lowered the glass bubble over his head, locking it. With only seconds to spare, he hopped to the opposite side of the machine, secured himself inside the second passenger bubble, and clapped his hands together in anticipation. "Let's give it a whirl!"

"This thing won't go too fast, will it?" whined Gershwin.

"Oh, no, not at all" pooh-poohed Edison. What a whopper of a lie; so huge in fact that he couldn't resist rolling his eyes at Emily. She started to protest then thought the better of it. There was no time and the less Gersh knew, the better. Their lives were in each other's hands. If Edison was right and a clue from the afterlife could save their skins, if knowledge really was power, then it was time to go to school.

Edison continued the countdown. "…three…two…one… voltage!"

Emily activated the machine. The laboratory buzzed with unleashed electricity and the resurrector started to revolve.

* * *

The boy was only seven years old, but he'd been given the most crucial task of any villager, even the most skilled warriors. He shimmied to the top of the tallest tree to blend in with the bark so he could see without being seen. He was as limber as he was brave and alert to any sign of the unordinary.

The island fell silent. Even the animals laid in wait. After all, this was their home, too. Because of the silence, it wasn't the boy's eyes that first detected the enemy, but his ears; a soft threshing of leather boots against the tall grass. He breathlessly scanned the landscape, pitting his sight against the night. The elements admired the boy's grit and provided him with a small act of charity. A brisk wind parted the clouds, revealing the shimmer of the moon; just for a moment, but a moment was enough. He saw them. A battalion of shadows, dark gray silhouetted against black. He cupped his palms to his mouth and released a yowl that floated on the night air. To the untrained ear, it was merely the sound of an animal. However, the Seminoles immediately recognized it as one of their own.

"The enemy is among us," whispered Papa Abaladi, yet he took no action.

"What are you waiting for?" asked John.

"The island must test them. To see if they are worthy or unworthy," explained the stone-faced chieftain.

John was perplexed. "Worthy of what?"

"Their lives."

* * *

The resurrector had risen up to fifty percent of its required velocity. Emily monitored the gauges intently. The generators were all 'in phase' and within the margins of safety. Safe perhaps, but still unnerving. For Gershwin, the sensation felt as if all the thrill rides at Coney Island had been rolled into one.

"I – have – a – nervous – stomach!" he shouted above the

bombast of the machine.

"Sorry!" the cagey inventor merrily apologized.

The machine's revolutions accelerated to seventy-five percent of velocity and the benchmark triggered the thousands of tuning forks that began spinning; the measured tremors of voltage stroking them to produce an unearthly whine. Emily covered her ears with a pair of rubber mufflers Edison had provided and watched the dials in anticipation as the RPMs inched up to eighty percent…eighty-five… At ninety percent, the steel panels surrounding the core of the machine split open to reveal spirals of swirling electricity that accelerated toward a climax.

* * *

Captain Krill scanned the island through the powerful lens of a terrain telescope, finally resting on the Seminole village. The scene appeared tranquil - but not for long. He was determined to shake things up.

The captain imperiously turned to his men, one hundred strong, fully-armed and primed for mayhem. He shot his right arm into the air, his monocle glinting with moonlight, and signaled his three advance teams. They moved out in a triangle formation toward the village.

However, to get there they had to survive the swamp. A goal easier ordered than accomplished, especially at night when the unsettling mixture of tall grass and waist-deep mire would be more disorienting than usual. The men were professional killers who had trained in a variety of climates and were well-equipped: guns, poison gas, flame-throwers, and more. Their manpower matched the native warriors one-on-one and their weaponry promised a decisive victory. However, they had not figured on two critical obstacles to their plan of attack. One was that the Seminoles would be fighting in spiritual union with their ancestors, which exponentially increased the power of one. The other was the participation of John Dawkins, a man who held no outward fear of death. Yet now, with Emily, he had someone to live for. It was a contradictory but potent combination.

The first advance team slogged into the heart of the swamp and before long they were up to their bellies in a fetid stew of water and mud. The second group of soldiers treaded warily through a dank arbor that was canopied by hanging vines. The third team had the lucky draw of a drier, more direct route to the village through a crag of rock that descended into a wash of thick underbrush. Oddly enough, it was the team with the easiest path that was the first to stray from formation.

One of the third team's rear guard soldiers, an intense young man named Rolf with an unhealthy obsession for the shoot-'em-up exploits of the Wild West, veered off to investigate what appeared to be a flickering light. As he advanced, the light was snuffed out, but a new element appeared – the cry of a baby.

Rolf warily rounded a corner and was surprised to discover a Seminole toddler stranded on top of a mound of white sand, crying for the parents who must have been separated from her in the rush to save their own lives. However, the sight of the helpless babe didn't summon pity in Rolf, but ambition.

"The only good Injun is a dead Injun," he muttered. He'd adopted the motto from devouring dozens of dime novels on the cowboy way, and now he had a chance to earn his spurs by making the first kill of what promised to be a victorious campaign. Rolf raised his rifle into firing position and took gleeful aim. Success would mean a medal on his chest, an increase in pay, and perhaps even a weekend leave in Heidelberg. He would see Rosie, his beautiful Rosie. Blond and plump with bee-stung lips. She'd spurned him before the war, but now she'd change her mind. How could she not? And if she still rejected him, he would show her who called the tune. He would make her love him. He would---

Alas, the wretched Rolf would do no more. His reverie proved fatal. For as his finger toyed with the trigger, the mound of sand beneath the bawling toddler rose up, revealing Long Tooth. The huge maw of the albino alligator opened wide and snared the wretched soldier, the jaws snapping shut around his spine with an audible crack of bone. The toddler's parents rushed up to bundle her away from the grisly scene. Rolf shrieked and waggled his bayonet with all the potency of a toothpick as the alligator's jaws sawed into his flesh.

Rolf's screams danced across the wind and reached the Seminole village where Papa Abaladi turned decisively to John.

"*Un*worthy."

On cue, the island sprung to life with the animals taking the initial line of defense. In the swamp, the legs of the first team were mangled by a swarm of alligators. In the arbor, the tranquil scene of hanging vines revealed itself as a ruse, for the foliage was only window-dressing for a cluster of snakes. They constricted their bodies around the necks of the second team and joined forces to strangle them up into the trees. As for the third team, the underbrush collapsed, dumping them into a pit teeming with wild boars, ravenous diners who nature had graciously equipped with the ready utensils of tusk and fang.

The chorus of shrieks from all three teams unnerved Captain Krill, and he damned himself for having underestimated both Edison and the Seminoles. He unleashed a roar of defiance, a rallying cry of bloodlust meant to inspire his troops and remind them their only claim of victory would be the total destruction of the village.

23

THE AFTERLIFE PART I

So far, the elements of the purgatory equation had performed as planned. However, as the velocity dial on the resurrector crept towards the launch trigger, Edison had to admit he was at a loss as to what actually might happen next. He surmised that our reality was separated from a variety of realities (death, time, alternate dimensions, etc.) by unseen walls of matter, as razor-thin as they were impenetrable. Occasionally elements of one realm seeped into another (ghosts, psychic phenomena, déjà vu, also etc.) but usually in brief encounters that were indistinct at best. Thus his goal to create a vehicle capable of penetrating the membranes separating these realms and establish a 'metaphysical highway' to the afterlife.

The velocity dial clicked onto 99. Was Edison afraid? He was. Yet his fear was balanced by an exhilarating sense of anticipation, rather like what an artist must feel when he overcomes the threat of the blank canvas and applies the first stroke of color. On the other hand, if something went terribly wrong, if he were to perish in his expedition to purgatory, at least he'd be memorialized as the only mortal in human history who'd had the benefit of a head start.

As for Gershwin, he dug his fingers into the arms of the passenger seat, determined to hang on for dear life. He discovered that any movement made him nauseous so he steeled himself and stared dead ahead.

The velocity dial hit 100%. Emily verified the RPMs and unleashed the core. A blast of voltage shot out from the churning pool of energy and magnetically enshrined the resurrector with a crackling shell of protective current. Aside from that initial volley of firepower, the machine continued to gyrate at a furious pace. However, inside the passenger bubbles something miraculous had occurred. The rings of the machine had achieved reverse synchronicity and in the blur of motion everything appeared to stop, as if floating in a frozen moment.

Then, with a furious cacophony that signaled the pillars of inner space being torn asunder, Edison and Gershwin plunged headlong into a cosmic void; the breakneck speed careening their passenger bubbles through a gauntlet of mind-bending phantasmagoria. Gershwin tried to retch, but the force of propulsion shoved the vomit back into his gullet. Even the hardy Edison was gratified he'd opted for a light dinner of tea and toast.

A pinprick of glittering light danced in the distance and within seconds they were at its door, only now it had expanded into a searing maw of white, hot energy. As the voyagers slammed into the wall of light a transformation occurred that not even Edison could have imagined. Their bodies began to deconstruct into swarming pools of molecules. The wall of light retracted into a tight funnel, what Edison would later refer to as 'the vanishing point,' and their molecules exploded, allowing them to pass through the restrictive entry and into the realm of the afterlife.

Edison quickly reconstructed into human form, elated to discover he had survived the journey. However, he was alone. No Gershwin, no machine, no constrictions of any kind. He was completely free to move about but to where? The landscape blossomed with amorphous life; a constantly evolving vista of form, color and sound. A clutch of fear clawed at his innards. He was lost and hadn't felt such sick panic since he was a boy.

A spiral of glittering jewels materialized in front of him. He studied the shimmering configuration. They were so tiny. So precious. He reached out tentatively to touch the dazzling prisms. They grew, expanding into a swirling curtain of color. As the curtain parted, Edison stood his ground, only to confront a figure as familiar as she was unexpected.

"Madame Blavatsky!" cried Edison. And damned if it wasn't her, looking exactly as she had at their brief but life-changing encounter some thirty years before.

The Madame nodded slyly. "Mr. Edison." She proffered a half-smile as tantalizing as it was enigmatic. "I told you it would be an adventure."

* * *

There was no one to greet Gershwin in his afterlife. As Edison had suspected, the purgatory experience might be different for everyone, specifically tailored to the subject's hopes and fears.

So he'd come all this way for what? Nothing, that's what. Swell. Then again, nothing was probably safer than something.

He placed his hands on his knees, twiddled his fingers, and waited patiently.

However, if Gershwin hadn't been blindfolded, he would have discovered he wasn't trapped in some solitary void but seated on the stage of a theater and illuminated by a star spot that slowly intensified from a limpid pastel to the brilliance of a hot pink. The searing light penetrated the fabric of his blindfold, giving the black cloth an iridescent quality. Gershwin dutifully lowered his head and shut his eyes.

Then it started. From the back of the darkened theatre a single hand began clapping. Then another set of palms joined in, encouraging the approval, then another and another, until the unseen audience awarded the young, unknown composer an ovation fit for a maestro. Gershwin broke into a grin, delighted by his reception, and blindly basked in the unanimous acclaim.

* * *

While the furious Captain Krill had been thoroughly blindsided by the animal kingdom's first-wave assault, he regained his bearing and ordered a counter-attack by the second unit to avenge their comrades who had fallen in such inglorious haste.

The invaders eliminated the alligators by pitching hand grenades into their gullets and blowing them into fragments of skin so puny that not even a single handbag could have been stitched from their remains. The arbor of snakes was incinerated by a trio of arsonists whose flame-throwers provided the serpents with the singular experience of shedding their skins before they had molted. The wild boars, although sated, remained trapped in a pit and became target practice for the marksmen who deliriously evened the score on behalf of their devoured comrades.

Naturally, some new casualties occurred. Once the alligators learned that grenades made for poor digestion, they effectively used their snouts, not to bite, but return the bombs to their senders. The remaining serpents hooked their fangs around the collarbones of the arsonists and yanked the frantic men into the treetops where the haywire streams of fire ignited their fuel canisters and engulfed the arbor in an inferno. Finally, the marksmen were so busy firing slap-happy, overkill shots into the pit, they failed to notice several of the deceased boars' four-footed brethren had remained outside the quarry. As a penalty for their short-sighted behavior they were roughly escorted down to the dining room for a second seating.

Despite the additional casualties, Captain Krill took cold comfort in the fact that the island's animals had been decimated as well. Obsessed with inflicting as much mayhem as possible, he ordered his remaining troops, some fifty in all, to charge the village.

* * *

"Here comes trouble," John alerted Papa Abaladi to the impending assault. However, the chieftain had turned his back on the marauding Germans and was gazing out to sea.

"Double trouble," offered Papa Abaladi, and John squinted, striving to see what new horrors awaited. A fleet of submarines? A convoy of troop ships invading from the west? No. It was something else, something not of man. Flashes of lightning illuminated the newest combatant to the melee: a tropical cyclone;

a tight, churning funnel of energy that was plowing across the gulf, gaining strength as it sucked up the warm ocean water and vomited it back out with a shattering force.

John steeled himself for the dual assault. He turned decisively to Papa Abaladi who nodded and gave the call: "*Totika!*" The circle of defense around the village erupted with spheres of hot light. They were fireballs, which the natives tucked into the metal catapult cradles and let fly on the advancing enemy. The Seminoles' aim was true, and several clusters of soldiers were instantly demolished. However, the light given off by the fireballs illuminated their positions and allowed the Germans to target their return fire. John and Papa Abaladi swung down from the observation platform to provide cover. John wrestled a machine gun off the body of a dead soldier and Papa Abaladi wielded his shark-tooth studded staff with deadly accuracy. The battle had been joined.

* * *

Edison gaped at the figure of Madame Blavatsky who, like the landscape surrounding her, ebbed and flowed in a constantly evolving form of shadow and substance. He blinked, steadied himself, and gathered his wits.

"Is this real?" he asked breathlessly.

"I am little more than a humbug," teased Madame Blavatsky with a wry arch of her eyebrow. "Why not consult a pillar of truth?"

A second spectral figure materialized in front of his eyes and took the form of the one man in whom Edison had always placed absolute confidence: Mark Twain.

"Samuel!" he cried.

"Is it real?" posed Twain. "I reckon it's real enough."

The two old friends clasped hands in greeting. The flesh wasn't exactly solid, noted Edison, but firm enough. It was him. "Tell me everything."

"All in good time," counseled Twain. "But right now you're in one hell of a fix!"

"Don't I know it – but how do I get out?"

Twain hem-hawed. "I'm not too savvy on all this scientific rigmarole."

Edison harrumphed in frustration and turned to Madame Blavatsky who shrugged. "Ditto."

"But I know just the feller to lend a hand," placated Twain. "He'll guarantee your invention's a blue-ribbon success."

"Who is it?" pestered Edison. It wasn't his intention to fuss but he'd made a difficult journey and he wanted to be greeted with answers instead of pleasantries.

Madame Blavatsky gestured and a figure emerged from the shimmering mist. It was Charley.

"Hello, Uncle."

Edison gasped as Charley embraced him. He returned the embrace and murmured, "My boy, my bright boy." This time there was no thwarted communication between spirit and matter but a genuine reunion. Edison stood back, scarcely believing his eyes. "Let me look at you." Charley indulged him. He was as he had been prior to his death: a lean youth with a shock of long, brown hair and a heart that was as determined as it was kind; kinder now than in life. After all, Charley had been no angel. Yet 'angel' now appeared to be his vocation.

Suddenly, Edison was flooded with the memory of shame. He had renounced the boy. How could he, a man who was different from others in so many ways, have disowned a nephew who was different from him in only one?

"Can you forgive a foolish old man?"

Charley fixed his gaze on Edison. "Forgive yourself, Uncle. Then all is forgiven."

Edison took his words to heart and was imbued with the joy of redemption, but Charley grasped his shoulders to ground him.

"There are three key elements you must master," he declared. Edison forced himself to focus. It was time to go to work.

"The first is that the afterlife exists on a parallel plane to life."

Edison nodded vigorously. He had theorized as much, but now spectral blueprints of the equation appeared before him and filtered into his brain, unleashing his capacity for comprehension into a whole new vista of intellect.

"The second key," continued Charley, "is that life and death aren't linear. They're circular and move in opposite directions."

Once again, the visual blueprints swirled around Edison's head. However, this theorem took more time to process, locking him in a kind of paralysis. Charley waited patiently. He prayed they would have enough time.

* * *

The applause for Gershwin had not abated. In fact, it had grown into a demanding wave of recognition with cries of "Bravo!" studding the ovation. If these kudos were truly for him, then who was he to deny this generous audience the communion of a curtain call? He stood and pulled off the blindfold. The theatre erupted in cheers, and two more spotlights joined the center spot as he bowed and embraced what could only be his coming success. Hadn't Edison said something about windows to the past and the future? Obviously, this was his future; the future he'd dreamt of so defiantly. He thrust his arms open wide and the audience rose to embrace him. So far, his young life had been one, long slog and, given the current circumstances, might be over before he got off the island. He was going to take advantage of this celebratory interlude and spend his remaining moments reveling in the acclaim.

Then he looked into the light.

It was not intentional. The light was so enshrining it was as if God himself were smiling down on him. But the look became a gaze and the gaze became a frozen stare as the future revealed itself. There was glory but misery as well, and the moment the images flashed before his eyes, Gershwin tried to blot them out of his brain. Yet the one thing he could not do was shut his eyes. A single tear crawled down his cheek. So there he stood, adulated and bound; horribly mesmerized as the things to come paraded obscenely before him.

* * *

The Seminole village had become a battlefield, with each new turn delivering a dilemma that either had to be vanquished or succumbed to. John and Papa Abaladi waded through the carnage, back to back, switching rapidly from offense to defense as the circumstances demanded; the only difference being that Papa

Abaladi relied solely on his razored staff to rout the enemy while John appropriated whatever weapon fell into his hands.

As for the gathering storm, it meted out an equal portion of obstacles to both sides. The stinging sheets of water added a clumsy layer of blindness to the Germans' assault. The Seminoles were forced to halt the barrage of fireballs when the fierce winds steered them off target and they crashed into a trio of huts, immolating them. Papa Abaladi realized it was time to change strategy. He grabbed John and pushed him toward the laboratory.

"You go. Save Edison."

"What about you?" he asked. "Your people?"

Papa Abaladi took John's measure. Here was a man who cared more for the safety of others than his own. That was a rare quality, no matter the shade of your skin. He clasped his forearm in gratitude.

"Seminoles are like swamp grass," replied the chieftain. "We bend."

With that, Papa Abaladi raised a conch shell and trumpeted a rallying cry. The natives halted whatever conflict they were engaged in and abruptly vanished. Had they abandoned the village? Yes and no. In anticipation of a threat to their way of life, the Seminoles had excavated a maze of tunnels beneath the village. There they'd be safe and able to covertly direct the battle to its outcome.

John raced to the laboratory. As he reached the building, someone clubbed him to his knees. He looked up and confronted two images of the same soldier. He shook his head, disoriented, but this was not a case of double-vision. It was his introduction to a pair of baby-faced Aryan twins, *both* evil, who exchanged cruel smiles and proceeded to batter John unmercifully, with one initiating a strike and the other repeating it. The roundelay of kicks and punches landed John flat on his back, only inches from the laboratory door and seconds from unconsciousness.

* * *

Emily anxiously monitored the puzzle of gauges and levers on the control panel. She had three immediate concerns. The first was that the mayhem outside the laboratory, weather-wise and other-wise, caused the walls to groan and buckle. Secondly, the metal base of the resurrector had scoured the wooden supports with such intense friction that a fire ignited. Finally, she prayed she'd be able to retrieve Edison and Gershwin in sound condition and armed with the miracle that would save them all. The experiment had ten seconds left.

* * *

John lay prostrate at the feet of the sadistic twins, who had grown winded from the fight and decided to turn John into a 'CC' – in military parlance, a 'closed casket' – a body so disfigured it couldn't be properly displayed to grieving loved ones. They raised their bayonets high to strike deep and skewer the cold steel through his eyes, when an errant bolt of lightning was lured to the wet metal and struck, searing through their weapons and electrocuting the venal siblings.

* * *

Edison opened his eyes. He was ready for the final part of the puzzle. Charley continued: "And the third key is---"

And then it happened. Mother Nature intruded, disrupting both worlds.

* * *

Although John was spared, the bolt of lightning surged through the jiggling, charred corpses of the twins and down into the laboratory, where it corrupted the control panel, flung Emily across the room, and slammed the resurrector to an abrupt stop.

* * *

Edison and Gershwin were sucked out of their respective purgatories at a sickening, dangerous speed. As they plummeted backwards through the vanishing point, their molecules became hideously scrambled and had to re-assemble again and again in a series of painful deformities until the frenzy ended and they returned to their proper forms.

* * *

John burst through the laboratory door and barricaded it behind him. As he started down the stairs he spotted Emily, who was crumpled in a corner. He took her limp body in his arms and shook her back to consciousness.

"John," she murmured. They embraced, steadied each other, and made their way toward the resurrector to pull Edison and Gershwin out of the machine. Both men were whole but disoriented; Gershwin strangely stunned and Edison babbling incoherently.

"The third key…I must have the third key…"

A rhythmic thud against the laboratory door cued John. Time to go! He pushed Emily and Gershwin through the hidden door in the wall that led to the escape tunnel.

"Hurry," urged John. "We'll be right behind …"

John turned back to Edison who sat vacantly in a chair, fingering Gershwin's discarded blindfold. He grimaced and shook his head. The poor boy. John urged him to his feet. There was no time for regrets. The Germans were at the door. Edison turned back for one final look at the laboratory. Would he ever know the meaning of the third key? He gritted his teeth and they made their escape.

* * *

Captain Krill stood at an admiring distance as his team secured the circumference of the laboratory and, with a tree trunk as a battering ram, proceeded to splinter the door. Edison would be his!

However, the area surrounding the laboratory had been camouflaged by a thin layer of sod laid over a track of wooden slats which, in turn, concealed a waist-deep moat of oil. On Papa Abaladi's command, the natives released the slats, toppling the soldiers into the pit of viscous fuel.

His warrior's mind quickly connecting the dots, Captain Krill screamed for his men to evacuate the pit – "*Schnell!*" – but he was too late. Papa Abaladi aimed a flaming arrow from his longbow and let fly. The arrow whistled through the air and hit its mark, igniting the ribbon of oil into a blazing snare of hellfire.

* * *

Emily pulled Gershwin through the tunnel's tight, murky path. She was exhausted, he even more so. Out of harm's immediate way, they stopped and collapsed. She hugged him tight. He stared straight ahead.

"I saw things. In the machine."

Emily nodded, distracted. "You can tell me later."

Gershwin shook his head and his voice trembled. "I think…I saw you. I think…" He pushed his fingers against his temples, trying to press the conflicting images into some kind of sense. "I think it's important."

Emily didn't doubt his pain or precognition but there was no time. "We've got to move."

Gershwin nodded, and they helped each other to their feet. As Emily turned to lead the way, she came face-to-face with someone she never dreamed she would see again.

Gaunt.

He grabbed Emily by the throat and lifted her off the ground. Gershwin rallied to defend her, but the giant swatted him into submission. Emily shouted for help and Gaunt smothered her cries by pressing his slab of a hand over her face, as he carried her out of the tunnel and into the churning storm.

24

FRIEND OR FOE

Following his resurrection from the smoking ruins of the Menlo Park laboratory, Gaunt set out on a quest to find Edison. After several dead ends, he paid a call to the great man's New Jersey offices. The terrified but defiantly officious Mr. Meadowcroft ordered Gaunt to put an end to his senseless mayhem, head south, and be quick about it. Surprisingly, Gaunt complied. Upon the giant's departure, the persnickety secretary immediately tried to warn Edison by telephone, telegram, and telegraph and, failing on all three counts, exited pell-mell as well on an extended sabbatical of his own – and as far north as possible.

At the end of a journey punctuated with numerous incidents of havoc, Gaunt found himself on Captiva prepared to meet his mentor. The question remained: Was Edison a friend or a foe? It was a conundrum Gaunt could not answer. The events at the laboratory had scrambled his mind and a capacity for integrated thinking had never been his strong suit. All Gaunt knew was that he had been mocked, tortured and left for dead. Yes, he had murdered in revenge. He didn't want to kill again, but he would, and gladly, if the circumstances so demanded. That's why it was so crucial he find Edison. Not only had the inventor provided him with a home, he'd served as a leash of conscience on the behemoth's unstable id. Until Edison could prove his devotion, Gaunt would do as he pleased and take what he wanted. Now, at this moment, he wanted Emily. He lurched through the wind-ripped swamp, ferrying her to a secluded place where he could indulge his forbidden desires.

* * *

John crooked Edison's arm across his shoulder and carried him down the stone stairway and into the tunnel. As they rounded a corner, they found Gershwin sprawled out on the ground and Emily gone. John eased Edison down to the floor and slapped Gershwin's semi-conscious face.

"Where's Emily?" John demanded evenly.

Gershwin rallied enough to point feebly toward the end of the tunnel.

"Gaunt…"

John bolted upright in shock. Gaunt was dead! He'd seen him collapse through the fiery floorboards. But what if…?

"Stay here," he advised Edison and raced down the narrow tunnel, his adrenaline surging. If Gaunt was alive and had tracked them, dear God! He'd seen how the giant had flung Harry Singer about the laboratory like a rag doll. He'd felt the monster's vise-like grip himself and still had the bruises to prove it. Emily was in terrible danger. They all were.

John's footfalls echoed down the tunnel and then grew silent. Gershwin turned to Edison and touched the old man's arm.

"Are you all right?"

Edison managed a nod. "I think so."

"I took off my blindfold." Gershwin began to weep, his tears hot with regret. "I'm sorry."

Edison clapped his hand on Gershwin's shoulder in a show of comfort. Then, with a tone that was as empathetic as it was curious, he asked, "What did you see?"

"The future." Gershwin wiped the tears from his face with the back of his hand.

Edison considered this. Then, breathlessly: "What happens?"

Gershwin screwed up his face and shook his head. "My mind's all jumbled up." He stared helplessly at Edison. "I can't remember."

"Consider that a blessing."

Gershwin nodded. "What did you see?"

Edison clenched his jaw. "Not enough."

* * *

John reached the tunnel's exit and, as he ventured into the storm, his movements devolved into slow motion. The winds had ratcheted into a howling barrier of fifty miles an hour. John blinkered his hands around his eyes and scanned the area for Gaunt. He spotted him, plodding into a hidden cove, Emily trapped in his arms. John took a running leap and the force of his assault startled Gaunt, who dropped Emily and tried to claw off his attacker.

Gaunt broke John's hold and hurled him to the ground. Before he could scramble to his feet to formulate some kind of defense, the giant was on him. Gaunt grasped his head between his huge hands and lifted him into the air. John could only summon a puny defense as the monster's fingers tightened around his skull, slowly crushing it.

Emily revived and attacked Gaunt, slugging at him impotently with her fists. He held John in the air with one hand and brushed her off with the other, although a brush for Gaunt was a wallop for Emily and she hit the ground hard. She summoned her strength and flung herself at his feet.

"Stop! I love him!" She repeated the phrase again and again, at first with tears and then, oddly enough, without – but fraught with an emotional insistence that penetrated the hulk's small brain, made him stop and, remarkably, think. It was the performance of her life because it wasn't acting. It was passion. It was real.

Gaunt looked down at Emily, chastened. She had been kind to him. He would return the kindness. He relcased John, who flopped to the ground. Emily rushed to his side. Gaunt watched the two of them and whined in envy as she cradled John and he revived. Suddenly the giant's wail ratcheted into a defensive snarl and they looked up to see what he saw – a half-dozen German soldiers who had them surrounded. The soldiers advanced, eager to inflict damage. They were well-armed but had no idea of the chaos they were swaggering into. Gaunt's metal eye began flashing blue/gold/blue/gold and with a blood-curdling howl, he hurled himself into the fray.

* * *

Edison felt the strength return to his arms and prayed that his legs had recovered sufficiently as well. He nodded to Gershwin and the two men helped each other up. The sound of swift, approaching footsteps was heard. They steeled themselves for any manner of adversary and were relieved when they discovered it was Papa Abaladi. He was startled by their ravaged condition but there was no time for commiseration.

"Storm is here - we must go!" The chieftain shepherded them down the tunnel and, as they navigated the twisting space, their gait steadied and they gained speed. Then they turned the next corner and ran into an impenetrable blockade – Captain Krill and his senior officers.

The captain greeted them with honeyed malevolence. "Mr. Edison. Again. But this time, for the last time."

Papa Abaladi leapt protectively in front of Edison and Gershwin and unleashed a warning cry as he defiantly thumped his shark-tooth studded staff on the stone floor. Captain Krill paused, raised his eyebrows in disbelief, and laughed out loud at the savage's temerity. His men chimed in with the requisite amount of supportive guffaws but their amusement was genuine. It would be a treat to see the captain toy with this 'redskin' and then decimate him.

Captain Krill peered at the chieftain's staff and delicately extended his monocle. "What a charming antiquc. May I take a closer look?"

"Watch out," warned Gershwin but it was too late. Captain Krill flung the razored weapon at Papa Abaladi, who only had time to wield his staff in a single stroke. The captain sneered, the soldiers howled, and Gershwin grabbed hold of the valiant Seminole so when he collapsed from the fatal blow he'd be spared the indignity of falling flat on his face.

However, Gershwin was surprised to find Papa Abaladi

was not bleeding and the deadly monocle had not retracted into Captain Krill's wrist compartment. Instead it was wedged safely in the chieftain's staff. He pounded it and the monocle popped out, the glass shattering on the stone floor.

Dumbfounded, Captain Krill looked down at his demolished weapon. His vision blurred. He blinked hard but the focus refused to return. His face felt flush. He touched his cheek, fingered the moisture, and drew back pinpricks of blood. Perplexed, he turned to his men whose mouths shot open in horror as their leader's skin erupted in a rash of dotted blood that rapidly seeped into parallel lines, revealing the angle at which Papa Abaladi's staff had cleaved his face into slabs of meat. The captain shrieked in agony as slices of his flesh began to slide off his skull and spatter onto the ground. Oddly, although there was no longer sound, the jawbone remained open in mid-scream until the torso collapsed in a heap. Papa Abaladi unleashed a murderous war-cry – *Chati!*– and raked his staff against the ceiling of the tunnel, rousing a colony of vampire bats who bared their blood-thirsty fangs and attacked the general's petrified men as they abandoned the tunnel.

Papa Abaladi guided Edison and Gershwin out of the tunnel and into the swamp. The cyclone was moments from striking land. Edison pulled his old friend in close. "Go to the cavern," he instructed. "We'll find the others and meet you there."

Papa Abaladi paused, unsure if the old man could survive the onslaught without him. Edison decisively waved him off and the chieftain, encouraged by the return of his friend's irascible nature, nodded sharply in agreement and disappeared into the swamp.

Before Edison and Gershwin could decide which route to take, an ungodly howl prompted their decision. They dashed through a windswept grove of oleander trees to discover a scene of unimaginable carnage. Gaunt stood in the center of a bloodbath. He had shredded the soldiers into a collage of ripped appendages and convulsing torsos. Yet he had been damaged as well. His body was studded with bullets, his face and chest charred and still smoking. He arched his head back in a howl of conquest that echoed through the screaming winds. It was a foolish boast, for his defeat had already been arranged. He was mired in a pool of quicksand, the tenacious kind of adversary he'd never battled before. Yet fight he must, for, as the ruptured bodies littered around him sank into the bog, Gaunt's attempts to raise his legs from the vise of quicksand only served to lock him into its clutches.

"Gaunt!" cried Edison. The hulk whimpered tremulously, like a child who has taken his first fall and is confused by how much pain he should register. Edison tried to rally the others to the rescue but they remained wary. Although Edison had professed Gaunt to be a harmless creature, his actions had proved otherwise, and they resisted the old man's cries for assistance.

A roar of wind blasted through the cove and several palm trees collapsed. One of the trees, a large cabbage palm, fell in a perpendicular direction with the roots still anchored to solid land and its thick fan fronds brushing the surface of the bog. Edison hopped onto the base of the trunk and began to slowly crawl towards Gaunt, whose wail ratcheted into a high-pitched squeal of panic as he continued to sink into the grasping bog.

Emily took pity on him. She urged John and Gershwin to come to his aid and they grudgingly agreed. John hacked off a vine and fashioned it into a lasso. While Gershwin secured the back end to a crag of rock, John hurled the lifeline out to Gaunt. On the second throw, the giant caught the lasso and looped it under his arms. The three of them pooled their strength, pulling as hard as they could to free the hulking creature, but his weight – and the suction of the quicksand – was too great.

They all shouted instructions at once. John urged Gaunt to lean forward so he could reel him in at an angle. Emily begged him to stop thrashing and relax. Gershwin advised Gaunt to lie on his back and float – it had worked for him. All the while, Edison continued to shimmy across the tapering trunk, and then the unstable fronds, placing himself in mortal danger. Gaunt registered none of this. For the first time in his life he was in the grip of something greater than his own might and he was lost, fighting frantically as the pit raised its hold on him; legs, thighs, stomach and now chest. He felt a hand grasp his – Edison! Gaunt took the old man's hand, patted it, and spoke Edison's name in gratitude. He had the answer he had hoped for – friend. They shared a silent moment of fellowship. Then an ear-splitting din caused both of them to confront the horizon.

The cyclone landed on shore with an incredible, pulverizing force. Gaunt considered the circumstances and, while he was not a thinking man, he knew his time was nigh – and that any further attempt at rescuing him might end the lives of his would-be redeemers as well. He let go of Edison's hand, transferred the lassoed vine from his body to the old inventor's and cinched the loop. Edison protested but Gaunt assumed a serene demeanor.

"You stay," declared Gaunt in a kind of benediction. "I go."

Edison reluctantly accepted Gaunt's decision and allowed John and the others to pull him back to solid ground. Once secured, he waved farewell to his old friend. John and Gershwin acknowledged his sacrifice, and Emily blew him a tearful kiss of thanks in gratitude for his mercy and affection.

Mercy and affection. These were not the attributes of a monster. In fact, it was rare that human beings exhibited such qualities, unless of course they had motive, self-serving or otherwise. Gaunt did not speculate. Edison was his friend. That was enough. As his head descended beneath the suffocating surface of the bog, his metal eye began to rotate; first gold, then blue, then a blur. But this time it spun not out of rage or fear, but from joy.

25

RELIANCE

Edison stoically led his battered crew through a wind-whipped grove of palm trees. Tears rimmed his eyes, but he did not look back. Their only salvation was to keep moving. A final push and they reached the mouth of a cavern. They entered the hollow of limestone to discover a towering ceiling daggered with stalactites. A winding path lit by torches cast an otherworldly glow against the icicles of rock.

"I only have one invention left," Edison informed John. "But it might aid in our escape."

John decisively shook his head. "The cyclone's on top of us. We'll never get off the island."

Undeterred, Edison led them through a tight, winding corridor of rock that opened onto a waterway. It featured a boat dock and a narrow canal that extended directly into the north side of the gulf. Papa Abaladi stood on the dock next to a large, shrouded object. At Edison's command, he pulled the tarpaulin off the oblong curiosity, revealing:

"The Reliance," he proclaimed. "My electric launch."

The trim vessel operated on electricity, which made for

a silent rather than roaring ride and, unlike ‘explosive motors’ (or ‘gasoline motors,’ as they would someday more shrewdly be marketed) that dumped up to a third of their fuel as waste, it created no pollution. All well and good, surmised John. But no amount of environmental benefits would be of use in their current predicament. Any attempt to breach the fury of the gulf on a 24-footer with a candy-cane striped canopy was madness.

However, John had not taken Edison’s penchant for innovative accessories into consideration. The hull of the launch had been lined with rows of propellers that transformed it from a Sunday afternoon excursion boat into a high-powered water craft capable of pinpoint handling and enormous speed.

“Quickly!” ordered Edison. They climbed onboard and strapped into their seats which were stationed in a single row, one behind the other.

Papa Abaladi bid farewell as Edison took the seat next to the throttle. The canopy split down the middle and re-fashioned itself into an aerodynamic shield around the launch. John fingered the material. Strangely, it wasn’t oil cloth but aluminum.

Edison punched the throttle and the launch shot out of the cavern with a speed that stunned them all. With a solid assist from the prevailing winds, the needle-shaped craft threaded a narrow path of least resistance through the turbulent waters of the gulf. Once they had reached the relative safety of the tempest’s back-end, Edison slowed the launch and brought it around. They watched in amazement as the cyclone ripped across the island and reached the laboratory. The powerful fists of the funnel dug deep into the earth and yanked the resurrector into the air, the muscular winds warping the machine with the same arbitrary disregard by which a toddler rips the petals off a daisy. As it spun drunkenly in the air, the resurrector served as a magnet, drawing all the crackling fingers of lightning to its core. First one strike, then another, then a dozen more as the bolts congregated into one mighty blast. The resurrector exploded, disintegrating into a clattering mist of metal.

Edison bolted up in shock. John steadied him. He noted that, while the inventor was in his sixty-eighth year, he'd never truly looked his age until now. His mouth flopped open in wordless grief, his eyes turned pink and wet with regret and, absent the natural exuberance that normally propelled him into the unknown, his body caved in on itself. The attack on his Menlo Park laboratory, the deaths of Harry and Gaunt, and now this irreversible loss.

"Thirty years of work…gone," he whispered. John and Emily tried to comfort him but he was inconsolable. "My greatest invention. All gone."

Gershwin felt someone should add a silver lining to the suffocating gloom. He remembered his mother's favorite maxim of dubious encouragement. "Look on the bright side," he offered. "At least nothing else can go wrong."

Fortune sometimes smiles on the fool. This was not one of those occasions. For no sooner had Gershwin uttered those fateful words then the next conveyance for their misadventures presented itself – a German submarine that broke through the waves and stranded the launch on the bridge of the U-boat.

Sailors poured out of the hold and roughly shanghaied them below. There was no point in fighting, no place to run. There was only surrender and the belief that, despite Mother Gershwin, things would continue to go wrong. Edison was the last to descend into the bowels of the submarine. He paused and watched in resignation as what was left of the resurrector sank into the swamp. Utterly defeated, he did something he hadn't done since he was a boy – he did as he was told – and joined the others below as the call to dive was sounded and the submarine disappeared into the dark, roiling waters.

26

WASHINGTON, D.C.

Washington, D.C. was dressed for war. The country had resisted the attire since the first outbreak of armed conflict in Europe four years ago. In 1916, the current occupant of the White House, President Woodrow Wilson, won re-election to his second term under the campaign slogan, *He Kept Us Out Of War!* Now, only two years later, war was inevitable. The United States would have preferred to maintain their neutrality for financial reasons if nothing else. It would be several years before another president would deathlessly declaim, 'The business of America is business!' but that was already the unspoken sentiment of the time. This sorry fact would have come as a surprise to the founding fathers who'd been naïve enough to suppose that the business of America was democracy.

The United States had developed a substantial trade relationship with Germany. Even Edison himself had established several lucrative contracts with Berlin. However, both man and country changed their tune when the Germans unilaterally declared their right to unrestricted submarine warfare as witnessed by the sinking of the Lusitania and even more importantly, with the revelation of an infamous communiqué known as 'The Zimmerman Telegram.'

Germany realized their unprecedented nautical misadventures might goad the United States into war. So a subterfuge was conceived by Alfred Zimmerman, their foreign minister, to delay America's engagement by embroiling it in a separate conflict all its own.. Zimmerman contacted President Carranza of Mexico and proposed their countries form an alliance. In return for Mexico's declaration of war against the United States, Germany would provide them with all the support they needed to achieve a re-conquest of their vanquished territories in Texas, New Mexico, and Arizona.

Unhappily for Zimmerman, President Carranza declined his generous offer. More unfortunately, the offer was intercepted by British Intelligence who passed it on to President Wilson. Infuriated, Wilson broadcast the bribe for the whole world to witness. Several months later, he went before Congress to ask for a declaration of war and received a thunderous endorsement. He took no pleasure in the acclaim. Wilson knew his edict was more than a call for national service. It was a death warrant for tens of thousands of young Americans. The outcome must be certain; victory of such a magnitude that it would ensure a lasting, postwar peace, and that a world conflict of this kind would never be permitted to happen again.

* * *

President Wilson emerged from a smoke-filled meeting in the cabinet room with his retinue of advisers clustered around him.

The day's war news was uneventful. General 'Black Jack' Pershing and his troops had arrived in France to provide the allies with the support they so desperately needed. However, the American forces were still in the process of assembling in sufficient numbers and had not yet entered the fight. The pros and cons between the president's brain trust remained split between an engagement of 'now' or 'later.' Wilson wisely relished the dispute. Presidential power exuded an intoxicant that often persuaded even the most individual voice to succumb to the chorus. He prized loyalty but only in public. In private, he wanted a vigorous debate with partisans, not parrots.

As Wilson approached the oval office, Joseph Tumulty, his earnest personal secretary, intercepted him, a blush of consternation on his freckled, Irish face.

"Mrs. Thomas Edison has arrived with an urgent message from her husband."

Tumulty was forced to fall into step with Wilson, who was in no mood to stop and far from inclined to accept what he assumed was Edison's apology for their combative telephone conversation of several weeks ago.

"Take the message and offer my regrets," responded Wilson. With that, he and his advisors returned to their deliberation.

Tumulty persisted. "She refuses to leave until she sees you. She insists that---"

Wilson broke his stride. It was rare of Tumulty to re-visit a minor edict. "Tell her I'm busy being president," ordered Wilson. "Then send her on her way." Wilson offered a curt nod and started back down the hallway, his advisers in lockstep.

Tumulty stayed where he stood and spoke out, louder than

usual. "She's invaded the oval office, sir."

Wilson stopped and laughed in surprise. He hadn't laughed in several days and it was a pleasant respite.

"She's very stubborn," concluded the abject Tumulty.

The president exhaled slowly and shook his head. Stubborn women were an inconvenience but one that he secretly admired.

"Damn suffragettes," muttered Baker, the Secretary of War.

"Hell-bent to get the vote," joined in McAdoo, the Secretary of the Treasury, who also happened to be the president's son-in-law. Ah, well. There was one in every family. Even the first family.

The only advisor not to disparage Mrs. Edison was Josephus Daniels, the Secretary of the Navy. A closet progressive with a bulldog face and a persuasive manner, he'd already notched a series of nautical advances, both major (introducing the service of women into the Navy) and minor (replacing all alcohol onboard ship with coffee, thus inaugurating the phrase, 'a cup of Joe.') Less successfully, he'd been the administration's leading advocate on behalf of Edison's innovative military inventions, and he welcomed the opportunity to witness the fireworks first-hand as the president and his men entered the oval office to confront a properly enraged Mina Edison.

"I am not a hell-bent suffragette," she brusquely advised, having overheard their demeaning conversation. "I am a lady and will be content to remain as such if you will behave like gentlemen."

Mina had been cooling her gabardine heels in the Hotel Washington for the past four days. There'd been no word from her husband and she'd been unable to gain an audience with the president through conventional means, so she wheedled her way in, using a potent mixture of charm and clout. President Wilson trotted out his honeyed southern accent to placate her. He'd come a long way since the Carolinas but found his folksy tone often disarmed bullheaded constituents and delighted the ladies.

"My apologies, dear madam. This war business…"

"Which is my business," sharply countered Mina, in no mood to be disarmed or delighted. "My husband charged me with delivering this message to you within three days' time. That was seven days ago."

She handed President Wilson a sealed envelope. He read the message with a growing concern he was unable to mask. "Where is Mr. Edison?" he asked.

"Vanished."

Wilson paused. There was no use alarming the lady. "I shouldn't worry. I'm sure he'll re-appear in due course." However, it was Wilson who was alarmed. To bolster his argument, Baker and McAdoo chimed in soothingly.

"He's probably holed up working on some new-fangled invention," said one.

"It is the way of the creative mind," added the other.

Mina offered them a sunny smile laced with disdain. "How wise of you gentlemen to enlighten me as to the habits of my own husband."

Secretary Daniels stifled a chuckle. He had thought of introducing himself as an ally of Edison's. It might have brought her a bit of solace in a roomful of strangers. However, her kind of grit didn't require solace, and his identity as an advocate might be better served discreetly.

She turned to go. "My mission is complete. You have the information. You will either take action or not." The men stood as

Mrs. Edison made for the door and then turned back sharply: "As a woman, it's true; my powers in this democracy are minimal. But if I should become a widow due to your incompetence…"

Mina burst into a heartbreaking display of distraught tears then coldly shut off the fraudulent waterworks with a savvy rise of her eyebrow.

"I will bring you to your knees."

Wilson gulped.

"Good day," she trilled brightly and then was gone.

The president turned grimly to his war trust. "Have there been any reports of an incursion off the Gulf Coast?"

An awkward silence. Daniels glanced at Secretary McAdoo who tightly shook his head in warning. Daniels proceeded in spite of his craven colleagues. "Yes, sir," he replied. "The sighting of a German submarine. Four days ago."

Wilson angrily pursed his mouth. "Why wasn't I informed?"

Secretary Baker stepped forward. He'd previously countermanded Daniels on this piece of intelligence and proceeded to do so again. "Mr. President, the source was completely unreliable," he preened. "A tribe of Seminole Indians."

"Nothing but ignorant savages," tittered McAdoo.

Wilson shot him a sharp look. "Not so ignorant as some in this room." Secretary McAdoo's laughter choked in his throat. It was hell being a son-in-law.

Wilson stared out into the Rose Garden as the winter sunset descended and the honor guard lowered the American flag. "The Germans have Edison. The last time we spoke he said he'd make a contribution to ending the war on his own terms. What might those terms be?" Wilson paused and turned to Secretary Daniels. "Joe?"

Daniels considered the various scenarios and settled on the most prudent course. “Alert General Pershing,” he advised. “Tell him to keep his eyes peeled and his powder dry.”

“Mr. President, no,” interceded Secretary Baker. “The First Division’s primed for battle. We must attack now!”

Wilson shook his head. “Let’s wait for the Germans to make the next move.”

Secretary Daniels nodded in agreement. It was a small, but welcome victory. “The Germans…or Edison?” he added wryly.

Wilson gave a small, hopeful laugh. “If I was a betting man? Edison.”

27

PRISONERS

In addition to his fame as a great inventor, Thomas Alva Edison had earned a reputation as a cantankerous old man. If that same adjective, which illustrates the mischief of dotage, could be applied to childhood it would have been an equally apt description of the young Tom Edison.

The baby in a family of six siblings who were either years older or had died prematurely, he was raised as an only child. Although frail and prone to illness, he was a relentlessly inquisitive toddler. While the active cultivation of the boy's imagination seemed promising, it soon translated into nothing but trouble.

Intrigued with the element of fire and its applications, young Tom proceeded to burn down the family barn. Consigned to a plodding education under the caned tutelage of one Reverend G.B. Engle, he promptly lit out as a runaway. Plagued by a series of ear infections that initiated his lifelong battle with deafness, the boy was confined to home where his mother, Nancy, schooled him. A good woman who took solace in her sufferings, Nancy's lesson plan placed a special emphasis on the Bible; a daily rumination on all the ways a bad boy could qualify for eternal damnation, with all of those ways being the stock-in-trade of young Tom Edison. He was, by turns, impatient, manipulative, slothful, and difficult. However, far worse than any of these unfortunate attributes was that no one in his immediate vicinity had enough horse sense to realize they were integral clues to the boy's potential brilliance.

Samuel Edison, a handsome jack-of-all-trades, prided himself as being as much a free-thinker as his wife was a disciplinarian. Yet even Sam had grown concerned about his son. The general consensus of the townspeople of Port Huron was that Tom was an addle-brained misfit, but Sam suspected his son's mind was simply too active for his body. On Tom's twelfth birthday, his father decreed the time had come for him to put aside childish ways and go to work. This was not Dickensian child labor. For small town boys without the grease of wealth to ease them into higher education, work was the rule. For Edison, work was a blessing. It was work that saved him.

He secured his first job hawking sundries on the train that ran between Port Huron and Detroit. He thrived in the hub-bub of humanity, and his mind was given free rein to take in all the aspects of life he encountered, like a sponge indiscriminately sucks up every speck of moisture within reach.

Edison soon graduated to his second job as a boy telegraph operator. In this esteemed profession he experienced what biographers often refer to as their subject's 'defining moment,' although the following incident would be underestimated as just another anecdote of youth when in fact it spurred and haunted him for the rest of his life.

One stormy evening, a Detroit shipping magnate offered

young Tom twenty-five dollars cash money to deliver an emergency message to one of his former captains with the condition that the missive be delivered before morning. The captain lived in the far countryside, some fourteen miles from the nearest telegraph station, so the boy would have to deliver the message on foot.

Eager for the money and the opportunity to impress his employer, he volunteered and set out with a single lantern to guide his way. The trek demanded that he pass through a shrouded forest and at the halfway mark, the dark clouds opened up and gave way to a deluge of pounding rain. Soon after, Edison stumbled over a thicket of tree roots, smashed the lantern, and lost the light. He was alone in the dark and petrified; every shadow an assassin, every sound a rapacious animal intent on devouring him. He stood frozen in sick fear and wept. Then pissed his pants. Then shat them. Finally, with nothing else to purge from his system, he took one step forward, then another, and on and on; propelled not just by fright but by the iron determination to subdue his fear and conquer it. He achieved the former, arriving at the captain's cabin by daybreak. But the latter? The conquering part? Not then. Not even now.

* * *

John was swaddled in a plush cocoon of shadows and never wanted to leave. Any notion of departure had to be gently strangled into surrender. The drugs had done their work. And yet… there was something tugging at him; murmurs that echoed into yelps of panic. John grew concerned that the cries were his and that this was a third-person variation of his recurring nightmare.

However, the nightmare was not his but someone else's. He woke up in darkness, tried to shake the morphine out of his brain and determine his surroundings. It was a pit, not of earth, but of stone; the cold, slate walls streaked with condensation. He followed the strands of light to their source. Above him, by some twelve feet, a few errant stars peeked through the bars of a metal grate. They twinkled promisingly but were too far out of reach to inspire any incentive except wonder. The yips of anguish sounded again, and John turned to discover the source was Edison, who lay curled on his side, his right hand pressed firmly against the floor as if holding something horrible at bay. John gently rustled the old man from his nightmare and Edison rolled over, disoriented, his fingertips speckled with blood.

"Dark…it's so dark…" whined Edison as he emerged from his drugged stupor.

John reached out to him. "It's John. I'm here," he offered comfortingly.

Edison grasped his arm and held on tight, his breath still ragged. "Are we alive?"

John propped him up and gestured toward the ceiling grate. "I think so," he replied. "See the stars."

Edison looked up and smiled as if those few hazy stars were the most beautiful sight he'd ever seen. They were. They always had been. "Stars," he marveled. A veil of haze parted, increasing the brilliance of the constellations and revealing the moon which lit up Edison's face with a soft, reassuring glow.

"Ever since I was a boy, I've been afraid of the dark."

It was a strange, sudden confession, and it made John uncomfortable because he expected in time it would make Edison uncomfortable. However, a response was warranted so he decided to offer one as bland as possible. “Everyone’s afraid of something.”

Edison chuckled wanly. “The dark’s more than just something. Night. Ignorance. Depression. Loneliness. Blindness. Death. All forms of darkness.” He sighed in wry resignation. “Foolish old me. All these years. All these inventions to hold back the dark.” He shook his head. “But it’s still dark. And I’m still afraid.”

John was silent. He had just witnessed the vulnerable child at the heart of a great man. He had no words.

Edison turned to him. “What are you afraid of, John?”

John avoided questions like this. They were usually posed in drunken parlor games and he had several responses at the ready: lions and tigers, an empty whiskey bottle, etc. However, this time the answer escaped from his subconscious so quickly it startled him.

“Life.”

Edison blanched at the unexpected response.

John continued: “It’s so arbitrary. No rhyme. No reason.”

Edison studied him pensively. “The loved ones you lost,” he recalled. “Who were they?”

“My parents,” replied John. Now the words became a struggle. “When they married, my father took on the family business. When I was seven, he lost it all. He killed himself.” He paused. “My mother was overcome with loss. She died three days later.”

“I’m so very sorry,” offered Edison.

Under normal conditions, this condolence would have ended the discussion. But John had tapped into a well of buried emotion. “He couldn’t live with himself,” he blurted out. “And she couldn’t live without him.” John dropped his head in misery and wrapped his arms around his knees to stave off the regret that wracked his body.

Edison patted a supportive hand on his shoulder. “There now…it’ll be light, soon enough.”

John nodded, choked back his emotion, and gazed up at the sky. “Just look at those stars.”

A moan sounded from the far end of the cell and John crawled over to investigate. Two more figures were balled up on the floor. Emily and Gershwin. Then he remembered everything. Captiva…the battle…the storm…the submarine…kidnapped by the Germans and finally the lullaby of the hypodermic that had submerged him into the long, lush sleep. He rustled Emily, bringing her face to his.

“John?” She arched her back as she brushed her lips lightly against his.

“I’m here.”

Emily purred in satisfaction and then sat upright in doped concern. “Where’s Gersh?”

Gershwin lay propped up against a wall, his mouth lolled open. He shook his head in a futile attempt to banish the hangover. “I’ll never drink again,” he vowed, mistaking the effects of morphine for one too many champagne cocktails.

Emily became suddenly, soberly aware of their dank circumstances. “Where the hell are we?”

“The question isn’t ‘where’ my dear,” observed Edison. “It’s ‘why.’ Why are we still alive?”

In the distance footsteps echoed. Leather against stone.

Three pairs of boots. Then the flicker of an approaching torchlight.

"We're about to find out," whispered John. A heavy key clanked into the lock. The metal door swung open, and a torch was shoved into the cell, exposing the captives' state of anxious disarray. Then the torch illuminated the silhouettes of three mysterious figures and, finally, the face of the man in the middle. He opened his mouth in a smile but the flames only accentuated his red tongue and sharp teeth, giving him the appearance of a ghoul. John peered at the face and realized he had seen it before. But where…when…? Then he knew.

"You!" exclaimed John.

General Skinehardt cocked his head in acknowledgement. "Small war, isn't it," he observed with caustic nonchalance. Skinehardt motioned, and the guards dragged the prisoners to their feet and out of the cell.

"You know this man?" muttered Edison as they were shoved down a long, dark corridor lined with empty cells.

John nodded. "He tried to kill me once."

They approached a guarded door that opened into a laboratory. They entered. Inside there were more guards and a solitary figure in a white lab coat hunched over a drafting table.

Skinehardt turned with a flourish, blinding them with his chest full of medals. "I am General Wilhelm Skinehardt. I know who you are. So there is no need for further introductions." Skinehardt paused sardonically. "Except one."

Skinehardt gestured to the figure who looked up from a scroll of blueprints, revealing himself to be…

"Harry!" exclaimed Edison.

"Mr. Singer?" echoed John.

Could it be? The persona presented to them appeared to be a doppelganger of a different color. Gone was the frizzy-haired, absent-minded demeanor of Edison's chief assistant. Instead, stood an icy, reptilian presence whose slicked back hair only served to emphasize a cadaverous skull and sharp, black eyes framed by dark sockets.

"Dear friends," he gurgled in malevolent amusement. "Not Harry Singer, I fear. But rather...*Herr Reisinger.*"

28

UBER RESURRECTUS

Comprehending all sides of an equation usually came easily to Edison but he was having a devil of a time wrapping his mind around this particular piece of subterfuge. Harry Singer had been his chief assistant for the past year and a half. If he'd also been an undercover operative for the Germans, it was obviously deep cover because Harry had arrived with a resume that boasted substantial recommendations. What Edison didn't realize was that Harry had established a long and profitable career in industrial espionage, going from one patron to another, cherry-picking only the key elements of a new creation, and then getting out while the going was good.

The theft of intellectual property was a given in the world of invention, rampant with ongoing duplicity and the constant jockeying for bragging and patent rights. Edison himself had fought tooth and nail with more than a few of his peers (Bell, Tesla, ad infinitum), and many of them reserved a bruised hatred for him. In truth, the 'new' was always somewhere up there, floating in the clouds with dozens of hands clamoring to pull it down into practicality. It was fate rather than fairness that usually parceled out the glittering prizes, and that only increased the shouting. In this fevered climate of recriminations, Harry's serial sabotage had gone unnoticed.

Edison had been completely hoodwinked. He was so startled by the deception that the only response he could summon was that of a wife whose marital honor has been compromised by an errant husband,

"Harry!" he declared in exasperation. "How could you?"

"I saw you die," protested John. "Gaunt threw you in the fire."

"Not in," corrected Reisinger. "Through. The wall collapsed. Minor injuries." He leaned forward. His eyebrows had been singed off and the right side of his face was badly blistered. These blemishes, along with the 'X' Captain Krill had carved into his cheek, provided him with an even more demented appearance than usual. He shrugged. "The price of doing business."

John and Edison were beginning to catch on, but Gershwin remained stupefied. "You were chained to the machine. We all were! How in the world did you---"

Herr Reisinger gleefully clapped his hands together. "A piece of pie."

"Cake," Gershwin corrected automatically. Then he remembered a similar, previous exchange and put it all together. "Wait a second. Krill. And you!"

"It's an old magician's trick" affirmed Emily. "Misdirection. You only show the audience what you want them to see. So when Krill cut up your face, he was really doing what?"

"Handing me a key," confirmed Reisinger. "We had to be certain."

"Certain of what?" demanded John.

"Of how much you knew," replied Reisinger. He grunted contemptuously. "Which was next to nothing." He pursed his lips together. "There was only one who suspected my real intentions."

"Gaunt," answered John. "That's why he tried to kill you."

Reisinger nodded curtly. "He saw. From his room above."

"Then he wasn't a murderer," realized Emily.

"He was a freak," mocked Reisinger.

Emily slapped him hard across the face, bursting his blisters. "*He was a fan!*" Reisinger screamed in pain as the guards restrained her.

"Enough!" commanded Skinehardt. "You are prisoners here. And this time, you will all die!" He paused with a malicious beat and then added, "Unless..."

The general gestured with a flourish, and the guards parted the rear doors of the laboratory. They split, opening into a towering airplane hangar that had been converted to accommodate a massive resurrector, nearly three times the size of Edison's original version and designed in a grandiose, uber-military style. The support struts had golden talons for feet, the tips on the thousands of tuning forks had been honed into daggers and the two passenger bubbles housed thrones of oak and velvet.

Everyone gaped at the gleaming monstrosity, especially Edison, who approached the machine as if in a trance. He was delighted to discover that his invention still lived, even in this bloated form, but remained utterly confused regarding Skinehardt's intentions. He was about to receive an education.

"Herr Reisinger is unrivaled in his talent for industrial espionage," stated General Skinehardt. "However, his gift for original invention is sadly lacking."

Reisinger burned silently. John made a mental note of the little man's fury and quickly scanned the hangar. It was barren with the exception of the machine, a grandiose control panel shaped like a pipe organ and an oversized, oblong boiler that, via an extensive network of floor and ceiling grates, evenly distributed the heat required to ensure the machine ran smoothly. More intriguingly, the windows had been blacked out and covered with canvas mats to deaden the sound. Obviously, Skinehardt and Reisinger didn't want some (all?) of their comrades to know what they were up to. Why not?

Suddenly, Edison realized why they were still alive. There were no other inventors in the hangar, only guards. "It doesn't work," he stated plainly. "You need me to fix it."

"So the Germans can win the war!" blurted Gershwin. He was suddenly seized by a patriotic fervor, they all were. Of course! That's why the Germans wanted the resurrector. To win the war!

"We're gonna kick your Kraut ass!" threatened Emily and the others loudly agreed.

General Skinehardt sighed indulgently and waited for the star-spangled din to peter out. "I agree. You *will* kick our Kraut ass." This admission startled them all into silence.

"Germany is exhausted," explained Skinehardt. "And you Americans are so…" He searched for the right word and found it. "Enthusiastic," he concluded with mild distaste. "My original plan was simply to acquire the blueprints for Mr. Edison's new weapons of war. The ones your own government so stupidly rejected. But when Herr Reisinger informed me of this marvelous machine…" He gestured to the resurrector. The burnished steel gleamed seductively. "I had to have it. Not for Germany. For me." His demeanor fell from delightful insouciance to the deadly serious. "I don't care who wins the war. As long as I profit from the peace."

Skinehardt was not a candid man by nature but he was telling the truth. He was too practiced a cynic to have bought the national goods lock, stock and barrel. When he achieved the rank of general, his entry into the inner sanctum of the high command proved to be a grotesque revelation. The Kaiser was a hapless relic and his generals nothing more than arrogant lackeys. Except for Ludendorff. He was a gifted, if mercurial, strategist – but was he good enough? The last four years suggested the answer was 'no.' Thus, Skinehardt's acquisition of the resurrector; his own gilded parachute to survive the coming post-war debacle, and one which would provide him with the happiest of landings.

"But why?" demanded Edison. "Why steal what I gladly would have shared with all the peoples of the world?" He paused and qualified: "For a small fee."

"Because you want to comfort the people," retorted Skinehardt. "I want to control them. War *is* hell." He whined in mock sympathy. "So many dead. So many yet to die. And all those millions left behind who never had a chance to say 'goodbye.' In such a universe of loss, a middle-man between our world and the next should prove indispensable. Perhaps in time, there will be no more need of countries. The only three certainties will be life and death and me."

"You're insane," John stated flatly.

"I'm a capitalist," corrected Skinehardt. "So, let us negotiate." He gestured to John and Edison. "You stay and complete the resurrector." Then he turned to Emily and Gershwin. "And you return to the bright lights of Broadway."

Gershwin's head popped up optimistically but Emily wasn't having it.

"Ix-nay," she shot back.

"Emmy," warned Gershwin.

"Ix-nay?" queried Skinehardt. "What is this 'ix-nay'?"

"I think she means no," explained Reisinger.

"It's an opening bid," countered Gershwin, trying to save the deal.

Skinehardt ignored this last and looked at Emily in amused indignation. "You don't trust me?"

"Trust you?" Emily horse-laughed. "Not for a million bucks."

"You see!" Gershwin gestured diplomatically. "Already we're talking price."

"Oh, wise up," interrupted Emily. "The only way he's going to send us home is in coffins."

As they squabbled, Reisinger murmured to Skinehardt: "So cynical."

Skinehardt nodded and half-smiled. "I admire that in a woman."

Gershwin threw up his hands in frustration and Emily rushed into John's arms. "I'm not going anywhere," she declared.

John held her tight. "Damn right."

It was an odd, stand-off moment and, surprisingly, the first one to step over the line in the sand was Edison. While the others were bickering, he'd approached the machine, inspected it closely and, satisfied, turned to quell his companions' fears and bring some Yankee pragmatism back to the table.

"Now children," he admonished, "let's not be rash. We *are* at a disadvantage. And it's a fair offer; fifty cents on the dollar, so to speak."

"Are you nuts?" exclaimed Emily.

Edison fixed her with an opaque stare. "The opposite of nuts, I assure you." He hoped she could read between the lines. She could. Emily nodded and turned to John, and in that unspoken moment, they decided to go all in with the cunning old conjuror.

John flexed his jaw. "See you soon."

"You bet your ass," replied Emily.

They embraced and kissed – a full, hard kiss – as if it was the last time they'd ever see each other because, moxie to the contrary, it might well be.

Skinehardt paused for a voyeuristic moment and then cocked his head to the guards. They yanked the lovers apart and goose-stepped Emily and Gershwin toward the exit. Emily paused in the doorway and took one final look at John. She started to step back in but Skinehardt intruded, gesturing 'ladies first.' Emily made her exit but it was bereft of any theatrical flourish. It was tentative and frightened. Skinehardt followed them out and firmly shut the door.

Reisinger swaggered over to Edison and John. He gestured imperiously toward the invention and blithely queried, "So. What do you think of *my* resurrector?"

It was all Edison could do to restrain himself. Harry or Herr, this overblown version of the resurrector exposed the psychological deficiencies of its two-faced, faux creator. Perhaps one of his Achilles' heels would serve as the key to their salvation. All in good time. For now, Edison forced a smile and assumed a fawning irony that his former assistant failed to detect.

"Harry," he proclaimed. "It's *definitely* you."

29

DEUS EX MACHINA

The guards escorted Emily and Gershwin across the airfield to a waiting staff car. On their left were a dozen shiny new attack planes and a dedicated crew of pilots and mechanics who appeared to be up against a mission deadline. On their right, the housekeeping staff at the chateau bustled about in anticipation of what promised to be a gala event; crisp linens, gleaming crystal, bouquets of fresh flowers, and a gourmet's menu of four-star food and drink. Emily nudged Gershwin in the ribs.

"Remind you of anything?" she asked in a low voice.

He nodded. "Opening night."

The messenger rode his bicycle up to General Skinehardt. He'd been eating breakfast in the mess hall when he was called to duty and the telegram he handed the general was speckled with bits of egg. Skinehardt flicked them off and read the telegram. More pressing business awaited. Before departing, he turned to a hawk-faced adjutant whose specialty was strangulation, and discreetly ordered, "Send them home to America…" He paused, savoring Emily's punch line. "…in coffins."

Emily and Gershwin drew closer to the car. The engine was running and exhaust belched into the chill morning air. Some of the pilots wolf-whistled at Emily and she stopped to flash her gams. Yet the cheesecake smile smeared across her face belied the small voice of instinct that repeated a warning – if she got into that car she'd never get out alive.

* * *

Edison continued his examination of the resurrector. Despite the inflated scope of this version, the basics appeared to be intact. However, John was less concerned about a short-term salvage job than he was in the long-term repercussions.

"If we fix it," he observed, "we're dead."

Edison concurred. The moment the Germans secured the machine's operational status, they'd be eliminated. However, Edison knew something that John – and Reisinger – did not. Over the years, he had instituted a policy of excluding one key facet from the design of every invention. He knew from regretful experience that success had many fathers and even more litigants. So he made it a policy to keep even the closest of his associates in a bit of darkness. It was a chore to maintain a nature so untrusting and Mina had warned him repeatedly that such duplicity smacked of being unchristian. However, in moments like this, he was delighted to be counted among the heathens.

There was a sudden commotion among the soldiers, and they hurried from the hangar into the corridor of adjoining cells where the windows hadn't been fully blacked out and still afforded a view of the airfield. Edison turned curiously to Reisinger who dismissively offered, "The *Deus ex Machina* has arrived."

Edison and John remained perplexed, so Reisinger waved them off to join the soldiers who were jostling each other to get a good look through the iron bars as an imperious hot-air balloon descended onto the airfield. The skin of the craft was illustrated with the face of the Greek God, Zeus, and carried an ornate gondola. Edison dropped his eyes, deep in thought. If the passenger was who he suspected, their presence might change everything. But for better or worse, he could not yet say.

* * *

The adjutant gestured for Emily to enter the staff car. As he slipped on a pair of skin-tight, black leather gloves, she saw his hands ripple with cords of sinew, vise-like muscles she doubted he'd gotten from picking edelweiss. Emily gulped but saw no other option than complete surrender when a cheer went up from the pilots. She spun around and saw the hot-air balloon floating down to the airfield. A bugle sounded, and the soldiers froze in salute as the flyboys tethered the balloon to the ground and provided a golden stairway for the craft's occupant to descend in the style to which he was accustomed. A diminutive, older man with an enormous, upturned white mustache emerged from the gondola, popped a tasseled commander's hat on his head, and acknowledged the soldiers' salutes.

Emily gasped. It was Kaiser Wilhelm! She knew him by sight from the newsreels but, more importantly, by his reputation as a ladies man. "Hang onto your hat," she confided to Gershwin, as she assumed her showgirl persona, waved broadly, and courageously went off-book: "Willy! Oh, Willy!"

Both the Kaiser and Skinehardt reacted sharply in confusion. However, Emily didn't wait for an invitation. She slipped out of the dumbfounded adjutant's grasp, bustled across the muddy field towards the Kaiser, and threw open her arms in reunion. "Willy! It's me!" Gershwin loped warily behind as she continued full steam ahead. Her assurance worked. No one, not even Skinehardt, knew whether to stop her or shoot her or what. She greeted the Kaiser and kissed him on the cheek. "It's your Emily!"

"Emily?" The face remained unfamiliar but was certainly attractive.

"Silly Willy!" she flirted outrageously. "How could you forget little me? 1913. Paris. The Folies Bergere! I was performing a rather naughty ditty and afterwards we shared an intimate *supper au deux*."

The Kaiser's face brightened. "Of course, my dear. Yes, I remember it well."

The old roué didn't remember a thing. Emily had never played Paris or suffered through a romantic interlude with the Kaiser. But she could have. The possibility was enough for his ego to substantiate her premise. He hoped he had enjoyed a fulfilling romp with her. Of course he had! Who said he hadn't?

"But, uh…what an unusual reunion," he qualified, noting her tatty appearance and beginning to question her presence on the military base.

Emily sensed his hesitation and, out of the corner of her eye, spotted General Skinehardt striding toward them. She heaved an enormous sigh of hardship. "An utter disaster. A European tour gone horribly wrong." She conspiratorially pulled Skinehardt into the scene. "The general's been an absolute darling. He saved us!"

"Yeah," added Gershwin, wise to her angle. "He's a regular resurrector."

Emily discreetly dug her nails into Skinehardt's arm. He realized he should never have revealed his plan in her presence but he had, and now she claimed him as her momentary hostage. He crooked his head in a courtly bow. "Anything for such a lady."

"Good man, Skinehardt," offered the Kaiser in hearty appreciation.

The general gripped Emily's arm in return. "But you'll be late for your train."

"Ah, we must be off," she gestured theatrically, stroked the Kaiser's cheek, and gave him the works. "What a delicious interlude. Farewell, my *liebchen*." She blew him a kiss and turned to go. She prayed he'd call her back within three seconds. If she reached four and he remained silent, she and Gershwin were goners. One...two...three…

"Why not stay the night?" invited the Kaiser.

Emily burst into a savvy smile and turned back to him, overcome with faux surprise.

He continued, encouraged. "Refresh yourself…sing for your supper, perhaps. Then afterwards we could rekindle…"

Emily playfully tweaked the upturned tips of his moustache. "You sly puss! Of course, I never perform without my accompanist, Mr. Gershwin."

Gershwin leaned into the Kaiser and pumped his hand. "Pleased to meet'cha."

The Kaiser had no idea of how completely he was being bamboozled. Skinehardt did. "Sir, I must insist…" He was already too late.

"Please show Miss, uh Miss…"

"Auburn," supplied Emily coquettishly.

"Auburn and, uh, company, to their quarters," directed the Kaiser. Skinehardt saw that further protest would be useless and clicked his heels in obedience.

"Until tonight," purred Emily as the Kaiser kissed her hand and ambled off, feeling years younger than when he had arrived.

"Clever girl," congratulated Skinehardt between clenched teeth.

"You bet your ass," Emily purred coyly as she blew a kiss to the Kaiser.

* * *

John and Edison watched in amazement as Emily entered the chateau with Gershwin in tow. "Wonderful woman!" exclaimed John, and Edison nodded in agreement.

They headed back to the hangar's main room to resume their diagnostic inspection of the resurrector when Edison glanced into an adjoining storage cell. He was startled to discover the space stocked to the ceiling with even more stolen bounty from the Menlo Park laboratory, including two of the H2Ohms, a full-size version of the magnetic torpedo net complete with jettison gun, and barrels of chemicals, including a tub of concentrated oleum.

Edison turned on the smirking Reisinger with a fury. "You son-of-a-bitching bastard! You robbed me blind!" He flew at him and, if not for the intercession of the guards, would have flattened the sniveling little traitor. The soldiers held Edison tight as the old man struggled furiously, and when John tried to intercede they slugged him to the floor and pinned him down, a dozen boots ground into his body.

Reisinger composed himself, imperiously approached Edison, and slapped him hard across the face. "I am no longer your underling!" he screamed. "Here, I am your God!" He took a step back and coldly ordered: "Now…invent. Or die."

30

MASTER PLAN

By mid-afternoon, Emily and Gershwin had enjoyed the most basic luxuries provided by warmth – a hot bath, a luncheon of roasted chicken and grilled vegetables and a fresh set of clothes still crisp from the press of an iron. Yet all that heat amounted to cold comfort, for they were locked up in a suite on the top floor of the chateau. Skinehardt had seen to that. He couldn't deny the Kaiser his folly of flesh but he was shrewd enough to negotiate the terms. Emily would be permitted to attend the evening's banquet, perform a few numbers, and then provide their supreme leader with whatever frolic he was capable of sustaining. After that, she'd be Skinehardt's property again, her and that piano man of hers, that Gershwin, and they'd be disposed of as previously arranged. Until then, they were his prisoners. It was a necessary precaution. There were too many eyes, too many competing agendas, too much at stake to risk the possibility that a pair of wild cards might escape from the deck.

Emily's suspicion that something big was cooking was dead-on. Touring cars had been arriving all afternoon, ferrying a variety of top brass with rainbows of stripes splashed across their chests.

Obviously, the chateau was the designated site for a meeting of the minds although as to the exact nature of their despicable agenda, who knew? Was it the resurrector? Had Edison's kidnapping triggered an international outcry? Or could it be something else? Whatever the reason she knew they had to find out and then get out.

Gershwin didn't mind being a prisoner as much as Emily, at least not at first. He felt like he'd been rolling in a gutter ever since Captiva and was delighted to savor the dual sensations of a full stomach pressed against a starched shirt. However, as he polished off the last drumstick, he began to suffer a sense of queasy guilt. As Emily scoured the suite, in search of an escape hatch, Gershwin grudgingly joined the quest.

"First you get us in, and now you want to get us out?" He tried to pry a window open. No dice. It had been nailed shut.

"It's called saving your ass one step at a time," Emily acknowledged. "Besides, we've got to help John."

"Again with Adonis," complained Gershwin.

Emily knew what she was about to say went wildly against her character and would make her sound like a chump. "Love!" she declared. "It's the sucker bet of all time. But I love him, Gersh."

Gershwin lowered his eyes and inadvertently blushed. "I know," he replied. He'd known since Menlo Park. He was jealous and he always would be, but he accepted her declaration, offered a crooked nod and smiled. He adored Emily without reservation and was happy she'd finally found the one thing in her life that had defiantly eluded her for so long. As for Emily, she was savvy enough to sense the grappling emotions behind his sweet smile and embraced him. He was someone special to her as well, and all the peril they'd been put through only confirmed her feelings. Gersh was that rare thing – a real friend.

A whirring noise interrupted the moment and, puzzled, they began to search for the source as the sound became louder. Their investigation revealed the noise was coming from behind the frame of a full-sized painting of buxom courtesans that graced the far wall. Gershwin touched the painting and it moved. It was bracketed to the wall on a hinge and opened to reveal the door to a dumbwaiter.

The door featured a horizontal slit in the center that split open from top to bottom, creating an entry space of approximately three by four feet. As the whirring grew louder, Gershwin poked his head into the shaft and saw the dumbwaiter descending from the roof garden. As it reached their floor, Emily pushed the stop button and they peered inside. The dumbwaiter featured an unusually large carriage space that Emily suspected that, on occasion, had been used to ferry more nefarious deliveries than breakfast in bed. This could work to their advantage. Struck by the same brainstorm, they crowded into the space. It proved to be a tight fit for two (although Gershwin judged it no worse than a balcony seat at the Hippodrome) but it would be a short ride. They hooked thumbs for luck and pressed the button to deliver them to freedom.

Alas, it was not to be. While the dumbwaiter descended past the grand salon, it also transported them from a rock to a hard place, for the chateau's main floor had been converted into a meeting hall. Emily and Gershwin cautiously parted the doors. They peered through a series of strategically placed holes that had been drilled into a life-sized painting of two noblemen charging into battle that decorously hid the dumbwaiter from view. They blinked through the slits in the canvas and witnessed a rare congregation – the Kaiser and his generals – who had assembled for a critical presentation.

General Ludendorff had been hard at work since the high command's previous conclave at the Reichstag. He ascended the improvised stage, complete with a curtained set in the shape of an oblong puppet theatre, to make his case.

The parameters of the conflict were changing rapidly. With Russia now temporarily, but effectively, out of the combat equation, Ludendorff determined Germany should shift the maximum number of troops to the Western Front and re-calibrate their presence from a stance of wary defense to aggressive offense. The campaign would begin in March, with the Germans moving from north to south. However, before the first chapter of this new offensive could debut, a prologue of sorts was required. Skinehardt's prior call to 'annihilate the Americans before it's too late' had been a sound one. So, without further delay, Ludendorff pulled back the curtain to reveal the scenario for his surprise attack on the Americans who were assembling just over the border in eastern France.

"Our Trojan Horse will be a zeppelin," explained Ludendorff as he pointed to a pint-sized craft that emerged from behind a stage curtain of cut-out clouds. It hovered on wires above a pool table whose green felt had been pressed into service as the French countryside and was populated by a division of toy soldiers. The Kaiser beamed excitedly, eager to see how the plot of this entertainment would unfold. Ludendorff managed to conceal his disdain. While the military class covertly recognized the general as the de-facto leader of Germany, he still needed the Kaiser's approval for such a momentous undertaking, and he hoped the play-acting of a Punch & Judy show would secure the old man's public blessing. He continued: "The hull of the craft will be covered with a net of electric lights."

Inside the cramped dumbwaiter, Emily and Gershwin listened breathlessly as Ludendorff detailed his despicable plan.

"The western flank will beam a fraudulent message of surrender to the Americans". One side of the model zeppelin lit up with the words: *We Surrender*. The Kaiser pursed his lips in anticipation as Ludendorff continued: "In the confusion, the eastern side will signal our fliers to…" The zeppelin pivoted, revealing a billboard of light that spelled out an opposing message: *Attack*.

Ludendorff paused to let the weight of his scheme resonate with the audience. A squadron of model planes came into view and spritzed the toy soldiers with lighter fluid. "The sleeping Americans will be massacred and their plans for expansion aborted."

The general tossed a match onto the battlefield, igniting a fire that swept across the pool table and dissolved the plastic soldiers into puddles of goo. He briskly summed up: "Thus paving the way for *das Kaiserschlacht* – the Kaiser's Battle," he paused theatrically, "which begins…tonight."

Emily gasped in horror, and Gershwin would have done the same but his mouth was bone-dry from a furious kind of fright he'd never experienced. The generals murmured appreciatively and applauded, even Skinehardt. It was a pre-emptive strike of such ruthlessness that its public relations value in dispiriting the Americans could fracture the Allied forces.

The Kaiser stood and the assembly fell silent. "This is my war to win but not my battle." He raised his glass in salute. "To the Ludendorff Offensive!"

They all enthusiastically joined him in tribute, although Ludendorff appeared more daunted than delighted by the Kaiser's endorsement. Now he owned it.

The generals downed their drinks and the meeting ended. Skinehardt stood in line to praise General Ludendorff, although not too much. "An intriguing plan," he observed. "It might work."

Ludendorff accepted the lukewarm kudos. Then: "There's a rumor you've become obsessed with some mysterious project of your own." He chortled deprecatingly. "Some…science fiction."

"It's not fiction," responded Skinehardt curtly. "It's fact."

"*Wunderbar*!" endorsed Ludendorff too broadly. "And when will you be making your contribution to the fatherland?"

"Soon," he replied tersely.

Ludendorff smiled dubiously and moved on. Skinehardt watched him go. He'd monitor Ludendorff's battle plan with a sharp eye. If it approached success, he'd climb onboard. If it veered into failure, he'd have the opportunity of proceeding with his plans for the resurrector – and much sooner than later.

The meeting room emptied with the exception of two overworked maids who took one look at the godawful mess that had been left behind and decided it was time for a cigarette break.

"Let's make a run for it," advised Gershwin.

Emily held him back. "We can't go now. We've got to stop them."

Gershwin gaped in disbelief. It was a diabolical scheme but the odds were staggeringly not in their favor. "You're a singer, I'm a piano player," he reminded her in exasperation. "What the hell can we do to stop a German invasion?"

Emily hesitated. She knew trying to throw a monkey wrench

into Ludendorff's plan was a million-to-one shot but she was convinced it was the best way for them to survive. She defiantly pressed the lift button on the dumbwaiter. What the hell could they do? Emily had the answer:

"We're gonna put on a show."

31

READINESS

Night came fast. Edison and John had been slaving over the resurrector all day long, fine-tuning the invention and adapting some of the components to Reisinger's pathological surge in the machine's size. Edison found himself oddly amused to discover "the bastard even stole my defects," a truth that became evident when the jettison lever in the passenger bubble jammed. He'd spent the better part of an hour on the release mechanism, but not so much working as thinking. John had called it. The minute the resurrector was operational, they'd be disposed of. He had considered and discarded dozens of potential scenarios when he noticed the thermostat on the boiler. The current temperature, as converted from the Celsius scale, was 72 degrees Fahrenheit; the acme of comfort on a cold winter's night and adequate for the operation of the machine. For his plan to succeed, however, he would need a greater intensity of heat and John's committed participation. The former could be easily obtained. The latter might prove more difficult because it would involve injury and the possibility of death. First, he had to get John alone to detail his plan without the guards' knowledge.

With a tragedian's skill that would have done the great Duse proud, Edison lifted the back of his hand to his forehead, bobbled on legs of rubber, and swooned to the floor in a dead faint. John rushed to his side.

Reisinger was enjoying a deluxe dinner of blood sausage, mustard potatoes and hot coffee when he looked up sharply and strutted toward them. "Why have you stopped?" he screeched.

John propped Edison up in his arms. "He's an old man," answered John. "He needs food and rest." In fact, John was so concerned about Edison's condition he failed to notice the inventor's reassuring wink.

Reisinger pursed his lips together in frustration. He was eager for the resurrector to be completed, but he had first-hand knowledge of Edison's odd constitution. After fifteen minutes or so he'd be back to the task at hand. He signaled a curt nod to the guards. They herded John and Edison into the storage cell, tossed in a minimal amount of bread and water, and locked them in. After they left, Edison revived from his stage faint and pulled John in close.

"This morning I thought we'd either have to fix the damned thing or blow it to kingdom come," he whispered confidentially and then shook his head. "Now there's a third way."

* * *

The guards were enjoying their own dinner in an adjoining storage cell. They had converted the space into a miniature mess hall where they supped on stew and day-old barn bread washed down with a mediocre ale. A philosopher might have hypothesized that they were prisoners as well, but at least their door remained unlocked and the bars on the windows were graced with ruffled curtains.

"Help!"

It was a sudden, sharp cry, and the guards recognized the voice belonged to Edison. They ran to the storage cell, dumbstruck to find John chasing Edison around the stacks of purloined inventions and supplies, catch him, and then try to throttle the life out of the helpless old man.

"You traitor!" John shouted at Edison. "You'd sell out your own country just to prove the damn thing works!"

The guards fumbled the key into the lock and rushed to Edison's defense. John escaped their grasp and began hurling anything he could to stave them off, finally up-ending the tub of concentrated oleum and dousing them with a thick coat of the white, oily powder. However, once John ran out of improvised weapons, the guards converged and viciously assaulted him.

"No, stop – don't hurt him!" Edison cried out in misery. Yet they continued to batter John, who had balled into a fetal position to deflect the brunt of their blows. Edison turned to Reisinger, who savored the gang assault with the appreciation of an armchair sadist. "Please, he doesn't understand how the world works," pleaded Edison. "Make them stop!"

"Why?" queried Reisinger.

Edison leaned in and played his trump card. "Because the resurrector…is ready."

* * *

Within moments, Reisinger had assembled everyone, even the bloodied but unbowed John, back into the hangar. "We shall begin immediately," he ordered and, as Edison suspected, refused to allow his men even the brief amount of time it would take to wash and change into new uniforms after their tussle with the keg of oleum.

"Shouldn't we wait for General Skinehardt?" quizzed Edison. "After all," he chided, "it's *his* machine."

"The machine is mine!" screeched Reisinger.

"Yes, yes, of course," soothed Edison in commiseration. "It's just that he's such a pushy fellow."

Reisinger grudgingly accepted the condolences. "Yah, well, we will see who pushes who. Proceed."

Edison nodded subserviently. As he assumed, Reisinger and Skinehardt were only associates of convenience and would sabotage each other at the first opportunity. This could be played to his advantage. He gestured grandly toward the nearest passenger bubble. "You will occupy the, uh, throne of honor and – "

Reisinger cut him off abruptly: "No."

"Surely you wish to be the first," explained Edison expansively. "After all, you've earned the right to triumph as the Columbus of this new world."

Reisinger considered the offer. Common sense would have prescribed a more cautious route. All inventions require an interval of rigorous testing, especially for one so unique. But Reisinger's grasping ego wouldn't allow reason to prevail. While Skinehardt had provided the funding for the enterprise, Reisinger had never agreed with his intended coronation as the 'middle-man to the masses' nonsense. Reisinger wasn't so much in it for the money but the glory that would belong to him and the fatherland. He was a company man and oblivious when it came to appreciating how an entrepreneur might profit once he had broken free from the red tape of corporate protocol. He scrutinized Edison and signaled his agreement with one, shrewd provision.

"Only if you join me. As my guest."

Edison pretended to hesitate. It was exactly the twisted quid pro quo he'd anticipated. "If you insist," he conceded, and then added his condition. "But John must man the controls."

Reisinger hooted derisively. "You take me for a fool?"

"He's learned his lesson. Besides, his participation is essential."

"And why is that?"

"He knows how to run the machine." Reisinger hesitated, and Edison pressed his case. "And he's the only one who can get us back."

"Very well," deigned Reisinger. He turned to Sergeant Buchan, a barrel-chested bully with an eager trigger-finger. "One wrong move, shoot to kill."

Reisinger doubted it would come to that. John was injured and unfit to launch a counter-attack. And if he tried? Buchan had trained under the late Captain Krill and was more than willing to inflict maximum damage on anyone remotely connected to his mentor's death. As for John, he'd taken the full measure of the sergeant. When he'd been assaulted by the guards, everyone got in a free punch, but Buchan had punched the hardest.

Edison began setting the dials and motioned for John to join him at the control panel. "Set the timer for ninety seconds, no more, no less," Edison advised in a husky whisper. Then he broke into a boisterous harangue to deflect any suspicions from their captors. “And someone must turn up the heat! All this cold air will put a drag on the RPMs.”

Reisinger felt comfortable enough but agreed that the machine would perform more reliably in a warmer environment. He gave the order and the engineer cranked the boiler’s gauge up to 75 degrees Fahrenheit.

“Higher,” ordered Edison.

Reisinger dismissively gestured for the temperature to be increased again. “As high as he wants,” commanded the reptilian little man as he climbed into one of the passenger bubbles. The engineer set the boiler to a destination heat of 82 degrees, and Reisinger impatiently rapped on the window, as eager for his ride to the dead zone to begin as a spoiled child on a merry-go-round that has yet to go-round.

Edison completed his calculations and fastened himself into his own passenger bubble. “Let’s give it a whirl.”

John stood at the control panel and gauged the rising capacity of the generators. Behind him Sergeant Buchan dug the nose of his gun into his spine as a reminder of the instant fate he’d suffer if anything went wrong with the experiment.

John and Edison exchanged knowing looks. “Generators primed and in phase,” confirmed John, and he started the resurrector. The machine rotated slowly at first, its maiden voyage spitting off a detritus of metal shavings. However, soon the groaning machine gave way to brisk, well-lubricated revolutions, and Reisinger shivered as the resurrector accelerated to a whiplash speed that made him dizzy with an ecstasy he’d only dreamed of. And now, the dream was coming true.

32

ENTRANCE

Gershwin paced nervously. The chateau's majordomo had provided him with grooming utensils and an oversized tuxedo, but despite the close shave on his face and the posh fabric against his skin, he felt as clammy and disheveled as he had beneath the ice. He and Emily had committed themselves to an incredibly dangerous course of action without the benefit of a detailed strategy. They were shooting without a script.

Emily entered the room and her appearance took Gershwin's breath away. Her sumptuous body was embraced by a silver satin evening gown that achieved the dual feat of being both elegant and provocative.

"So how do I look?" she asked flatly, breaking the spell.

"Dressed to kill," pronounced Gershwin.

Emily grinned. "That's the idea."

A staccato rap on the door signaled a visitor. Emily quickly rehearsed a series of devastating poses, committed to one, and signaled for Gershwin to open the door. General Skinehardt appeared in the doorway, attired in his formal military dress, his chest festooned with a rash of medals. It was rare for Skinehardt to betray any emotion he didn't wish to expose, but the sight of Emily made him gulp like a schoolboy confronting his first crush. Exquisite? Glorious? Primal? He couldn't find the proper word to explain Emily's effect on him. If only he had accepted the invitation from Dr. Richard von Krafft-Ebing to join him for an exploratory session in the new science of psychology. In time, the good doctor would have divined the appropriate term from his dictionary of *psychopathia sexualis*. The word was 'edible.'

The general stiffly extended his white-gloved hand. "*Fraulein*," he beckoned.

Emily took a breath, unleashed her most dazzling smile, and whispered an encouraging "Curtain up," to Gershwin as she linked her arm in Skinehardt's and they regally descended to the grand salon.

The salon, mused Gershwin, looked, well, grand. Cream-colored plaster walls were accented with crown moldings of golden cherubs scantily swathed in pink ribbons. A dozen waiters deftly strolled through the assembly, bearing trays of champagne and sumptuous hors d'oeuvres. At the far end of the room, on a petite, circular stage framed by a trio of curtained picture windows, sat a black grand piano. The stage was surrounded by rows of golden Chiavari chairs to accommodate the arriving audience for the evening's entertainment.

Gershwin knew he'd lived a relatively sheltered life but doubted that he'd ever witnessed such a motley congregation of what might charitably be referred to as 'old money.' Wealth was the only desirable attribute they possessed. Apart from the generals, the Kaiser's guests consisted of corrupt collaborators from the local aristocracy who had abandoned the national honor to suckle at Germany's tit. Everything about them seemed ancient, from their habits to their hates. The men bobbled like whiskered relics, committed to maintaining the status quo but only as it applied to their status. The women were former beauties; once vibrant, now decrepit, plastered with powder and paint that did little to recapture their youth but, instead, mocked its memory. It was not a good house.

Emily accurately gauged the unspoken but potent cross-currents of greed, envy and lust percolating in the room. Skinehardt presented her to the Kaiser and, as the elderly monarch greeted her effusively, she began the delicate work of defusing the competing agendas so she could navigate the social maze without incident. Gershwin lingered in the background and smiled proudly, impressed by Emily's uncanny ability to command center stage no matter where she stood.

Smitten, General Ludendorff sidled over to Skinehardt and offered his endorsement. "She's magnificent!" he exclaimed, as the wattles of his double chin flirted with the iron cross draped beneath his neck.

"Yes," replied Skinehardt. Then, as Ludendorff moved in for a closer look, he provided an afterthought which no one, not even Gershwin, could hear.

"I think…I'll keep her."

33

THE AFTERLIFE PART II

John monitored the control panel intently as the resurrector's velocity level climbed to 75% and triggered the thousands of tuning forks which crescendoed to an ear-piercing whine. When the velocity gauge hit 100%, all of the soldiers, even Sergeant Buchan, looked on in astonishment as John confirmed the RPMs and unleashed the core. A blast of electricity enshrined the machine with a skin of voltage.

Inside the passenger bubbles, Edison and Reisinger had achieved the floating, frozen moment of reverse synchronicity. Then they were hurled through inner space, careening toward the dot of light that quickly expanded into a wall of blinding white. Their physical forms deconstructed into a swarm of molecules and, as the light retracted, allowed them to pass through the vanishing point and into the afterlife.

Edison's body quickly reconstructed itself and the curtain of shimmering mist parted yet again, revealing the figures of Madame

Blavatsky, Twain, and his nephew, Charley, who acted as if no time had passed since their last reunion. Edison urgently embraced them. "Dear friends, I need your help," he pleaded. "The fate of my greatest invention hangs in the balance!"

"What invention is that?" posed Madame Blavatsky.

"Why, the resurrector, of course!" sputtered Edison. Good God, hadn't the blasted seer been paying attention?

Madame Blavatsky offered a wry smile. Could it be that, after all these years, Edison had come to believe in, but not see the true nature of his creations? Ah, well. There was still time. She glanced at Twain and Charley. They nodded. The spirits were willing.

"What is the third key?" pressed Edison.

The three specters evolved into a mass of amorphous equations and whirled themselves into Edison's mind. "The third key," offered Twain. "Life dominates death..." continued Charley. "But if you reverse the process…" Then Madame Blavatsky concluded the lesson by warning: "Death will dominate life."

* * *

Reisinger's purgatory experience was less an instruction and more of a revel. As his physical form re-assembled, the machine's oak and velvet passenger chair transformed into a golden throne and he found himself dressed as a Roman emperor. Then it began, at first only with sound. Chimes were heard, followed by the seductive wail of a flute. Sight followed. Unlike Edison's evolving vistas, Reisinger's afterlife was draped in billowing, translucent silks. Touch came last and with it, the denizens of Reisinger's afterlife: a harem of adolescent boys and girls, all of them pink and supple and as close to nudity as the wisps of their tunics would allow, all of them hungry to worship at the altar of their master's flesh.

Reisinger leaned back imperiously, straddled one scrawny leg over the arm of the throne and sucked a hit of air into his lungs. It was thick with clots of gluttony and lust. Another snort of breath, then another. He was swollen with the dull bloat of power and gazed with opaque eyes at the young, expectant faces surrounding him. They were waiting on his command, lips licked in anticipation, eager drool beginning to puddle out of their open mouths. Reisinger bared his teeth in a smile of wanton desire. He crooked a single finger of permission and the revels erupted in an orgy of indulgence so debauched it would have brought a blush to the cheeks of the lowest degenerate. In this pocket universe, Reisinger was the supreme ruler, and any action was determined solely by his appetites. He could do whatever he desired, without conscience or repercussion. And so he did.

* * *

The witnesses in the hangar were unable to observe Edison's lesson in metaphysics or Reisinger's revels of the flesh. They had no notion as to what might be occurring in the parallel dimension of purgatory, so they had to content themselves with the wail of the tuning forks and the dizzying revolutions of the great invention. John checked the timer – ten seconds left – and shot a quick glance at the boiler. The temperature gauge read 79 degrees Fahrenheit. At the five second mark, Sergeant Buchan punched the base of John's spine with the butt of his rifle. Time. John grasped the control levers and evenly dragged them down, slowly reducing the machine's speed.

Inside the dead zone, Edison felt the pull of the earthly dimension and offered a heartfelt farewell to his dear ones. The spirits spun around him, offering good will and Godspeed as Edison erupted into a hive of molecules and was sucked back though the vanishing point.

Reisinger was in no mood for farewells. He was immersed in an orgiastic gaiety that, until now, had only existed in his darkest imaginings. As his form began to deconstruct, he tried to halt his departure by clinging to his zealous playmates, but was yanked into a million pieces and propelled through the vanishing point at a furious, frustrating speed.

The resurrector slowed to a stop, and John helped Edison out of the machine. The elderly inventor was discombobulated but, unlike before, his impediment was only one of physical balance, not mental agility. He watched craftily as the guards tried to retrieve Reisinger from his passenger bubble, but the impudent little tyrant would have none of it. If it was possible to be both blissful and manic at the same time, Reisinger had achieved such a state. The experiment had been an epoch-making triumph, far beyond his wildest expectations.

"Extraordinary!" he crowed.

"Would you like to go again?" asked Edison with sly innocence.

"Yes!" demanded Reisinger. "At once!"

Edison feigned exhaustion. "I'm afraid I'm spent," he muttered feebly. "Perhaps someone else could take my place. Perhaps one of your men?"

Reisinger considered the potential candidates. "No." He pointed a bony finger at John. "He will go."

"As you wish," Edison complied. It was as he had expected. Reisinger was unwilling to share the experience of the resurrector with any living man. Since both Edison and John would soon be dead, they were the only acceptable nominees.

Edison quickly prepared John for the journey. He popped him into the passenger bubble and bent down covertly.

"I know you'll be tempted," he whispered, "but *do not* complete the experiment. Once you see the vanishing point, abort." Edison grabbed the jettison lever. "And pull hard. The damned thing sticks."

"What about you?" John asked. He knew the wily old inventor had a card up his sleeve and hoped it was an ace. He gestured to the guards who were tending to the impatient Reisinger. "If anything goes wrong, they'll kill you."

Edison chuckled at John's concern. "I have the third key," he confided. "Besides, don't you know what happens when oleum combines with water?"

John shrugged and shook his head. Chemistry had never been his strong suit. Edison gestured to the boiler, where the temperature gauge hovered at 80 degrees, and revealed the answer.

"It turns to acid."

John's mouth dropped open in happy surprise.

Edison beamed raffishly. "Have a nice trip!"

The cagey inventor ambled over to the control panel and, while Sergeant Buchan and his men were otherwise engaged with Reisinger's petulant demands, reversed the polarity of the resurrector. He commanded silence with a throaty cry of "Engage!" The guards stood back as the outer frame and the gimbal began to turn, but this time, in *opposite directions*.

34

SHOWTIME

Emily's designated role at the Kaiser's pre-dinner soiree was 'leading lady,' a part for which she was expertly cast. She was a natural enchantress, captivating the men without unduly threatening the women. Her winning formula was based on a bit of wisdom she'd picked up from the Madame of a Hoboken whorehouse: A prostitute's ultimate skill lay in making men feel like boys and boys feel like men. Emily found this advice to be useful in dealing with the male sex in general and theatrical producers in particular. Despite her unanimous popularity, she remained conscious of the two linchpins to her continued survival, the Kaiser and General Skinehardt, and wisely stoked flattery as necessary.

Gershwin's part in this little drama is what was known in the trade as the 'juvenile.' Usually the hero's best friend, the juvenile provides a fair amount of comic relief and often inadvertently points the way toward the theme's resolution before retiring into the background. As waiters deftly waltzed silver trays of champagne to the melodies of Brahms, Gershwin dawdled on the fringe of the reception. It wasn't that the guests were dismissive of his presence. They considered him 'the help,' but help with talent.

As for Gershwin, he was appalled by these horrible people and afraid if he opened his mouth in a moment of candor, he might never close it.

That theory was put to the test by a Dowager Countess named Gusterman. Now in her dotage, she was a shrill scarecrow dripping in so many pearls they hung around her neck like chains. In her youth, she'd achieved the notorious reputation as a skinflint who'd purloined her title due to a talent for knowing the price of everything and everyone. Yet this gift for chiseling could not save her from committing the unpardonable fashion felony of wearing a headdress of peacock feathers in an ill-fated attempt to camouflage the bald patch on her unusually bulbous head. As the other guests had long ago grown bored with her standard line of nonsense, she decided to cultivate the accompanist with small talk.

"Ach, Munich!" she reminisced. "You should have seen Munich in the old days!"

"Why?" asked Gershwin.

The countess heaved a sigh of nostalgic reverie. "The glorious parties. The fascinating people. The excitement of the times." Then came the topper. "And there weren't any Jews," she added, trying to pick a sliver of shellfish from between her yellowed teeth.

Gershwin stared at her hard. "No Jews?"

"A few, here and there," she qualified, oblivious. "But nowhere near the hordes one finds nowadays."

"What have you got against the Jews?" asked Gershwin.

"My dear young man!" she tittered in surprise. "The Jews are nothing more than filthy, money-grubbing vermin."

"Oh, really?" replied Gershwin with a deceptive lilt in his voice.

"It's a fact of life. Everyone says so. Everyone. But, I don't suppose *I* have anything against the Jews. Not *personally*."

"You do now," quipped Gershwin. He tripped a waiter, who crashed a tray of champagne flutes over the countess's head. She shrieked in soaked effrontery, demanding retribution and towels. However, Gershwin was rescued by two mercies: timing and the mob; 'timing' because a wave of applause greeted Emily as she took to the stage, and 'the mob' due to the fact that, while everyone else might dislike the Jews, they disliked Countess Gusterman even more.

Gershwin swiftly took his seat on the piano bench and pounded out the opening chords to Emily's act. It was time to shut up and sing.

35

99% PERSPIRATION

Reisinger was so excited at the prospect of a return trip to his debauched paradise in purgatory that he failed to notice Edison had reversed the polarity of the resurrector. There was another reason for his lack of attention. He had instructed Sergeant Buchan that, once he safely returned from his second expedition to the dead zone, Edison was to be exterminated.

The sergeant watched as the old inventor puttered diligently at the control panel, monitoring the various levers and gauges and increasing the velocity lever to full tilt. He doubted Edison knew of his imminent fate but, if he was so wise, surely he sensed something. Yet he whistled a happy tune. So calm in the face of such mortal danger. So cool, considering the stifling heat of the hangar. More than stifling, smothering. Why, the temperature must be over 80 degrees…

Suddenly, Sergeant Buchan realized something was wrong.

The outer frame and the gimbal of the resurrector were moving in the opposite directions from the first go-round. He was no inventor, but even he realized that 'opposite' could prove problematic. He fumbled for his English. "Nein!" he exclaimed with growing panic. "Stop the machine, you must!"

"It's too late for that," Edison answered amiably.

The sergeant struck him, knocking the old inventor to the floor. Edison wiped a trickle of blood from the corner of his mouth and staggered to his feet, only to find himself surrounded by the snouts of a dozen guns. The tenor of the tuning forks shifted; instead of a collective whine, the air was sliced with what sounded like a cacophony of shrieks.

"Do it you will!" ordered the sergeant.

"I most certainly will not!" retorted Edison defiantly.

The sergeant paused, uncertain how to resolve this unexpected act of insubordination. Then a happy thought came to mind. Why should he care if the experiment was a failure or not? Reisinger had proceeded without General Skinehardt's approval and would have to suffer whatever consequences came his way. As for Edison, he was no longer necessary. The sergeant would kill him in retribution for his betrayal and he, the heroic Buchan, would be prized by Skinehardt for his indispensable loyalty. It might mean a rise in rank and pay! He chuckled to himself. He was a better tactician than his superiors had judged. He could afford to be generous in victory.

"Then now you will die," he stated. "Do you have any words to last?" He meant 'last words,' but Edison had already deciphered the scrambled syntax.

"Indeed I do," he began, hedging for a few more precious

seconds. "Words of wisdom that I hope every last one of you young hooligans will take to heart." Edison glanced at the temperature gauge on the boiler. Eight-two degrees. "Genius," he proclaimed, "is one percent inspiration…" The guards stared at the crazy old man, ready to fire, but curious as to what might come next. Edison surveyed the lot of them. Their underarms were damp and beads of sweat were breaking out on their faces. "And ninety-nine percent…" Edison paused, transfixed, as a plump rivulet of sweat rolled down the sergeant's temple and came to rest directly over a smear of oleum that covered his jugular vein.

"Perspiration."

Sergeant Buchan pressed his revolver against Edison's forehead but before he could pull the trigger he heard a pop. Had one of his men fired first? No, Edison was still standing. Then what could have…? His eyes shifted from side to side and he spied a spray of blood rhythmically spurting across the room. He felt a sharp sting on his neck and a vacancy in his knees. He brought his hand to the side of his face. It was blood, and the blood belonged to him, for the concentrated oleum had combined with his sweat, triggered an exothermic reaction, and transformed into sulfuric acid. The acid breached the hull of his vein, and his blood spewed across the shocked faces of his men. He tried to stanch the flow but failed, and unleashed the uncomprehending wail of a toddler. The cry would have to serve as his own 'words to last,' for he could only manage a few crazy-legged maneuvers before he fell down dead.

The shock of Sergeant Buchan's demise had jolted the other guards into such a state of disbelief that they'd ignored the curdling symptoms of their own fate. No more. They panicked as their eyes, faces, hands, any part of their bodies contaminated with the oleum, burned horribly in a sizzling bath of acid. Edison deftly removed himself from their frenzied circle and offered up a silent prayer that death would come quickly for the wretched men.

They scattered in shrieking agony, with the exception of one, a former wrestler named Franz, who had developed a high tolerance for pain during his time in the ring. He ignored the hot blood bubbling up from beneath his flesh and charged Edison. He shoved him back against Reisinger's laboratory table, determined to strangle the life out of the old conjuror. Edison tried to break his hold, failed, and fumbled through the place setting from Reisinger's dinner for something, anything, to defend himself. A fork? Out of reach. A knife? It clattered to the floor. Then he happened upon the perfect weapon. He grabbed a bowl of sugar and smashed it against the grappler's skull.

Franz started back in surprise and then laughed cruelly. "You think you can stop me with some sweet?"

"Well," judged Edison, "yes."

Franz grunted and moved in to finish him off when the combination of sulfuric acid and sugar ignited a new chemical reaction. His face began to fume, the heat peeling off his skin, and the blood turned brown, then black, and erupted in an oozing crust of pure carbon. Like fast-rising yeast, the carbon overwhelmed his features and, as he clutched his head in agony, it drooled through his fingers. Disoriented, he blindly stumbled into the whizzing rings of the resurrector. The machine snagged his torso and the blades cleaved him so thoroughly he was reduced to a pile of ground chuck laced with khaki.

* * *

Although this melee of carnage was taking place only steps away from them, John and Reisinger were unaware of any disturbance. They had reached the intersection of maximum velocity and reverse synchronicity; plunging toward the vanishing point that, if Edison's equation was correct, would also be the point of no return. John reached for the jettison lever and flexed his fingers around the release rod. He hesitated. He was tempted. To learn the secrets of the afterlife…who wouldn't be? Or perhaps to discover there were no secrets after all. As the pin of light enlarged into a wall of blinding brilliance John remembered Edison's warning and made a decision. He would confront the mysteries of the dead on death's timetable, not his own. At peace, he gripped the jettison lever and pulled.

It stuck. He pulled again, yanking harder, but two inner slats of metal had shifted, grinding together, and refused to give way. John feverishly rattled the lever and the housing as the horizon of light began to retract into a funnel. While Reisinger hyperventilated in giddy terror, as if he was approaching the pinnacle of a roller coaster just before the rush of the corkscrew descent, John put his back into budging the lever. He could not. Sick with panic, he realized the beads of sweat dripping onto his chest weren't sweat but pieces of his body beginning to devolve into a swarm of molecules.

As Edison had prayed for the demise of the soldiers to be quick, John offered up a prayer of his own. However, his desire wasn't for death but for life. Ironic. Now he coveted the thing he had most feared. He had a life, and Emily to live it with. As the funnel of light began to close, his prayer was answered. The mysterious shadow appeared once again, embraced his body, and momentarily forged his molecules back into solid flesh. John clutched the jettison lever for one last pull. As he desperately strained his entire being against the lever, the shadow wrapped tightly around him, as if to aid him in lifting the release. The lever gave way and the shadow split into two faces John recognized.

His parents.

There was no time for a reunion, only a split-second of floating wonder before John slammed through inner space and blasted back into the hangar. The passenger bubble ejected from the machine, broke through the cocoon of electricity, and pin-balled off the walls, until it came to a stop. Edison rushed toward the bubble. It was seared with scars, making it impossible to peer inside and see if John was alive. Edison tried the lock – jammed – grabbed a discarded pistol and shot off the hinges. He flung open the door and John lurched out, gasping for breath. Edison dragged him from the bubble, and the two men tumbled onto the floor.

As John revived, Edison awkwardly got to his feet and stumbled to the control panel. He grasped the handles of the RPM levers and evenly slowed the machine down to a stop. However, as he disarmed the controls, he was interrupted by the piercing squeals of bullets whizzing past his ears. Edison spun around to confront a baby-faced, blonde soldier, badly injured, but as determined as he was terrified. Edison froze in the bullseye of the young soldier's sights when John tackled him to safety. The soldier unloaded his weapon, the bullets eating into the control panel and severing the levers from the housing. As the soldier frantically attempted to reload, John grabbed a gun from the floor, pulled Edison to his side, and fired wildly to cover their escape.

They raced down the corridor of cells until Edison

abruptly stopped and returned to the space being used to store his inventions – the H2Ohms, the magnetic torpedo net and the tubs of chemicals. John joined him and quickly signaled his agreement. The embezzled bounty would help them even the odds and might guarantee their freedom.

* * *

As for Reisinger, his molecules had been sucked through the funnel, and he found his re-assembled-self back on the golden throne in the palace of silk and fur. This time, however, there was no sound of chimes, no scent of warm musk and no adolescent harem. Instead, the plush furnishings melted away, revealing a barren landscape enshrined by an ominous, roiling sky that bristled with green tentacles of infection.

"Edison!" shouted Reisinger. "Stop the experiment. Something's gone wrong!" His cries echoed back in return as if his own commands were mocking him. He waited and listened. Nothing. Infuriated by this lack of obedience, he ordered, "Sergeant! Kill him!" Again, emptiness. Reisinger staggered to the top of a hill and scoured the horizon for a sign of hope. He was alone. He bleated out pitifully, "Someone? Anyone? Help."

It was the third time in a row a prayer had been expressed and, like the others, an answer was granted. However, Reisinger should have been more specific in his request, for he was not graced by the presence of one of his nubile playmates. Instead he turned to confront the last person he would have expected to find in his own, private purgatory – although the individual in question was most assuredly dead.

Gaunt.

36

SWANEE

Emily purposefully delivered a slow-tempo version of her current Ziegfeld Follies finale:

...yes, the most priceless adornment
A girl can acquire
Is the love of the man
She truly adores.

Gershwin buttoned the number with an elegant flourish, and the audience applauded appreciatively. Emily acknowledged their approval, and then turned her back to them to take a sip of water. She had only planned three numbers but was already on her fifth. Skinehardt's aggressive monitoring of the performance had convinced her that while she might be safe until morning, the minute the singing stopped was the moment Gershwin would be 'disappeared.' She knew she had to do something to save him, stop Skinehardt, find John and Edison, and warn Black Jack Pershing and the American First Division that an attack was imminent.

Who was she kidding? She was no Mata Hari, only an ornament. For all she knew, John and Edison might already be dead, and if they were alive, had no way of knowing whether she and Gershwin were still in the compound. She was out of ideas – and material.

Emily took a second sip of water and looked at the wall of semi-circular picture windows that served as her backdrop. The windows were framed in gold velvet with sheer, white under-curtains. She gazed out onto the airfield through a part in the fabric and was surprised to see two figures scuttling out of a hangar. She took a closer look –and while she couldn't make out their faces, their forms were familiar: one tall and athletic, the other shorter and pear-shaped. Then they were swallowed up by the darkness. But she didn't need any more proof. She knew. John and Edison were alive!

Emily had to let him know she was still here. Thinking fast, she unlocked the center windows and flung them open. General Skinehardt stiffened to attention. Was she trying to escape? If so, he'd have to shoot her, and that would be a pity.

Emily turned to the audience, touched the back of her hand to her forehead, and gestured in explanation: "A bit of air." Skinehardt uncoiled. However, Emily was not faint but resolute. The air wasn't meant to revive her but relay her location to John on the winds of song.

"Finally, I'd like to perform, "Swanee," a number written by Mr. Gershwin." Gershwin looked up in surprise. "It's a new song but I guarantee…" she paused in emphasis, "…you'll never forget it."

Gershwin shut his open mouth, turned to the audience and stammered, "Uh…lyrics by Irving Caesar."

The still-damp Countess Gusterman turned to a hard-ofhearing baron who was forced to rely on an ear-horn. “Another Jew,” she crassly whispered. The baron nodded sympathetically and then pivoted his ear-horn away from the countess and toward the stage. Jew or not, he enjoyed a good tune.

Gershwin began to play, recital-style, and Emily trilled:

Swanee,
How I love you, how I love you,
My dear old Swanee...

Skinehardt studied Emily. She was up to something, the clever minx. Whatever could it be? He would enjoy finding out.

* * *

John and Edison moved stealthily across the grounds of the military base, crouching in pockets of darkness as sentries raked the grounds with searchlights from atop their watchtower. In moments like this, Edison was sorry he’d ever invented the damned electric light. He and John had to become one with the night and were well-equipped to realize that goal. They’d armed themselves with a pair of H2Ohms and skirted through the compound until they were positioned as closely as possible to the tower that served as the surveillance outpost for the hangar. As the two searchlights danced toward them they opened silent fire, unloading the weapons’ dual artillery of water and electricity. The sentries collapsed, stunned into an unconscious state that Edison predicted would last at least ten minutes or so; more than enough time for them to escape and make themselves scarce in the Luxembourg countryside. John fired a second volley for good measure and then short-circuited the searchlights to guarantee a cover of darkness as they made their way to the main gate.

* * *

Emily sang out, working the room to keep one eye on the audience and the other on the open window. A flurry of sparks erupted from the center of the compound. It must be John! She continued with greater insistence:

The folks up north –

She slapped the lid of the piano, producing a reverberating whack that jolted Gershwin.

Will –

Another slap, harder. Gershwin increased the tempo. Emily continued to beat the piano lid on every syllable, rousing the audience from its polite stupor:

See me no more
When I get to that Swanee shore –

"Everybody sing!" commanded Emily and the guests joined in, timidly at first and then with a growing sense of boisterous fun. Speed, sound and shock – weren't those the ingredients of Edison's purgatory equation? Damn right! If it worked for him, maybe it would play for her.

* * *

John and Edison were at the main gate when they heard voices wafting across the night air. Singing. John turned curiously to locate the source. The chateau. He saw a bank of lighted windows on the second floor. He could barely make out the words, but inside the jumble of sound was a voice he recognized:

Swanee, Swanee,
I'm coming home to Swanee.

John grinned excitedly and turned to Edison. "Emily."

Edison noted the tinkling accompaniment and nodded. "And Mr. Gershwin."

They reversed direction and high-tailed it to the chateau.

* * *

The injured young soldier in the laboratory limped to his feet and inspected the control panel. The various handles and buttons had been mostly demolished, thanks to his frantic handiwork, and the resurrector came to a stop. The soldier approached the passenger bubble that contained Herr Reisinger. He knocked tentatively on the transparent housing but Reisinger did not stir. He seemed to be frozen, trapped in some sort of suspended animation. The soldier pounded this time, but there was still no response. He started to pry off the lock to the bubble when the machine began to move, click by click, until it was slowly revolving. For while Edison had stopped the resurrector, the soldier's gunfire had not only blown off the controls, but locked the levers back to their full-on position. Thanks to him, the machine hadn't stopped – it had only stalled – and now, as he desperately tried to correct his horrible error, the resurrector's revolutions began to pick up speed.

Why did this matter? The only victim of the soldier's error appeared to be Reisinger. Yet if the reversal of the machine's polarity insured that 'death will dominate life,' in a broader sense that edict could impact not only the one inside the machine, but the many on the outside.

It could – and would. For the seed had inadvertently been sown to guarantee a metaphysical calamity that would threaten them all – and all of mankind in the bargain.

37

THE AFTERLIFE PART III

Reisinger reeled through the afterlife, fueled by a sick, heart-pounding fear. He was able to evade the lumbering Gaunt and, once he put some distance between himself and the monster, scanned the landscape for any sign of hope. There was none to give. The earth was pocked with geysers of brimstone; the sky a slab of unforgiving gray, riven with clouds of pestilence. These were the bowels of purgatory. He had entered the waiting room for Hell.

He wept, not out of regret, but terror. Yet even these selfish tears appeared to be rewarded with a sop of mercy when, in the distance, an isolated oasis appeared. Reisinger ran toward the vision and found it to be real. It was a circle of land, rich and green with a bubbling spring and a red tent in the shape of a fez that welcomed him as a sanctuary from the scouring winds. He reacted with even greater joy when he discovered the oasis was populated with the members of his harem, the painted boys and girls whose former lasciviousness had been gelded by fear. However, when they saw Reisinger had returned to them, they burst into a grateful babbling of welcome and bowed down to his magnificence. Reisinger calculated there would be safety in numbers, so he abandoned his concerns and prepared to be idolized.

The youngest of the girls, a freckled red-head of ten, scuttled toward Reisinger and dropped to her knees. He puffed up his scrawny chest in majesty and extended his hand. The girl took it, her head bowed in subservient communion, for that was the true nature of this twisted worship – an unholy Eucharist. Jesus Christ had urged his disciples 'this is my body, take and eat.' If Reisinger was to be a deity in this land of the dead, he realized he had to give good value for the trade. The girl's mouth puckered in tribute against the back of his hand.

What happened next was as unexpected as it was excruciating. The touch of the child's lips burned like a blow torch and not only scalded Reisinger's hand but ate through to the bone, soldering the surrounding flesh. Reisinger gagged in shock and withdrew his hand, clutching it to discover he could see clean through the wound, like an eye-hole in a peep show.

The girl shuddered and threw back her head in a yowl of unexpected, primal pleasure. After decades of death, she had tasted the nectar of life again, and the memory made her ravenous for more. Her eyes rolled back in a white glaze and her mouth jawed open in a jabber of wont. She reached out once again. Reisinger drew back and cast his furtive eyes from one to the other to the next of his former playmates as they rose up and moved toward him, their hands outstretched, flicking their tongues like vipers through their pouting lips, starved for their own taste of life.

Reisinger scurried through the shape-shifting landscape,

shrieking wildly as the nimble youths pursued him with an insouciance that would have been more appropriate for a game of tag, if the consequence of being 'it' wasn't so horrifying. The adrenaline coursing through his veins gave Reisinger the edge of speed and he paused, turning back to see how far he had gone, when he felt a force grab him by the scruff of the neck and lift him off the ground. It was Gaunt. However, the giant did not harm Reisinger but merely held him high, like laundry on a line, as one by one, the boys and girls congregated around the altar of his flesh. Gaunt grunted and thrust the squirming, squealing Reisinger out for their edification. They began at his feet, ripping off the shoes and socks and lapping their tongues against his skin, drinking in as much life as possible. It was delicious. He cried out for mercy but none was given for, with each taste of life, his young disciples demanded more. Gaunt lowered his shrieking body into the ravenous huddle and Reisinger flailed in agony, like a wild animal impaled on a hot spit, as the denizens of the afterlife ate him alive.

38

IMPLOSION

The messenger returned to the military base from an evening's leave. He'd ridden his bicycle to the nearby village. There was an inn on the outskirts of town with good *groestl* and a *linzer torte* that, while nowhere near as delectable a confection as his late mother used to make, was a damned sight better than the slop they served in the mess hall. An extra incentive was that the innkeeper offered a sizeable discount to the military on food and drink as well as the services of his two corpulent daughters, May and June, who entertained upstairs at intervals of fifteen minutes a pop. Occupation, mused the messenger, made pimps and whores of the populace. Not all, of course, but enough. It illustrated a valuable lesson in economics. When pressed, the rules of commerce adapted seamlessly and shamelessly to accommodate the fluctuating market.

He was late. He'd become sick with liquor and was forced to stop on the dirt road to vomit out the soup of schnapps and raspberry jam. By the time he reached the camp, it was after-hours, so instead of going through the main gate he approached a service entrance in the rear. A friend was on guard duty and let him pass in exchange for a pack of smokes. ‘A pack of smokes;’ a sample of slang he’d picked up from some American tourists during his time in Vienna, before the war, and he liked the snappish sound of it. No doubt he would hear more phrases like it in the coming months. Many more. Little matter. He was amused by the Americans. So open and so closed at the same time. It would be intriguing to see how they adapted to the business model of pimp and whore.

The messenger’s route took him past Skinehardt’s secret hangar, and he was surprised to find no sentries were posted. How could this be? He tentatively approached and rapped on the hangar’s main entrance, a wide set of sliding doors made of corrugated steel. No answer. Most unusual. He rapped again and listened. From behind the padded walls, he heard an insistent, high-pitched wail and the angry clatter of metal.

He tried the doors. They were unlocked but jammed. He steadied himself, grabbed the handles and yanked the doors open. The lifeless body of the young blond soldier tumbled out, fell on top of him, and slammed them both to the ground. Startled and repulsed, the messenger shoved the dead soldier off of him and scampered to his feet. His breath heaving in shock, he stared at the corpse. The arms and legs had been broken, with each appendage splayed out at a sickening, left-facing angle. It was as if the soldier had tried to escape from the hangar but had been interrupted, and diabolically so. Who would have done such a thing? Who? Or what?

The messenger warily entered the central chamber of the hangar where he discovered the wholesale slaughter of the guards. Their broken bodies were littered haphazardly across the floor like so many mannequins, and a towering machine in the middle of the room was spinning so violently it shook the hangar's foundation. The resurrector! He stood frozen in a combination of fright and fascination as the spills of blood began to slowly move toward the bizarre invention, coaxed across the floor by some weird force of gravity. The machine sucked the blood into its maw, quivered with a satisfied moan, and then clamored for more. However, it was not until the actual bodies began to drag across the floor and fly into the core of the machine that the messenger snapped out of his dunderheaded trance and sounded the alarm.

* * *

With Gershwin enthusiastically matching her every note of the way, Emily proceeded to sell the finale to the rollicking sing-a-long for all she was worth:

Your wandering child
Will wander no more...

An aide made his way to General Skinehardt. He had a sheen of panic on his face that no amount of military bearing could hide, and Skinchardt instantly knew something had gone horribly wrong. The aide relayed the catastrophe with a terse whisper: "Edison escaped, Reisinger missing, the machine's out of control."

Emily thrust her arms open wide and, in a sure, strong voice, brought it home:

When I get to that Swanee shore!

The audience cheered as Skinehardt, propelled by sick fury, stalked to the stage and flung open the curtains to the picture windows. What he revealed astonished the entire assembly. The hangar was crowned with a cluster of black lightning. As a team of soldiers converged on the building, the dark voltage revolved ominously, growing in force.

Ludendorff sidled up to Skinehardt and noted accusingly, "Science fiction."

Skinehardt spun furiously back on the room. Many would feel his wrath, but he would start with Emily. She would do. "Arrest that woman!" he commanded.

The guards apprehended Emily, but the Kaiser protested their actions and a general uproar ignited. It was the perfect preamble to herald the entrance of John and Edison, who launched into the grand salon and sprayed the room with their H2Ohms.

The not-so-bright old things dropped first, more out of surprise than injury, as the potent mixture of water and electricity spiraled out from the weapons' nozzles and doused them into submission. The soldiers required a more concentrated blast from the H2Ohms but, once struck, were easily incapacitated. The generals, being generals, let the soldiers do their fighting for them and took cover, but were eventually found out and subdued. The Kaiser's bodyguards stuffed the doddering despot into a closet and rejoined the fray just as John's H2Ohm ran out of water. Without the conductor of liquid, the weapon was little more than a cattle prod, and that's exactly how he used it, stunning and clubbing the guards until, backed up against the bar, he grabbed a magnum of champagne, refueled, and unleashed a barrage that smashed them to the floor.

Skinehardt fared better than the others. He immediately realized that Edison's inventions couldn't be bested by conventional weapons but might be countered by other, more traditional means. He slugged Gershwin and grabbed Emily, holding her in front of him as a shield. Edison fired off a few shots at Skinehardt, but the general ducked, foiling Edison, who inadvertently zapped Emily. She absorbed the full brunt of the current and collapsed, unconscious, in Skinehardt's arms. He threw her over his shoulder and escaped down the stairway. Before John and Edison could join the chase, a team of reinforcements arrived and effectively blocked their path by cordoning off the grand salon and securing the chateau.

Under fire from below, John and Edison crawled to Gershwin's side. He was groggy but conscious. They pulled him to safety as canisters of gas clattered onto the marble floor and began flooding the room with noxious fumes.

"Chlorine gas!" exclaimed Edison, and he was right to be alarmed for it was an agonizing poison that smelled like newly mown hay but caused asphyxiation, blindness, and death. The men quickly tore a tablecloth into makeshift masks to stave off its gruesome effects.

John ran to the windows. The moment his face appeared, shots rang out from below. He scanned the room for another option and found none. "We're trapped."

"Like rats," added Gershwin.

"You got any ideas?" asked John.

Edison shook his head, fresh out. They turned to Gershwin who shrugged and then was struck with a sudden inspiration.

"As a matter of fact…yeah."

* * *

The messenger watched, mesmerized, as a group of soldiers stormed the hangar, and then cautiously approached the resurrector. It was revolving at an extraordinary speed, fueled by the bodies of the dead guards, including the tangled corpse of the young soldier which somersaulted across the floor and into the machine's avaricious gullet. The sphere contracted, as if swallowing, and then shuddered, expanding in size. The rivets in the support struts popped out like corks, and the base collapsed in a shambles of warped metal as the resurrector began the terrifying transformation from a machine to a black ball of pure energy.

The soldiers panicked and opened fire. The resurrector groaned in audible fury and retaliated by jettisoning its thousands of tuning forks. The messenger hit the ground, barely escaping injury. But the platoon was eviscerated by the flying metal tongs and the men, lifeless or not, were snared into the insatiable maw of the whirling globe and swallowed whole.

Tempted by the horrible lure of the resurrector, yet grounded with the common sense of self-preservation, the messenger chained himself to the frame of the boiler that had been welded into the foundation of the hangar. He sensed his role as a witness to the dark side's birth into the realm of the living. Terrified but fascinated, he moved in closer to study the abomination and see if there was some way to harness its' mayhem.

* * *

As the hangar pulsed with blasts of dark light and a cacophony of screams, Skinehardt realized the time had come to bid farewell to Plan A and embrace Plan B. He spotted the waiting zeppelin in the distance. The soldiers who surrounded the tethered vehicle were diverted to the assault on the chateau, and the craft was abandoned except for the airship's captain, a roly-poly, ruddy-faced officer in his sixties named Gunter, who was looking forward to the completion of his run and then a return home to the benefits of a warm fire and a cold bottle. Skinehardt arrived at the underbelly of the airship, dumped the still-dazed Emily into the craft's command car, and leapt inside, disrupting the captain's protocol by demanding: "Prepare for departure."

"What is this?" sputtered Captain Gunter. "What about my crew? Where's General Ludendorff?"

Skinehardt withdrew a pistol and shoved the muzzle under the captain's whiskered chins. "Ludendorff is out, I am in, and we are off!"

* * *

Commandant Henke rushed into the chateau, an officer's coat slung over his dressing gown and the tassel of his nightcap bobbing coyly from beneath his helmet. He had been summoned to fill the breach of authority laid bare by the bizarre attack. Truth be told, he was pleased by this ruinous turn of events. Ever since Skinehardt and his team had arrived on the base, they'd usurped his authority. Granted, it was the general's right of rank, but there was no call to have been such a belittling bastard about it. Why, Skinehardt had even ordered that he be excluded from the evening's festivities. Outrageous! Now Henke had a chance to prove his mettle in front of the Kaiser and the high command. He called for silence.

A faint voice echoed from above. “Help,” wheezed the voice between fits of a racking cough. “I surrender.” It was Edison.

“Descend. And slowly,” ordered the commandant. Had he already won the battle without having to engage?

Edison wobbled down the stairway. Although he clasped a swatch of table linen over his face, it appeared the chlorine gas had dealt him an injurious blow. He reached the stairwell and two guards apprehended him.

“Hah! Guilty as charged,” declared Henke triumphantly.

“Oh, no, please, no sir, not guilty,” pleaded Edison. He pointed to the life-sized portrait of the two warring noblemen that fronted the dumbwaiter and added flatly: “Framed.”

On cue, John and Gershwin surreally crashed out from behind the canvas. The Germans pivoted sharply but it was too late. The two flesh-and-blood warriors unloaded their H2Ohms, mowing down Henke and his flummoxed men before any of them could click their triggers.

As Edison and Gershwin tip-toed over the fallen soldiers, John raced out of the chateau in search of Emily. He feverishly scanned the grounds of the base. She was nowhere to be found. Then, a shout – it was Emily’s voice. Then a second shout that was muffled in mid-yelp. It came from the direction of the zeppelin that was primed for takeoff; the few remaining landing tethers slipping out of the soggy earth. John sprinted toward the zeppelin in a parallel direction and spotted Skinehardt shoving Emily into the hold as the zeppelin lifted into the air. John stopped, aimed, and fired the H2Ohm. It was a sure shot and would have disabled Skinehardt but the blast fell short, only striking the shell of the command car and causing the control dials to temporarily spike.

The shot had an unintended consequence as well. Skinehardt spotted John, withdrew his pistol, and fired. The zeppelin's awkward ascent threw Skinehardt's aim off target and the bullet slugged into the H2Ohm, saving John's life. However, the shot pierced the weapon's electrical housing and triggered a surge of reserve power that shivered through his body and slammed him to the ground.

As the zeppelin soared into the sky, the landing tethers skittered across the frosted grass and a loop of rope snagged around John's ankle. It tugged, cinched into a knot, and pulled, dragging him foot-first into the air where he dangled unconscious, his limbs splayed open like a wishbone.

* * *

Edison and Gershwin victoriously emerged from the chateau only to confront an even greater challenge. The hangar that housed the resurrector was surrounded by ominous rings of dark, pulsating light. Edison ran toward the hangar with Gershwin following reluctantly behind. Given the increasing number of soldiers in the vicinity it was a foolish move, but the astonishing display of haywire metaphysics proved to be so great that friend and foe stood paralyzed as one.

Edison hurried into the hangar, and then stopped in shock. "But…I shut it down," he murmured, "what in the name of….?" Suddenly, he knew. While reversing the polarity of the machine had saved John and condemned Reisinger, it inadvertently established the possibility of an even greater threat, for the resurrector had transformed into a churning ball of dead energy, and the more it gulped into its starving maw, the larger it grew. The only way to stop it, if it wasn't too late, was to sever the source of its power before it evolved even further into a self-sustaining entity. If that happened, Edison surmised, the world might cease to exist.

Only two people realized the extent of the wayward machine's potential for Armageddon – Edison, theoretically, and the messenger, instinctively. Yes, he was still alive, still secured to the boiler, and striving against the force of the resurrector to reach the control panel in time, for now he knew there was no harnessing this monstrosity. The only option was to shut the damned thing down.

Edison sensed what the messenger was trying to accomplish and moved to assist him but Gershwin held the old inventor back. The dark side of purgatory would not bow down before his genius, and he'd be consumed by the swirling black mass, just as the hangar itself was being demolished to satisfy its limitless hunger.

The walls split apart, the roof peeled back like the lid on a tin of beef, and the bric-a-brac of metal and glass sailed into the mouth of the roiling sphere. The messenger survived the bedlam and continued tortuously toward the control panel, the mooring of which began to pry loose from its foundation, the bolts slowly twisting up from their sockets.

The Kaiser and General Ludendorff, both dazed and injured, limped towards the shell of the hangar and, along with the cowed soldiers, watched in astonishment as the messenger struggled against the supernatural assault. Just as he reached the control panel it was ripped asunder, and the force slammed him to the ground. However, it also revealed the unholy orb's one remaining and, for the moment, essential connection to the living world – an industrial electrical plug the size of a man's arm that fed directly into the cement floor and was secured by four metal prongs.

The messenger roused himself but was disoriented and, suddenly, fearful. Edison noted both his fear and the instrument of their possible salvation. He broke away from Gershwin and reached out to the messenger.

"The power source," he cried, pointing to the electrical connection.

The messenger looked up at Edison, startled by the inventor's presence and their eyes met in a brief, fateful moment. Edison sharply gestured again to the electrical connection.

"Sever it! Now!"

The messenger understood and nodded intently.

As Edison strained toward the outlet to help him, he felt his feet slipping out from beneath him as the pull of the resurrector flexed its claws to entrap him in its clutches. Gershwin saw what was happening, leapt to Edison's side, and dragged him back to safety. Together they watched as the messenger reached the outlet and, one by one, tripped the prongs. As the maelstrom reached peak force, he grabbed hold of the plug's cord, wrapped it around his forearms and pulled upward with all his might. Slowly, torturously, the metal pins in the plug squeezed loose from the socket. The messenger appeared to freeze in the midst of the struggle, even lose ground. He summoned all his strength for one final pull and the plug shot out of the socket, severing the power that fueled the infernal machine.

The swirling mass shrieked as though mortally wounded, for it had been. It slowly ground to a halt, began to rotate in the opposite direction and then, miraculously, perceptibly shrink.

"What's happening?" wondered Gershwin.

"It's imploding," responded Edison. He was right. As the globe reduced in size, the cocoon of dark energy around the hangar dissipated. Yet no one moved. The only one who dared approach the dwindling mass was the messenger who, while exhausted, remained hypnotized by the churning sphere of calamity that had now deflated to a circumference of six by six. As the messenger drew forward he thought he heard what sounded like a voice, the tone faint but insistent. He bent down, crooking his ear to better hear as the spinning orb slowed to a stop. He drew closer. Then closer still.

In a flash, a shrieking cadaver of bone and shredded flesh jolted out from the sphere and grasped hold of his right arm. The messenger howled in terror, his body rigid in petrification, and the other onlookers echoed his screams. Edison's fear was tempered with grisly insight, for he alone recognized the mangled hank of gristle was all that remained of Herr Reisinger.

The ghoul spotted Edison, stared at him damningly, and cursed his name.

The messenger tried desperately to shake loose from the frenzied cadaver's grip but the hideous thing would not let go and dug its bones into his right forearm, mixing its black blood with his. Then something even more bizarre occurred. Two, four, eight, and then a dozen supple, child-like arms reached out from the orb, wrapped themselves around Reisinger's howling form and dragged him back into the dead zone.

The globe began to spin again, faster and faster, until it shriveled to the size of a medicine ball and then exploded in an ocean of blood, vomiting all the life it had consumed back into the living world. The force of the blast slammed the messenger to the floor where he lay, sodden, and seemingly dead.

Edison was tempted to go to his aid, but Gershwin yanked him out of the hangar as the Germans secured the area. Besides, someone else was in greater need of their assistance. Gershwin pointed skyward. As the zeppelin soared past, they spotted John hanging precariously from one of the craft's landing tethers.

"The zeppelin!" insisted Gershwin. "It's leading a surprise attack against the Americans. Tonight! We've got to do something!"

Edison thought hard, pacing, processing the elements of the dilemma as rapidly as possible to discover a plan of action that might save them all, but what? What? Suddenly, his dour face brightened, flushed with inspiration, and he uttered the one word he swore had never, ever, crossed his lips.

"Eureka!"

The wily inventor hurried off to the airfield.

"I knew it!" Gershwin proclaimed and danced after him.

* * *

Ludendorff and the Kaiser surveyed the bizarre wreckage. What unholy mischief had Skinehardt been tinkering with? Where was Skinehardt, anyway? The more questions they considered, the more confused they became. The messenger was lifted onto a stretcher by two orderlies. He passed by them, drenched with the rot of blood and meat but still alive. His glazed eyes were open but unresponsive, and his purgatory encounter appeared to have robbed him of his sight.

"I cannot see…not see…not see…" he moaned deliriously

as the orderlies carried him off to the infirmary.

"I've never known such daring," offered the Kaiser.

"Or insanity," countered Ludendorff dryly. He gestured to a guard. "Who is that soldier?" The guard retrieved the messenger's I.D. tag from a pool of blood and wiped it clean. The name was legible but unfamiliar.

"His name is Hitler."

39

ATTACK

General John Joseph Pershing excelled at the impossible.

Following his graduation from West Point, the future commander of the American Expeditionary Forces was assigned to the New Mexico Territory and, after proving his mettle, was awarded command of the 10th Cavalry, a 'Buffalo Soldiers' Regiment composed of African-Americans. Pershing's time among the minorities taught him a skill rare among men, military or otherwise – empathy. That unique ability propelled him into the key leadership role for a variety of successful international campaigns: the Philippine-American War, the Sino-Russian War and even, by God, the pursuit of Pancho Villa. It also earned him the moniker of 'Black Jack,' a nickname first employed by his critics to mock his democratic nature and then, over time, adopted by an adoring public as a sign of respect.

In 1917, President Wilson was in the market for a miracle worker. To prepare the nation for a decisive entry into World War I, a standing army of twenty-seven thousand men had to be transformed into a fighting force of over two million professional soldiers and in no time flat. It was a Herculean task, but Pershing accepted the challenge. Upon his arrival in France with the First Division, that challenge increased exponentially. The French and British troops had been decimated by four long years of conflict and were desperate for a fresh supply of manpower. For them, soldiers had become little more than numbers to be entered into the abacus of war. It took all of Pershing's considerable powers of diplomacy to mollify the Allies while buying the necessary time to keep the Americans on the fringe of the battle so they could cultivate their clout.

So here he sat, just east of Lorraine, overseeing some two hundred thousand troops. Within ninety days their number would swell to over a million. Until then, his orders were to wait. Pershing had received Wilson's odd communiqué regarding Edison (what the devil was old Tom doing in the middle of this mess?) and believed the 'interlude of inaction' was a blessing that would prove decisive in the war's outcome. However, his soldier's instinct was on high alert. It was one thing to keep your powder dry. It was another to be a sitting duck.

The moon beamed a milky light down onto the American base camp. The First Division had retired for the night. Pershing, however, was still at work in his command tent, when a young staff officer arrived with a status report.

"All quiet on the western front, sir," he claimed with assurance.

Black Jack looked up from his paperwork, cast a knowing eye at the officer, and gave a shrewd snort. "Don't bet on it, bucko."

* * *

John thought he was in heaven. As he soared through a quilt of billowing clouds, the dulcet tones of a harp echoed around him. Although the clouds were the genuine article, he soon realized the 'harp' was the sound of blood rushing through his temples. Closer inspection revealed he was some 3,000 feet above the earth and upside down to boot. It wasn't heaven. Not yet. John jackknifed his torso and grabbed the knot in the tether rope to right himself. He gazed upward and saw the zeppelin looming above him, blotting out the stars. He gathered the line of rope into his hands and began the formidable climb to the hull.

* * *

The zeppelin was secure and on schedule. Skinehardt left Captain Gunter to his navigational duties and entered the darkened hold where he coolly inspected Emily's unconscious, trussed-up body. She had cracked her head when he shoved her inside and tied her wrists to a ceiling pipe, leaving her in a position that was as vulnerable as it was salacious. He lit a long, brown cigarette, inhaled deeply, and blew a halo of smoke into her face. The acrid scent of tobacco roused her. Emily recovered her bearings quickly and struggled uselessly against her bondage. A bright orange dot in the darkness signaled someone's presence.

"Where am I?"

Skinehardt stepped forward, parting the scrim of smoke. "We are aloft," he answered. "And on course to pay a visit to your countrymen."

"What about the resurrector?" countered Emily "Wasn't that supposed to be your big meal ticket?"

"That is no longer a viable business opportunity," he replied dryly. "But as the hero who single-handedly saved the Ludendorff Offensive, no, make that the Skinehardt Offensive, who knows? I might even become Kaiser myself." He leaned in, inhaling her scent. She smelled of peaches and sweat. "Until then, let us take succor in each other's company…"

He kissed Emily roughly, his mouth plunging over hers. She froze for a moment, only certain that the phrase 'Skinehardt Offensive' had the ring of truth to it on a variety of levels. However, instead of truth she opted for a reverse strategy and responded to his kiss, suggesting in husky patches of breath, "I'm a lot better at 'succor' when I'm untied."

Skinehardt started to loosen her bonds and then stopped. He surveyed the curves of her figure. His hands roamed over the bodice of her dress and ripped at the fabric. She responded with an unexpected start that brought him a perverse jolt of pleasure. "I prefer my women…restrained," he murmured in a guttural sigh of lust and buried his face in her breasts. Emily screamed. Sometimes a good, loud scream slammed on the brakes, but not this time. She struggled impotently and then, furious at his taken liberties, locked her legs around his waist, bent forward, and bit down, chewing her teeth into the ridge of his ear and drawing blood. Skinehardt bolted upright, cradled his ear in pain, and slapped Emily hard, the only concession to her femininity being that his palm was open instead of closed into a fist. The fist would come next if she didn't behave.

A timid, timely interruption by Captain Gunter interrupted the foreplay. "We're at the ready, sir," he advised. In truth, they weren't. Even at a speed of sixty miles per hour they were still some distance off. But the captain didn't care for this Skinehardt fellow, and he didn't appreciate having his airship despoiled as a white slaver's bordello. He was outclassed by the general in youth, size and rank but he was the only one on board who could pilot a zeppelin, so there it was. He retreated but left the door to the hold open. Skinehardt pulled back, stanching the blood from his ear.

"Don't fret, my sweet," he hissed. "There'll be plenty of time for us after the war." He bared his teeth in a playful sneer. "Which should be…any minute."

He swept out of the hold, locking the door behind him. Emily struggled mightily against the ropes and then paused, spent. Suddenly, she recalled an old employer and one of the methods he used in his arsenal of legerdemain.

"Houdini!" she gratefully acknowledged.

Instead of yanking on the ropes, she gently shimmied the knots back and forth. Slowly, they began to give way.

* * *

The zeppelin emerged from the clouds and crossed into French territory. Skinehardt peered through his binoculars and could make out the flickering signs of life in the First Division's training camp. "On my command," he instructed Captain Gunter.

* * *

John had reached the hull of the zeppelin. He was surprised to find it covered with a sturdy net of electric bulbs. He used the netting to climb up the side of the craft and was making progress when, suddenly, the left side of the hull burst into a wall of light so blinding it nearly repelled him into the atmosphere. What John couldn't make out in the blast of light was the message broadcast across the hull that shot out like a beacon to the American sentries below.

WE SURRENDER

* * *

The camp was bugled to chaotic attention. General Pershing leapt to his feet and raced outside. He grabbed a pair of binoculars from the sentry who'd first spotted the airborne message and took a long, perplexed look at the strange sight. "Damnedest white flag I've ever seen," he muttered. Then, after a moment he added curiously: "The second 'R' is moving."

And it was, for the 'R' included John, whose shifting outline against the illuminated letter gave it the animated appearance of a kicking leg. Pershing thought hard. If this was a surrender it was one for the history books.

* * *

"Stop engines," ordered Skinehardt. The captain complied. Being dead in the air would enhance their petition of helplessness. Skinehardt paused, savoring the moment, and then cried out, "Eastern hull," with a husky fervor that signaled what he now believed history would record as the pivotal moment in the Great War. The captain pulled a second lever and the other side of the hull lit up with a different message broadcast for a strictly German audience.

ATTACK!

* * *

Across the border, a German sentry spotted the electric command and relayed the order to attack. Curtains of camouflage netting were stripped away, revealing a dozen Junkers CL-1's, the fatherland's state-of-the-art aircraft, made entirely of metal, solidly-armored, and designed specifically to attack troops on the ground with everything from machine guns to racks of fragmentation grenades. It was the war's most sophisticated killing machine and primed for its maiden voyage. A crewman waved the planes forward. They rumbled down a trio of runways, lifted into the air, and headed straight for the unsuspecting Americans.

* * *

Skinehardt shivered with anticipation. He was on the verge of a triumph. He paced the bridge and inspected the craft's reflective mirrors; first the western hull (*We Surrender*), then the eastern hull (*Attack!*), then the western hull again, and that's when he spotted John, still alive, and hefting himself toward the top of the zeppelin. Skinehardt seethed in bottled fury. As far as history was concerned, Mr. Dawkins was forgotten but not yet gone. He would show him the exit.

* * *

John reached the top of the zeppelin, exhausted but relieved to be on semi-solid ground. He allowed himself the luxury of a few jagged breaths, pulled himself up, and stumbled toward the hatch. He tripped on the electric netting and sprawled across the canvas skin of the aircraft. He'd dislocated an ankle but, with no time to waste, painfully twisted it back into place. A shadow fell over him. It was Skinehardt, who was armed with a fire axe. The blade whistled through the air and John reared back, narrowly avoiding its blunt force. As Skinehardt swung again and again. John evaded the slashing assault and landed against a repair kit that popped open, revealing a supply of tools. John grabbed a rigging knife and charged Skinehardt, the two combatants thrusting and chopping at each other with an escalating fury. A gust of wind rocked the zeppelin and, after an awkward series of parries and thrusts, they came together in a face-to-face clinch.

"Why won't you die?" gasped the exasperated Skinehardt.

"Die?" replied John, with a second-wind grin. "Hell, I just got here!"

* * *

The captain righted the zeppelin's position. He was too old to be out so late on such a cold night and was dreaming of his wife's pork chops when he heard a polite but insistent tapping from inside the hold. It couldn't be the girl, could it? It must be that Skinehardt bastard. Curious, he opened the door and walked right into a haymaker that knocked him across the rudder wheel and into tomorrow morning. Emily shook her hand in pain; she'd forgotten how much it hurt to hit someone hard. She dropped to the captain's side, grabbed his gun, and tried to rouse him. No response. She rustled him again, this time more roughly, but he was down for the count. "Come on," she begged. "You've got to land this thing. Wake up!"

* * *

John drove his knife into Skinehardt's hand. He let out a yowl and dropped his axe which skittered across the hull until it caught in the electrical netting. Infuriated, Skinehardt head-butted John in the chest, and the two men grappled ferociously.

* * *

General Pershing and his men were glued to their binoculars, watching the bizarre fight silhouetted against the moonlight. Although the soldiers had no idea who the two pugilists were, they were already laying odds. It was shaping up to be the damnedest match since Benny Leonard KO'd Sailor Kirke in one. As for Pershing, the fight had stopped being a curiosity. It was a warning.

"Your orders, sir?" asked a by-the-book staff officer.

"Battle stations," replied Black Jack succinctly.

Suddenly a cry went up from one of the sentries and all eyes shifted to the south. The clouds shimmered with a golden glow and parted like a celestial curtain to provide a suitably dramatic entrance. Son-of-a-bitch. It was the Kaiser's balloon!

However, the balloon wasn't manned by a clutch of

nefarious Germans but by Edison and Gershwin, who had turned their 'eureka' moment into a last-ditch effort to save the day. At first it appeared they might have a measure of success in their favor but they immediately encountered two obstacles. The first was that the balloon was more difficult to maneuver than they'd imagined and the gondola rocked drunkenly across the sky. The second challenge proved far more desperate. The First Division had no idea that they were the good guys, and Pershing's cry of 'Prepare to fire!' was a preamble to blasting them out of the sky. Edison turned over the navigation duties to Gershwin and hoped that another 'eureka' moment might save their skins.

An assembly of stokes mortars were trained on the balloon "Ready….Aim…" commanded the general. Then suddenly, just before the artillery was unleashed to light up the sky, Pershing cried, "Hold your fire!"

"But, sir…" protested the staff officer, "they'll get away!"

Pershing's gaze stayed fixed on the balloon. He'd made the right call. "What is that?"

The young officer watched intently as the skin of the balloon, decorated with the art nouveau figure of Zeus, was illuminated with bursts of light; some briefly, others for a longer duration. He turned to Pershing in disbelief. "It's Morse code."

Edison! He had employed his boyhood training as a telegraph operator to adapt from an aural to a visual means of communication. The message?

I – T – S – A – T – R – A – P

"It's a trap!" shouted the officer.

"Not anymore," responded Black Jack who gestured grandly to the sky and cackled commandingly. "Go get 'em, boys!"

40

AUF WIEDERSEHEN

Although John and Skinehardt were locked in deadly combat, the sight of Edison riding to the rescue in the Kaiser's balloon interrupted their struggle. It also gave Skinehardt an edge. A gust of wind buffeted the airship and thc zeppelin bucked. The axe that had snagged in the electrical rigging of the craft cut loose, slid across the hull, and landed within inches of Skinehardt's reach. While John remained focused on Edison's arrival, Skinehardt broke free and scooped up the axe, raising it high to strikc deep.

"*Auf Wiedersehen,*" bid the general. The blade was poised to sink into John's chest, when a gunshot intruded. The bullet blasted the axe out of Skinehardt's hand and sent it pin-wheeling down to earth. Both men turned to discover Emily behind the refuge of the captain's gun.

"The show's not over." She delivered the line with a surety that quickly evaporated, for the airship lurched again, this time so precariously that the gun flew out of her hands and she followed, landing on her rump and sliding down the rear of the zeppelin.

John valiantly dove after her and, as she slipped over the hull, managed to grab her around the waist, while his other hand clung tightly to the aircraft's fin.

"They're in trouble," cried Gershwin as Edison tried mightily to ascend the craft toward their friends' aid as fast as possible, but it would not be fast enough. The burner was low on fuel and they'd begun to lose ballast.

John and Emily looked up as Skinehardt calmly stalked toward their dangling perch and ground the heel of his boot onto John's hand, delicately at first and then with bone-breaking force. "*Auf Wiedersehen*. Again."

Emily hung onto John. She looked deeply into his eyes and he into hers. They had no fear except fear for each other. He winced. The combination of the pain from his crushed hand and the hanging weight of their bodies was becoming too much for him to bear. Yet the hurt that cut deepest was his failure to save the woman he loved, the woman who had so immediately become his forever.

"It looks like we're going to die in each other's arms," he apologized.

"I can't think of a better place," confessed Emily.

Neither could he. After all, this moment was the rest of their lives and they were together. How many lovers could depart on such a glorious finale? They kissed each other deeply and John's grip slid from beneath the villain's boot, freeing his hand for a last embrace as they plummeted to the earth below.

Skinehardt opened his mouth to protest, but no words came, only a hollow groan. He was stunned, cheated by their sacrifice, and could only stand, limp and empty, as they surrendered to their fate. Until…

They felt something surround them – a hard mesh – and then a sharp yank that knocked the wind out of their lungs and rattled their heads. They looked up in wonder to discover their descent had been interrupted by Edison's magnetic torpedo net, which worked perfectly well as a conventional net. The unlikely agent who had assured their deliverance with one crack shot of the jettison gun was Gershwin – no longer a mere juvenile but a definitive man of action.

As Edison manned the motorized winch which gathered the net and returned them to the safety of the gondola, they all shouted in joy at beating the odds and being alive.

All except Skinehardt, who refused to let this heresy stand. He slammed back into the hold, hot with vengeance, and ransacked the supply locker for a more appropriate weapon of mayhem and selected a machine gun. He sniggered maniacally. Overkill? Yes, but it was what the high drama of the moment demanded. His reverie was interrupted by the bone-rattling explosions from a dogfight. He raced up the circular stairway through the skeleton of the zeppelin and emerged to witness a squadron of American fighters fully engaged with the German air force whose secret attack was, thanks to Edison, now an open book.

In truth, the Germans had been careless. The lynchpin of their assault had been surprise and they'd anticipated a peaceful valley of sleeping soldiers primed for slaughter. Once that key advantage had been yanked out from under them they had nothing to fall back on but a conventional plan of attack, and that was severely hampered by the aggressive defense of the American forces. The German squadron leader knew the mission was as good as lost when his select team of seasoned fliers was overwhelmed by twice as many of the enemy aircraft. The Americans weren't yet flying aces but they were more than game. After months of hanging fire, it felt good to be men again.

Skinehardt's prediction had been correct. The Americans would win the war and their unassailable weapon would be their 'enthusiasm.' As the dogfights played out around him in screaming tailspins and balls of fires, he saw his dreams of omnipotent glory fritter away. The resurrector was gone. The Skinehardt Offensive – make that the Ludendorff Offensive – had been compromised before it ever began. Even his promise of a carnal interlude with Emily had been foiled. And all because of Thomas Alva Edison!

Where was that damnable old man? He prowled the top of the zeppelin, intent on penetrating the scrims of smoke and flame. There! Sailing below the western hull but still within range. He sneered in consolation. He might not be acclaimed as the master of the world but history would be forced to accord him a berth of infamy as the man who murdered the 'Wizard of Menlo Park.' Murderer. Despite the rank and the medals and the cultivated cynicism that suggested a higher station, 'murderer' was his true identity. It always had been. To secure his firing stance, he wedged his leather boots beneath the electrical netting and split some wires in the process but paid them no mind. Skinehardt took aim and unloaded his machine gun at the balloon.

The hail of bullets compounded what was already a perilous situation. Edison had achieved his two objectives: to warn the Americans and to rescue his friends. His only goal now was to get clear – and fast – but the directional propellers on the balloon had been shattered and the craft refused to do more than drift. They took cover as Skinehardt's second round of ammunition blasted the air around them. The skin of the balloon was badly compromised, and Edison compensated by opening the sputtering burner valve to full. Other than that, there was nothing to be done. Except…

John grabbed the remaining H2Ohm. "Have you got any juice left?" Edison checked the surge level. It was a hair above empty.

"Enough for one shot," he responded dubiously. John nodded. He accepted the odds. He'd make the shot count.

Skinehardt stopped his assault long enough to reload. As he did, John sprung up from the gondola of the balloon, aimed the H2Ohm, and fired. The blast hit Skinehardt in the chest but the voltage was too low to do any real damage and only fazed him. He chortled sadistically and prepared to empty the fresh payload into his helpless quarry.

And then the unexpected occurred…

The weak strain of current re-charged off the metal from Skinehardt's chest full of medals, sparked the exposed wires at his feet, and infected the hull's electrical netting. The general tried to stamp out the contamination of sparks but it was too late. The chain reaction of short-circuiting current could not be stopped.

John sensed what might happen next. Edison knew it - but even with the propellers there was no way they could get far enough away from the zeppelin to avoid being consumed by the coming conflagration. He was out of 'eureka' moments. Thankfully, John wasn't.

"Strap yourselves in," he commanded. They did so, confused. "We can't fly," explained John, "but we can damn well drop." And with that he shut off the burner valve. The interior of the balloon collapsed and the gondola fell away from the zeppelin, accelerating its descent until it was plummeting to earth.

Skinehardt panicked as the haywire electricity blew out the engine compartment's main battery and triggered a fire that spread across the surface of the zeppelin, devouring the skin of the hull and eating into the chambers of hydrogen and blau gas below. The detonations erupted in a domino effect that climaxed into the one thing Skinehardt feared most. Failure. His cries were only silenced when the blasts reached critical mass and the zeppelin exploded in a shuddering vista of flames, ripping his body asunder into a million pieces of thwarted flesh.

John ducked for cover as a wave of debris from the zeppelin shot through the air and rocked the gondola with a violent assault. He peered through the slats in the stern and saw the zeppelin's captain gallantly going down with his ship, singing a hymn to the fatherland as the aluminum frame of the aircraft curled beneath the command car like the crooked legs of a dying spider.

With the explosion of the zeppelin, General Pershing and his troops broke into a chorus of hurrahs and the American fliers returned, plowing a victory lap through the clouds. "By Christ," mused Black Jack, as he chewed on a cigar, "this is one helluva way to start a war."

John re-ignited the burner valve. It broke the balloon's deadfall and allowed the craft to drift limply towards land. Exhilarated by the thrill of unexpected victory, the four friends embraced each other. They had hop-scotched over a gauntlet of disasters, saved the First Division and foiled the German high command. But most important of all, they were still standing.

41

THEY CAN'T TAKE THAT AWAY FROM ME

Stories of such daring usually end here. The guilty are punished, the good are rewarded and lovers are reunited for all time. However, this was not a conventional tale, and there were sorrowful twists that fate had not yet revealed.

Emily's euphoria at her triumphant reunion with John had been so great she failed to notice an injury had occurred. It wasn't until John fingered an unexpected wetness at the small of her back, and retrieved a hand smeared with blood, that she felt a sick roll in her stomach and her legs gave way.

"Oh, no…" she murmured.

She had been struck from behind by a thin aluminum rod that was one of the minor bones in the skeleton of the zeppelin. The sliver of metal had hit her with such force that it passed clean through her body, leaving two neat holes on both sides of her abdomen. It scrambled her insides, rupturing organs and unleashing a gush of internal bleeding that none of them could stanch, not the practiced Edison, nor the stricken Gershwin, nor the defiant John. Emily was not privy to these forensic details, as they were determined at a later date. It was only her dying of which she was certain.

John held her tightly as Edison yanked a swatch of bunting from the gondola and fashioned it into a tourniquet. The flow of blood slowed but he feared it was too late.

"You rest easy now," he brightly prescribed, more to reassure himself and the others than his patient. "Those Army doctors will have you fixed up in no time."

Emily touched his hand in gratitude. "You're a swell inventor…but a lousy liar."

"Emmy," pleaded Gershwin, "don't go." The tears came quickly, splashing onto his cheeks. "You're my muse."

Emily smiled wanly, hooked her thumb in his, and fixed with him a look that abandoned all pretense. "Go. Be my genius," she commanded.

Gershwin nodded tearfully and then turned away, unsure of how he would be able to face the future without her. A future he began to recall; a future that started now. "I remember," he whispered.

Emily shuddered. John refused to let her go. He had suffered everything up till this moment with all the iron resolve his masculinity had bred into him. But now, faced with the loss of love and hope, he was a little boy again, bereft and inconsolable. "No, no, no. Stay with me. Stay."

Emily stroked his arm and weakly murmured: "*The love of the man she truly adores…*"

She arched her back, trying to rise up to kiss him goodbye. John bent down and touched his lips to hers. She smiled and cupped his face in her hand. "Oh, John. Who could ask for anything more?"

Emily's eyes opened wide, gazing into a void that only she could see. "Me?" she asked meekly. Then she laughed; a laugh that was filled with the surprising satisfaction of a happy ending. "You bet your ass." And then she died.

Wracked with loss, John embraced her lifeless body.

Edison tried to comfort him. "My boy, I realize how impossible this is for you to understand but someday you'll both be together. Someday you'll---"

John shot him a look of such pure devastation that the platitudes choked in Edison's throat. "I don't give a goddamn about someday," he declared, shaking his head in a stiff agony. "I need her now!"

Edison didn't attempt to dissuade him. On this night, there was nothing but death. Death and silence. A haunting silence that remained with them all, long after the balloon had tumbled down to earth and their lives had unraveled into the future.

Epilogue

WHIRL

1931

There is a device used in motion pictures to signify the passage of time and the term for that process is *montage*. It can consist of the seasons evolving, with winter melting into spring, the pages of a calendar being ripped away by the winds of change, or the hands of a clock spinning wildly toward some future engagement. How odd that this cinematic device was so akin to real life. For with the benefit of hindsight, time really did fly. At least, that's what John thought come these thirteen years later. Everything and nothing had changed. Of the former, he had found a home in the astronomy department at Harvard University and was currently in residence as an associate professor. The campus served as a refuge; an easy confinement for a confirmed bachelor who had grown accustomed to being at home in his head.

On first sight, John looked remarkably the same. Although

he had recently celebrated his 34th birthday, his body was still stoked with muscle, a rich thatch of amber hair remained on his head and his strong, handsome face now sported what he thought was a rakish moustache. He was 'the cat's pajamas' or 'the bee's knees' or whatever the co-ed lingo of the day might be. But once those moon-struck sophomores took a second, longer look, they saw that, for all his virility, John seemed old-fashioned, if not downright old. There was a veneer of resignation about him that verged dangerously on retirement. He was a success who had given up.

So what was he doing standing in front of the entrance to Thomas Edison, Inc. on a freezing New Year's Eve just a few minutes shy of midnight? Frankly, he had no idea. He'd been summoned by Mr. Edison and, out of respect for old times' sake, had kept the appointment. It was not an imposition. He had no other plans. He absentmindedly scanned the early edition of the New York Times and stoically endured the cold. He was curious. That's why he had come. He hadn't been curious in a long time.

A limousine swerved up to the curb and, as the door opened, a celebratory burst of light and laughter spilled onto the street. Gershwin untangled himself from a bevy of chorus girls, promised a quick return, and shut the door, leaving the chorines to entertain themselves with gin and jazz. He was no longer a callow accompanist but an acclaimed composer whose light melodies were punctuated with deep yearning. He had become the person he most hoped to be. True, the hairline had receded and the features were more pronounced, but the trifecta of talent, fame and wealth had assured that wherever he went a party would follow. He took solace in this, for 'the party' guaranteed that, while he might often be lonely, he would rarely be alone.

Gershwin embraced John with a genuine warmth that took him aback. He responded as best he could with a manly pat on the back. They took an appreciative stock of one another as old friends do after an absence of so many years. John gestured toward the entrance of the building and Gershwin preceded him inside. John tossed his newspaper into a trash bin. Below the fold of the front page, a headline read:

HITLER PLEDGES NAZI PARTY
TO RE-UNITE GERMANY

The Great War, as history has confirmed, was a triumph for good. The entrance of the United States into the theatre of war proved to be the crucial turning point. Despite the bungled 'surprise attack' on Pershing's First Division, Ludendorff continued with the plans for his offensive, but the Allies bested the Germans at every turn. With the situation worsening and the collapse of Bulgaria, Ludendorff was forced to resign on October 27, 1918. The Armistice was signed soon afterwards and a cease fire declared on the eleventh day of the eleventh month at eleven a.m.

The leaders on both sides met with checkered fates. To avoid prosecution as a war criminal, the Kaiser fled to Holland where he spent his dwindling days as a recluse. President Wilson suffered a massive stroke and served out the remainder of his second term as an invalid. His cherished dream of creating a League of Nations to cement a future of peace was defeated by the Republican-led Senate. As for the Allies, the postwar treaty they approved was so cruelly punitive to the Germans that it sowed the desperate seeds crucial for the rise of the Nazi Party, paving the way for yet another Great War.

Thus, Hitler. After his encounter with the dark side of purgatory he was removed to a military sanitarium in Pasewalk and treated for his blindness. The true nature of the messenger's bizarre encounter with the afterlife was never revealed, and the baffled doctors explained his malady as a psychosomatic complication due to war hysteria. In time, Hitler's sight returned, he found work as a police spy, and was assigned to infiltrate the DAP, the German Workers Party. He became fascinated by the organization and one of its proponents, a wealthy occultist named Dietrich Eckart. Hitler confided his encounter with the dead zone to Eckart, and the dark magician seduced the young man into such a powerfully intimate mentorship that Hitler embraced the organization and later transformed its tenets into the bulwark of the Nazi Party. With an irresistible mixture of defiant nationalism, paranoid superiority and virulent anti-Semitism, the party proved to be Hitler's ticket to the top. Within two years he would be Fuhrer.

However, this was the province of the future. The present belonged to John and Gershwin, strolling down Edison's long hallway of inventions. John whistled a familiar tune: "Someone To Watch Over Me."

"It's my favorite," he offered.

Gershwin smiled, flattered. "Thanks. Mine too."

They reached the old inventor's private office and entered. They were alone, and the once-cluttered rotunda was empty except for Edison's desk and, on top of it, the miniature model of the resurrector.

"What's all this about?" asked Gershwin.

"All I know is what he wrote in his letter." He withdrew a piece of thick white stock with a feeble but insistent scrawl.

Thomas A. Edison
Requests the pleasure of your company
At one minute to midnight on December 31st, 1931

"Strange, isn't it?" observed Gershwin.

"What's really strange is he died in October."

"Why do you think he wanted us here? After all these years?"

John shrugged. It was the very question he'd asked himself after receiving the odd invitation. Upon their return from Europe, Edison swore both men to secrecy regarding the resurrector and the fantastic events surrounding its creation and demise. They agreed to an oath of silence and, with the exception of an occasional greeting card during the holidays or a break-a-leg telegram on opening night, thcy went their separate ways.

Some years later, an intrepid reporter for the New York *Sun* by the name of Kempton pursued a buried trail of innuendo and contradictions that suggested Edison had created a phonographic device that could communicate with the dearly departed and that the machine was somehow tied to the claim that he'd vanished during the winter of 1918. But where – and why? When Edison was confronted with the scattershot evidence, he freely admitted he had once held a passing interest in the possibility of creating such a machine, but it was nothing more than a public relations pipe dream. As for the winter of 1918, he hadn't disappeared. He'd merely sought the solace of isolation by spending the month of February in Key West. Fishing. For grouper. The reporter sensed evasion, but Mrs. Edison staunchly vouched for his claim and the issue was quietly put to rest. Yet here they were and the question remained. Why?

"Maybe for one last experiment," speculated John.

Gershwin traced a finger across the great man's desk. It was layered with dust. "A failed experiment by the looks of it," he sniffed. He looked up at John. "Not a day goes by that I don't think of Emily."

"The same," replied John quietly.

"She sings to me," confessed Gershwin.

He pressed his hand to his temple and winced in pain. John reached out in concern but Gershwin waved him off. "It's another one of these damned headaches. Getting worse all the time. Maybe some fresh air…" He gestured towards the exit and departed.

"I'll be along," John called out and turned back into the office to say, what, 'goodbye?' He sighed, unusually disappointed. It's not that he expected anything but, oh, how he'd hoped for something. He gave a melancholy spin to the sphere and turned to go.

And then something *did* happen.

The spinning model picked up speed and, as if possessed, began to shoot off rings of energy that expanded, opening a portal to the afterlife. A whirlwind of light and matter coalesced to reveal the spectral figure of Thomas Alva Edison!

John gaped at the vision, astonished. "It can't be."

"But it is!" responded Edison.

John exhaled sharply, his voice thick with growing revelation. "You did it," he gasped. "The resurrector works!"

Edison smiled. "Only this one time. There will be no more

resurrectors."

"Why not?" John asked plaintively.

"Because I was wrong. People need the unknown to conquer their fears," replied Edison. "Just as I finally conquered mine."

"But…" sputtered John. "It's your greatest invention!"

Edison shook his head. "Not the resurrector. Not the phonograph nor the moving pictures, not even the electric light. Wonderful contraptions, yes, but merely machines. You see, John, my greatest invention was my life. The same as any man's. The same as yours. If only you had the gumption to live it." Edison placed a supportive hand on his shoulder. "It's time to believe again."

"I'm a scientist," John replied evasively. "I need proof."

Edison chuckled and declaimed: "The two most important days in a man's life are the day he's born – and the day he finds out why." He shook his head, bemused. "You still won't admit to why."

"I'm a scientist-"

"You're no scientist," chided Edison.

John stood his ground. "Yes, I am! I'm an associate professor of astronomy at Harvard University and ---"

Edison flung his arms open wide. "You're a born hero!" he proclaimed and then drove home the lesson: "And your job, sir, is to save the world."

John was caught up short, finally face-to-face with his own truth. "I thought I did," he replied sadly.

"Hah," harrumphed Edison. "Beginner's luck." The old inventor leaned in slyly. "Did you really think destiny was done with you?"

"I need proof," John offered plaintively.

"No, my boy," counseled Edison kindly. "You need faith. How else can you create something out of nothing? Or light up the world?" He winked slyly. "Or fly to the moon?"

"I don't know how."

"Oh, all it takes is a bit of inspiration. Maybe a little something like…this."

Edison snapped his fingers. A second amorphous spirit emerged and swirled about the room. As the specter became whole, John came undone.

"Emily," he whispered hoarsely.

She smiled widely. "You bet your ass!"

The long-lost lovers approached each other in wonder. Emily drew him in close and they kissed, at first tentatively and then with mounting passion. She broke the kiss, stepped back and looked at him bluntly.

"Now do you believe?"

"He'd better," admonished Edison as the revolutions of the model began to slow. "If he doesn't, he won't be ready."

"Ready for what?" asked John.

"Our next adventure," answered Emily with a mysterious smile.

"What? When?"

"Soon enough," advised Edison. He extended his hand to Emily. She kissed the dazed John on the cheek and joined him as the model drunkenly curled onto its outer ring.

"Is this real?" he asked.

Edison gestured expansively. "It's all real! Isn't that wonderful?" Then: "But if it's physical proof you need, I suppose we could arrange a little demonstration for you and young Mr. Gershwin to remember us by."

As their visages faded, Emily pressed forward urgently.

"John? One more thing."

"Yes?" he replied, his level of urgency meeting hers.

"Your moustache?" she deadpanned. "Shave."

And with that the spirits disappeared, evaporating into the stale air of the empty office. There was a moment of awed silence as John took stock of his faculties. Had the visitation been genuine or some queer manifestation of his subconscious? He was beginning to doubt his own eyes when the lights in the room flared to a blinding intensity and the bulbs crackled with the ominous hum of overloaded energy. John grabbed the sphere and backed out of the room, lurching down the long hallway as all of Edison's inventions came to life behind their lead glass cases; the telegraph repeaters clattering, the film projector screening *Fred Ott's Sneeze*, and the phonograph blaring a cockeyed version of *Mary Had A Little Lamb* – all of them conspiring to urge John forward.

Outside, he grabbed Gershwin, who was startled to discover the sidewalk lights were ablaze with white-hot lumens that seemed to be prodding them down the street. John dragged Gershwin along the boulevard and found the same inexplicable phenomenon was occurring everywhere. Street lamps, household lights, neon signs; anything charged with electricity had increased in wattage to an extraordinary, blinding intensity. Pedestrians were flabbergasted by the spectacle, dazed motorists rear-ended one another, and a tenor of giddy panic invaded the streets.

John pulled Gershwin off the main drag and they ran with rollicking abandon toward a bluff that overlooked Manhattan.

As they raced into view, they were greeted by a radiant glow and astonished by what the skyline revealed. All the lights of the city had combined as one, forming a dazzling beacon that shot like a fist up into the sky.

"I'll do it," John promised softly.

"Do what?" demanded Gershwin.

John looked up in silent thanks and nodded decisively. "I'll give it a whirl."

The two old friends stood as one, their arms slung around each other, as the city sparkled magically beneath them. It made for a glorious, trumpeting finale. But like all fanfares of triumph, the experienced ear could discern a minor chord of caution. For a Pandora's Box of mayhem had accidentally been cracked open, and the long-term ramifications of the purgatory equation were only now beginning to assert themselves. A new adventure was in the offing, but one fraught with greater peril to the pillars of civilization than anyone – including the great Thomas Alva Edison – could have ever dreamed possible.

THE END

Although Thomas Edison and the

Purgatory Equation is a work of fiction,

the chronology of events is based on fact.

The majority of inventions that appear in these pages

– the hover tubes, the magnetic torpedo net and the H2Ohms,

etc. – were created in theory, if not fully realized,

by Thomas Alva Edison.

As for the resurrector, only one known remnant is said to remain:

an early, 'spirit-box' model housed in storage

at the Smithsonian Institution.

THE AUTHOR

WISHES TO THANK:

My late, much-missed colleagues, Mary Anne Page and David Stevens, who were present at the inception of the Edison Trilogy and generously provided enthusiastic encouragement as well as sound critical insight.

James Webber, who offered his valuable perspective at numerous stages of this project's development.

Richard Kilroy for his exquisite, evocative cover illustrations.

Larry Dean Harris and Lorraine Marchand for their early, unstinting words of praise.

Kevin Horton, Anthony Sarchiapone, James Fitzpatrick, Ansley Fones, Tracy Stopler, Brandon Mariano, and the gang at Ferrisville Publications who enhanced the potential of my work every step of the way.

John Hanc, my old Emerson College pal, who's not only a great friend, but the 'literary consigliere,' who assembled the team and provided a steady, savvy hand in navigating the publishing arena.

Finally, my gratitude to the namesake of this enterprise, Thomas Alva Edison. It has been a privilege to spend time in his company, if only from the distance of historical fiction. For while this is a work of invention, it has been shaped by the tenets of Edison's character: the joy of thinking, work above riches, disciplined modesty (but not too much), and his resolute belief that 'when you think you've exhausted all possibilities, remember this: you haven't.'

ABOUT THE AUTHOR

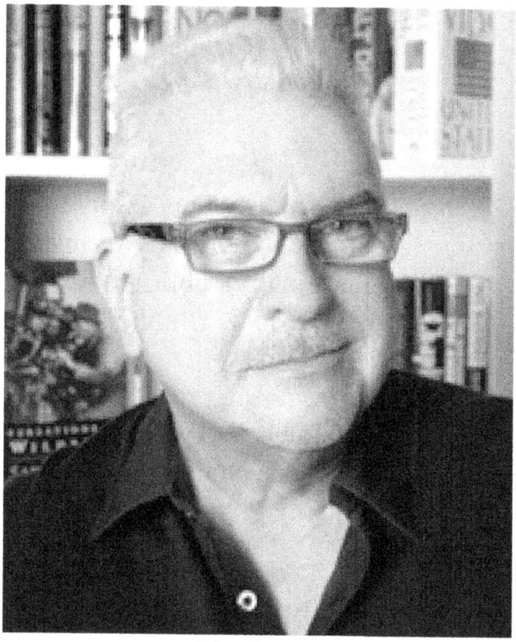

Matt Rose Photography 2021

A former advertising executive, David Church has written for publications as wildly diverse as *Soap Opera Digest* and *Interview*, authored an environmental children's book, *Larue and the Brown Sky* (illustrations by Toby Bluth), co-authored the award-winning, cult musical, *Judy's Scary Little Christmas* (with James Webber and Joe Patrick Ward), and developed a variety of films for United Artists, CBS and NBC, including *Psychic Housewife* and *Saving Grace*. He first became fascinated with the idea of Thomas Edison as the unlikely hero of a historical (science) fiction novel, when he accidentally discovered the Wizard of Menlo Park's decades-long passion for creating a machine that would communicate with the dead. David is a member of the Dramatists Guild and the Writer's Guild of America, and lives and works in Southern California.

CREDIT WHERE CREDIT IS DUE

SWANEE
Music by George Gershwin
Lyrics by Irving Caesar
Originally Published by T.B. Harms 1919
(Public Domain)

WAY DOWN UPON THE SWANEE RIVER
Music and Lyrics by Stephen Foster
Originally Published by Firth, Pond & Co. 1835
(Public Domain)

THE LOVE OF THE MAN SHE TRULY ADORES
Lyrics by David Church, 2021

THE EDISON TRILOGY WILL CONTINUE WITH:

THOMAS EDISON
AND THE
LAZARUS VESSEL

NOVEMBER 2022

Made in the USA
Middletown, DE
11 February 2022

60336211R00186